I0451639

Also by Adam L. Penenberg:

<u>Fiction</u>

Trial & Terror
A fast-paced legal thriller

<u>Non-fiction</u>

Blood Highways
The True Story behind the Ford-Firestone
Killing Machine

Viral Loop
From Facebook to Twitter, How Today's Smartest
Businesses Grow Themselves

Spooked
(with Marc Barry)
Espionage in Corporate America

VIRTUALLY TRUE

ADAM L. PENENBERG

WAYZGOOSE PRESS

Published in the United States by Wayzgoose Press.

Edited by Dorothy Zemach.
Cover design by DJ Rogers.
Book design by Maureen Cutajar.

ISBN 13: 978-1-938757-00-6
ISBN 10: 1938757009

For the Penengirls:
Charlotte, Lila, & Sophie

VIRTUALLY TRUE

Praise for *Virtually True*:

In Virtually True Adam Penenberg brings his considerable experience as a tech reporter to create a near future world that is both utterly disturbing and entirely believable. This is a fantastic novel, completely absorbing and full of memorable characters and fascinating ideas.

—David Liss, author of
The Twelfth Enchantment and *A Conspiracy of Paper*

Hero reporter True Ailey might ply his craft many decades in the future, with a bomb-proof self-cleaning suit taking the place of a grubby trench coat, but his readiness to risk life, love, and sanity to uncover the truth behind a deadly earthquake traces a clear path back to Woodward and Bernstein. Likewise, the relentless (and constantly delightful) twists and turns of *Virtually True* are every bit as gripping as any real-life journalistic exposé, only with the advantage of being set in a rich, perfectly imagined dystopian future.

Already a celebrated defender of journalistic fact, Adam Penenberg's debut novel proves he has equal mastery of the fictional realm. One part masterpiece of journalistic fiction, one part sci-fi masterclass, *Virtually True* grabs you by the throat from the opening lines and refuses to let go until long after a finale that's earth-shattering in more ways than one.

—Paul Carr, author of
The Upgrade: A Cautionary Tale of Life Without Reservations
and founder of Not Safe For Work Corporation

To live in the futuristic Republic of Luzonia is to live in a world of wrist-top devices, raw data run amok, orgasmic chewing gum, clone armies raised in vats, death by genetic-coded missile, and fluidly interpreted time. And if you're a journalist in that world, a journalist battling reality in search of truth, you're dodging a lot more than e-rain—you're investigating the very nature of free will. In *Virtually True*, the imagination fires, the dialogue crackles. Adam Penenberg's deeply imaginative novel is a wild ride of techno-subterfuge rooted in the eternally human quest for identity and justice.

—Paige Williams, author of
The Ghost and narrative writing instructor,
the Nieman Foundation for Journalism, Harvard University

PART ONE

TRUE

CHAPTER 1

It's late, the hours leaning closer to dawn than midnight, the sky soaked gunmetal gray by desperate city lights. And it's tomorrow, not yesterday, in Luzonia—a republic recently gouged out of a war-ravaged peninsula, a land weeping monsoon tears on the other side of Greenwich Mean.

Inside Bar 24-7, True Ailey sniffs the sweaty air, asking himself why he agreed to meet here. Like the surrounding city and country, it's a place that's dysfunctional, dangerous, brimming with prostitutes with unripe berry eyes and naked except for bar codes tattooed on their wrists (a government regulation), hustlers, fortune hunters, drug dealers and addicts, alcoholics, soldiers on leave, guerrillas from Southeast Asia's post-millennium ethnic cleansing wars; all of them scarred, True sees, with that distant look, like they've seen more than you.

Bar bravado in a score of languages flows over and around him, accompanied by plastic music. True's first foray into Bar 24-7, a landmark that never closes—has never closed, even for a nanosecond—in 20 years. Dots, blobs, and dashes of light dance around the room, spelling patterns on the walls and ceiling. *Is there a message, a symbol in there?* He cuts through the crowd, not meeting stares of lust or challenge, catching glimpses of infrared corneal transplants, robotic arms that can slice and chop mere mortals like himself, plastic skin grafts melted over burn wounds, bulging stacks of artificial muscle uncamouflageable under camouflage.

He's juiced, adrenaline coursing. Intuition is 60,000 times faster than thought but equally accurate; that and that alone will help him navigate this violence-infested sea. True moves quickly, arms pinioned to his sides, hands palm-side up: *No threat here, Jack,* in the universal language of the body. Like riding a cresting wave of pure information or shooting through clouds of 3-D data, numbers, digital images, sound that is not sound but waves, raw data factored by DNA computers.

But before these points are points they are trillions of dots squished together, each dot made up of trillions of other dots, veering off on tangents and funneled back into minuscule shapes that combine with other shapes to make the patterns that produce the dots that form these points that can be plotted so that one day True can interpret them.

At least, that's how he looks at it.

There. Alone at a table. Staring at True with onyx-tinted eyes and hair, slick designer ringlets chiming by his ears. The affluence of the clothes contrasts with the texture of his skin, which is dry, and spotted as crushed moth wings.

Images slash through True. The memory of awaiting his own execution: the shivering steel of a gun barrel brushing his temple, the click of an empty chamber. Then another: the fear of dying when he wasn't ready. Then a familiar voice. Reprieve.

He swings his leg over the back of an empty chair, sits.

"You're late," the man says.

True shakes his head. "Right on time."

He grabs True's wrist, twists it in order to better view the screen. "My internal clock's not in synch. It's this damned urban lifestyle. In the jungle I tell time just by looking at the sun."

True unearths the slightest traces of a Pakistani accent buried beneath many lands, many years of estrangement. "Aslam, you're one multi-talented zealot." Glances at Aslam's wrist-top, notes its complexities. A brand-new model, twice the RAM of True's, with built-in surveillance hardware, debugging software, weapons detector, DNA check, a cornucopia of video monitors and microphones. True's seen the commercials. "What's wrong with your wrist-top?"

"Just got it."

"So?"

Aslam hedges. "I don't know how to set the clock."

True smiles. A sitcom moment. "Well, it's hard to stay up on the latest technology."

Across the planet, from within the tiny nooks and crannies that pass for new republics to the monstrous regional trade alliances subjugating the world's economy, the words *latest technology* are ever splattered in ad copy and mooed in jingles. But the words have become essentially meaningless, day-old technology as stale as yesterday's aspirations or yesteryear's inspirations.

"What's with the new businessman look?" A suit with a roll of six buttons, equipped with UV shield. True fingers the lapel, shiny black and aqua-colored beads with super tensile strengths. "Bullet- and laser-proof?"

"Bomb-resistant, too, a few unk-unks aside."

Unk-unks—*unknown unknowns*. True imagines Aslam taking part in some contentious board meetings. "I suppose it'd depend on the bomb." True watches Aslam drain the dregs of his drink. A bloody Caesar, ostensibly. "I thought the Koran forbids alcohol."

"Please. It's been a rough day." Aslam smiles and slaps True's back. Walks his fingers down his spine. "You're skinny as hell, although that didn't stop every bar girl in this zone from giving you the once over."

"Why'd you want to rendez here?"

"I've always wondered. Why'd your parents order you with avocado eyes? Don't people assume they're lenses?"

"You're not worried about being marked?"

"What for? Copping enemies of the state's bad for business. Besides, I've left the insurgency."

"I was wondering, since I never saw you in a suit before."

"Camouflage isn't a suit?"

Aslam stepping off a precipice. His face has been stung by the sun's unfiltered rays, ravaged by countless bouts with melanoma. Reflected in Aslam's eyes, True can almost see replays of battles—violent orange and black explosions cracking holes in the earth. War exacted a tremendous toll. True wonders if he's the same man he left behind, years before, in Kathmandu, where his mind floated skyward in a hashish haze.

Aslam lights a *bidi*, slips the smoldering end into his mouth, a security from years of smoking in jungle cloak. Puffing oblong rings, "The world is changing, changing in ways you can't imagine." Taps his chest. "Look at me, True, how I've changed."

Except for the suit, designer 'do,' and flowery cologne, he's the same. True tells him so.

"Okay. I left because things were crashing. We were starving, our weapons were shit, we weren't claiming any new ground—or converts—and couldn't count on support."

True knows this, that the economies of Arab nations crashed with the recent discovery of alternative energy sources, solar cells, cold fusion, and fuel concocted from corn, wheat, barley, household garbage. No oil exports, no income; no income, no weapons, no training, no insurgency. He lets silence pressure Aslam for an explanation.

"I was headhunted. Jacked into major legitimate business. Better than eating roots and shitting in the woods."

It's inconceivable to True that the man of a dozen insurgencies would now be shimmying up the corporate ladder. "You? Hired for *corp* work? As what? Head of guerilla marketing?"

"Never mind. It's you we've come to discuss."

"Who've you sold out to?"

"Fuck you."

"I'll rephrase the Q. Who do you work for now?"

"Can't say."

"Why not?"

"It doesn't matter to you yet."

But it does. True's a journalist who's shot off the data runway so many times he isn't sure he ever left; smoked targets for scillions of bits of raw data, the lifeblood of his profession, and this helped him crack stories, spill news to an info-addicted world. More than once he became entangled in webs of information that took on a coherent shape only later, mega-bits of evidence that helped him uncover conspiracies, odd factoids here and there that were the springboard to a major epiphany, uncrunched numbers disproving statistics, a verbal slip, a gesture out of place, a break with habit that led to pay dirt. The trick is to keep pressing, suck up a crumb here or there until you can make sense of it.

Aslam's eyes fall on a VR weapons game. A pudgy tourist in khaki is leading an assault, missiles and stealth planes cloaked invisible until firing. Out of the jungle a few weeks and already Aslam's eyes are giving him away.

"So," True says, "you've booted into a gig with a weapons contractor."

Aslam's eyebrows modulate. "Forget me. I've got something for you."

"What? A scoop? You've left the insurgency and converted to Judaism? Now *that* would be a ratings star."

"Just because you're going to burn in hell doesn't mean I will. No. A business proposition." Aslam's eyes, effervescent, back on the urge. "Listen, True. The world's changing. Corporate power is still on the rise. Want my advice? Hitch on now. Soon government won't govern shit."

"Government already doesn't govern shit."

"So you know the way of the world. War is being revolutionized. Some of the new technologies in advanced stages of R & D are bound to change the global balance of power."

"So?"

"Some of the technologies are bad. Real bad. One corporation monopolizes them, that's major trouble for the rest."

"What's some corporate battle technology got to do with me?"

"My idea. We need a digithead who can suss out some info. I said I knew the *modeiant* one." Aslam coughs, extinguishes his *bidi*. "An ice cream habit." Clears his throat. "I should nix the nic from my life."

"Why don't you quit?"

"No discipline." Aslam stands, smoothes his suit. "I'll get some drinks."

Long strides to the bar. True covers Aslam with his eyes, ready to counter possible threats, but Aslam doesn't seem worried. The bartender stands behind a hole protected by impenetrable clear plastic: money goes in; drinks, drugs come out. Barbed wire winds double helixes throughout the see-through shield, more decorative than functional. On stage, whores feasting on hardcore kink, all types in addition to the usual balloon-breasted amazons—freaks with skin tinted across the ROYGBIV spectrum, female bodybuilts with Popeye forearms and rice-terrace abs, chicks with dicks, dykes, gays, contortionists.

In this age of bargain beauty they strive to fill a niche, and when market forces dictate a change, the cost is a few tricks, a few hours of surgery, a few years lopped off a meaningless life. At the game center, a virtual siren beckons through a haze of incense and sex oils, her body rounder, skin a touch more radiant, curly jet-black hair glistening. More real, more alluring to True than the surrounding pros, whose by-the-hour leers he parries by pretending to read from his wrist-top.

Aslam hands True a Kamikaze.

"Ah, a tragic drink." True sips, remembers days past when fiery drinks like this would KO his taste buds. Now, only a faint tingle. "Comes with a vomit-proof warranty. Goes down, fucks you up, is guaranteed not to return."

"You're going to accept this gig. Want to know the terms?"

"I don't vet out data unless it's for a story."

"Why not? Your journo career's maxed out. You fucked up, you're stuck in Loser-onia, and you'll never be able to re-boot your career. The network is waiting for you to just make one little shitty-assed error so they can delete you from their payroll. Pretty soon you'll be sitting home in some coffin apartment, hooked up to VR games, subsisting on government checks, jerking off to virtual babes."

There's something disturbing about hearing your life so perfectly described, True thinks, as if Aslam read his mind, was there the whole time, experienced the impotence of watching everything important to True combust. But Aslam was snaking through jungles furthering the cause of insurrection, was not around during this ugly time, was not witness to the destruction of True's mind. "How do you know all this?"

"*Donnez-moi un break.* I know more about you than you can imagine."

"Like what?"

"Like first of all, you *will* data-retrieve for us. Assured. I also know what happened to you, how you ended up in the hospital an emotional bulimic. I also know what WWTV has planned for you. Believe me, my friend, you will not chill to the tune of it."

"Tell me how you know."

"I have a whole computer model on you, all known information, and not just the stuff in your dossier. I know all the times during the Pakistani-Indian war you chugged yogurt to cool out the spices when you shit. I've seen your dreams. I know what happened to the woman in your life."

True's cheeks turn the color of roast pork. "What happened to her?"

"That can wait. You see, I do know what it will take to get you to chase down the gravy train. And I can't afford to dick around. I'm giving you a chance to leave this dead-end journo job, make some serious bucks, tell that shit anchor boss of yours to fuck off."

"The model tells you under the right circumstances I'll work for you?"

"*Précisément.*"

"Why me?"

"Because you're the best. Not just because I think so. Computer says so too."

"Flattering."

Aslam slaps the table, like enough of this bullshit. "So when you going infospace for us?"

"Like I said. I'm not going."

Aslam pokes a splinty finger into True's chest. "It's not like you've been prospering. Look at your clothes. Look at you: You're still a handsome gene-machine, that I grant you, but you're thirty-five, passed *Go* more than a few times and none the healthier for it."

True's gaze slides down his chin, his body, around slender arms and legs. Has to agree his is not the body of a prosperous man.

"How can you reject this more-than-generous offer?" Aslam's Pakistani lilt is more pronounced in anger.

"I don't work for corporations."

"Well fuck you very much. What do you call WWTV?" Aslam scratches his arm, rolls up his sleeve to unveil a circular cicatrix on his arm and shoulder; the shape of the Ouroboros, True thinks, the tail-biting snake, the ancient symbol for eternal disintegration and rebirth.

"What happened? It looks like a laser wound."

"The usual bullshit band-aid cuts and scrapes." Aslam stares ahead, silent so long True thinks he may have forgotten about him. "A laser wound, but not what you think. You can't imagine." Traces the scar full circle. "You know, you *will* work for us. Just a matter of a few more clock ticks. It'll take more than money to sway you, I know, but you'll see reason eventually."

"I am seeing reason. Besides, there's an ethics problem."

"There are no ethics in journalism."

True, caught in a pale lie, doesn't argue.

"How'd you know I work for a military contractor?"

"Who else would hire an ex-jungle insurgent?"

"You know, this weapon remains secret, the world will be irrevocably changed."

"There was a time I would have jumped at this, feeding off the danger. But I don't have the tools anymore. Since getting out of the hospital all I feel like doing is getting by, focusing on the day-to-day, not the grand scheme of things. It's hard enough waking up every day."

"Bullshit excuses. If you don't hurry, it'll be too late."

"It already is."

Aslam sips the Kamikaze, swishes it around his mouth, glares hard at True. "Sometimes, no matter how many times I tell myself not to feel anything, I can't help myself. Months ago, before I left the insurgency, we set up camp near a river, and a little girl from a friendly village nearby, she must have been about nine, would bring us food. One day she ran off too far, and it was several hours before we realized she'd disappeared. The next morning we found her. She'd been captured by some ethnics, tied up and stretched over bamboo seeds. But these were not the regular variety of bamboo. They were the kind that grow very quickly, overnight.

"She was still breathing but the stalks had begun to climb through. And we were faced with a no-win: If we lifted her off, she'd die—there was extensive organ damage—and if we left

her, she'd die anyway. Know what she said when I held a pistol
to her head?"

True waits.

"She told me she wanted to stand one last time."

"What happened?"

"She died." Aslam crunches an ice cube. "But she took
control of the little life she had left. Will you?"

"No."

"True, you've given up the struggle. What happened? You
once said there's a whole world to be conquered with each act
and statement."

True knows Aslam's lying. "We've been through a lot together."

"Yes."

"I saved your life."

Aslam sputters.

True says, "OK. You saved my life. And suffered terribly
for it." There: the toxic guilt that poisons their friendship, that
split-second decision that resulted in a half-dozen years of sep-
aration—yet still, in many ways, bonds them together. True
hopes Aslam's ready to bridge it.

But not this time. Instead, "Aren't journalists supposed to
keep their facts straight?"

True, torn between relief and the desire to let go of the
past, takes Aslam's lead. "It's the unpleasant memories. Twice
a year I get a monumental case of the runs, thanks to your cro-
nies' bowel-busting Moghul meals. But I'd wager your computer model told you that already. Don't put too much stock in
it. You think it takes everything into account, but it can't. Trust
me, reality is some messy business."

They finish their Kamikazes, wash down another with another with another. True's numb, a warm herring-boned crack of optimism spreading through him. He's comfortable and confident in altered states. The room throbs with fourth-world tongues mixing with benzene melodies. Mercenaries play Blade Roulette, a game where contestants splay the fingers of one hand on the table, stab at the empty between, the winner the fastest to go three (pain-free) revolutions. Standing on tiptoes, peering over shoulders, Indian Dhobis flip paper dollar gliders into a betting pool, each sheet folded uniquely—into triangles, pentagonal stars, birds of prey, creased in much the way their ancestors marked laundry on the banks of the Ganges. Threats, insults, blood thick with aggression.

Time to lock up the evening. On the way out True and Aslam run a gauntlet of narc dealers (many of whom are ex-U.N. peacekeepers), smugglers, travelers, and freelance guerrillas, the usual flotsam and jetsam living on the edge of a world teetering on the brink. Their shuffling whispers: Shrooms, VR FREEze, Cum Gum (*Chew for that 2-minute orgasm!*), Speed Cocktail. Aslam's wrist-top pulses blood (read: potential danger). His computer scans the DNA of the dealers and ran background checks. Aslam doesn't seem alarmed. He's probably packing enough portable weaponry to wipe out a small country anyway.

Outside, the street is yawning. A robot cleaner—German foreign aid—scrubs the sidewalk in front of People Protectors, one in a worldwide chain of security equipment stores. Vendors are setting up stalls. Sell flimsy sneakers, pirated video game programs, recycled clothing, perfume, noodles soaking in tripe and peanut sauce, day-old baby chicks fried on a stick. True decides to take advantage of the early hour and record some local color. Maybe save himself the trouble of creaking awake at the crack of dawn sometime.

The wrist-top digitizes, reproduces everything in a 360-degree arc, including himself. True notices a Luzonian beggar in the small-scale gram replica. Young, maybe eleven, her front teeth a little large for her mouth, her cheeks hollow, stomach distended. A tattered t-shirt hangs down and clings to her ankles. True reads the shirt's motto: *Brown Tasty Cola*, a local soft drink. Free advertising serving as clothing for the impoverished.

She hugs Aslam's leg and he gently unclenches her. She grabs his pinky with two tiny hands. Aslam leads her to 24-7's back alleyway where a drunk tourist is relieving himself, a stream of yellow soaking building concrete, unaware of a corpse heaped over a pile of garbage. Something is burning, probably pollution from a factory on a frenetic export drive, melting rubber and plastic for soles in order to meet the insatiable global appetite for sneakers. Or maybe the smell emanates from the wood-burning stoves the Luzonians crank up each morning. It's possible someone commandeered wood from a factory's dumpsters, is at this very moment searing toxic waste into the family feed.

True can hear their conversation. She asks for money. Her father is sick. The family starving. They want a chance at a better life. Or is it he's heard this same woeful tale so often he now overdubs his own dialog? Aslam pats her head. Hands her some money.

The wind whips up and clears the air. True films a street scene—beyond, a church's burnt-out shell, charred black and long ago stripped of valuables, next to a bomb crater between two low-slung buildings, held together by human ingenuity alone. He walks away from the bar, filming, the holoscreen floating at eye level.

Although his back is turned, True can see the light on Aslam's wrist-top bleed red and his face drain of color. A flash of light, a surging, stinging sound, jet propulsion, coming around the corner. Aslam tries to leap out of the way, pulls the girl to the ground with him.

A muffled explosion. True watches Aslam heaved against Bar 24-7 brick while the girl, tourist, and cadaver are shredded by the blast; Aslam, due to his bomb-resistant garb, is in one piece. Later, True won't remember tripping over his own feet as he rushes to Aslam, but the wrist-top records this, as it did his gargling scream. He does remember sliding to his knees, cradling his friend's head in his lap.

"I can't breathe." Aslam gags. A swatch of metal cloth is lodged in his neck.

"I'll get a doctor."

"No." Aslam's lips quivering, squeezed blue. "Too late."

"She'll fix you up."

"No. Too much damage. Inside." Aslam shuts his eyes, corners crinkling.

"Aslam?"

A jewel of water rolls down Aslam's nose, across his lips, drips onto the sidewalk. He looks up. "True, you have to help."

"Save your strength."

"The weapon. Not what you think." Aslam's in shock. Tries to continue, but True can't decipher it. Manages, "I'll contact you. I promise."

"How?"

"It depends."

"On?"

"You." Aslam silently mouths, "God is great." One last shudder.

There will be no more breaths, no more tears, no more memories, no more wars. Aslam's life no more. Memories: Aslam saving True's life, later trudging over veiny Himalayan passes to Lhasa, then Kathmandu. The sensation of sticky blood on his hands urges him to reality. He shakes Aslam, seeks a pulse, signs of life, knows he won't find any.

True runs his finger along the Ouroboros scar, wonders if Aslam will ever rise again.

Aslam, staring through one eye straight to heaven, doesn't seem to know.

And True does something he hasn't for a long time.

He cries.

CHAPTER 2

Nerula's police station is Luzonia's last male bastion. Thirteen years of warfare and ethnic strife have whittled away the population of draft-age males, first those between 17 and 35, then 15 to 45, finally anyone over 11. And while these men and boys, in order to carve out a sectarian Catholic state on this clammy Southeast Asian peninsula, surged into the jungle to kill and be killed, the nation's women remained tied to the land, taking advantage of their growing numbers to wrest control of the nation's government and businesses.

But not of the police, True thinks. He's standing with Officer Pidge, five foot nothing, greasy hair resembling the tip of a used Q-tip, knives, pistols, grenades, poison gas pellets pinned to a filthy uniform.

"Bong Bong?" True asks.

Pidge sings. "Bong Bong. Ha ha. Bong Bong."

Nerula's chief of police. Bong Bong heads a city-wide baksheesh racket, fleecing tourists, aid workers, and journos alike.

No need for surveillance technology because Bong Bong cows Nerulan hotel operators and bartenders; all hustlers, dealers, and beggars; every vendor and copyright pirate. They are his eyes and ears, and for this, they are afforded life. At times the pressure to please Bong Bong is so great, desperate Luzonians are ever-sneaking up on the unsuspecting, slipping small blocks of hash, packets of methyl-A, or wadded up balls of low-grade weed into their pockets, then turning them in.

Bong Bong is squatting behind a desk. He has an oblong-shaped head, weary eyes, and a face riddled in spiky acne. Luzonians say he looks like a pineapple but smells like a *durian*, the local toejam-scented fruit. He's watching an old rerun, black and white, about a fat Nazi being screamed at by another Nazi called Klink. Bong Bong haws and mutters something. When he sees True, he cups his hands behind his head. Cop casual.

"Come in." Bong Bong points to one of two chairs.

True sits.

Bong Bong giggles. "No. I change my minds. There." Gestures to the other chair.

True remains seated, a sideways *z*. Bong Bong launches an aside at Pidge, who harmonizes his giggles with those of his superior.

True's had enough. "Who killed him?"

Bong Bong's eyes pop. After a time he snaps his fingers. "Drink?"

True mouths "No," holds Bong Bong's eyes; then, allowing the cop to claim this inconsequential victory, averts his gaze. Satisfied, Bong Bong skims an ink-smeared page from his desktop, reads it aloud, slowly, torturously, mispronouncing some words, misusing others. "You have indentified victim by Aslam Qadar Aziz, citizen of Pakistan. Correct?"

True nods.

"When there was this Pak-land. Right?"

True says nothing.

"Muslim insurgent. Enemy of Luzonia. What is an American journalist doing with such a man?"

True remains wrapped in silence, just winging it, looking for the best way to handle things. Thus far he's drawn a blank. Looks to Bong Bong for inspiration. Finds only nausea.

"Name?"

No point in lying. "True Ailey."

Bong Bong slides over a crumpled wrapper, flips him a pen, and makes a scribbly gesture. True smoothes the grease-soaked paper—*It's Bigmcbuffaloburger Day*, it says in spiraling, copyright-infringed lettering—and scrawls his name.

"Not talking-a-tive, eh?" Bong Bong snatches the paper away and Pidge takes his position at the computer console. Bong Bong reads, "Ailey. A." A pause as Pidge searches for the right letter, then pounds it. Bong Bong moves on. "I." Pause. "L-E-Y." Long pause. "Comma. True. T-R-U-E."

The computer has taken a beating, perhaps due to Pidge's typing style, less hunt-and-peck than search-and-destroy. The printer sputters, and after some silent pleading from Pidge, spits out what True assumes is his dossier.

Bong Bong reads: "Sixty-seven years old. Occupatient: model. Specialitylizing in lingerie." True thinks it telling the one difficult word Bong Bong pronounced correctly is *lingerie*. "Now retired, living in England." Bong Bong snaps his eyes away from the paper—focuses on True. "It says female. You're not female." Bong Bong looks closer. "Are you?"

True reads the paper upside down. "It says Trude, not True. He made a mistake."

Bong Bong bellows a stream of Luzonian invective at Pidge, who retypes True's name. The screen wheezes then freezes. Bong Bong kicks the computer and it whirs back to life. Lo! True's dossier. After skimming the printout, Bong Bong reads, "True Ailey, journalist, age-ed thirty-three, employ-yed by WWTV. Hey! I seen you around lots of times. You were a news guy for Indo-Pakistan war?"

"Pakistan-Indian war." True's thinking of Aslam.

True's mind shifts back to driving along the border on the Pakistani side, guns, missiles, tanks poised to fire. A battle on fast forward, True seeking refuge, speeding to a rock face where he runs into a unit of Pakistani soldiers. The steely scent of war; True visualizes himself being tethered to the ground, stretched tightly over quick-sprouting seeds of bamboo, waiting for the blades to tear through.

But that never happened. True is fighting memories now as they impinge on other memories, some true, others just TV stories or fantasies or nightmares. The walls separating them are being breached, pushed to their limit by the stress of Aslam's death. True battles his way back to reality but can't shake the image of Aslam's neck with the lapel of his bomb-resistant shirt razored in, choking his life away.

Bong Bong is talking. "…stupid war. Nuclear bums. And you the only journalist alive from this war. Here in Luzonia, a hero is a man who fights until he dies."

"A lot of heroes here, then." The electricity crackles, sizzling meat, lights brown to black and then back to dingy yellow. "Who do you think killed him?"

"Who? This, this—" Bong Bong picks up the paper, "Aslam Aziz? I dunno."

"How about the girl?"

"How can I know who is she? Thousands and hundereds of girls disappear, *poof*"—he demonstrates—"into begging and prostititution world."

"If you find out who she is, then you might find out why she died. And Aslam, too."

"It is not important to me to instigate this Pak. If I seen him here, I kill him myself."

"If you take me back to 24-7, I might be able to scrounge up a trace of her DNA. Then we could run an identity check."

"This country has not just concreted a civil war for nothing. You think we have informations like that laid around?"

"How about missing children reports?"

Bong Bong waves his hand lazily. "It's the story of a lovely lady. Too many, *too* too many, to check."

"Maybe her parents are looking for her."

"She could have been absentiated weeks, for years."

"What about her clothes?"

"I did not seen her."

"She wore adspace. Brown Tasty Cola. When were those shirts distributed?"

"Situation, a situation is murky, just like your career." Bong Bong looks over the rest of True's dossier. "Too bad you did not pay intention to your evocation. I see here you"— Bong Bong curls two sets of fingers to make the point he's quoting—"suspended for lack of attention—ah, it is attention, not intention, I mistook. Wait. I have commented my faux past, right?"

"Sure."

"—to work. Ab-sen-tee-ism a chronic concern. Sub*ject*, or is it *sub*ject hospitaled?"

"*Sub*ject and hospitalized."

Bong Bong's voice hitches closer to alto than tenor. "English is difficult, not like Luzonian."

"Uh, huh."

"In Luzonian, you wish to tabulate your digits, you know what, addition the 's' or two 's'."

"Make a word plural."

"You say two times. One 'enemy of the state' is 'enemy of the state.' Two 'enemy of the state' is 'two enemy of the—'"

"Before we run out of time, how about an autopsy on Aslam?"

"In Luzonian, there's this same word for yesterday and tomorrow." Bong Bong sighs. "Nobody cares about time."

"Please, the autop—"

"—and no word for 'please.' It takes too much time to talk it." Bong Bong's face is robust, like a tomato.

"The autopsy. How about it?"

"He's dead. You think this is the U.S. of A. and I say, 'Autopsy! Autopsy! Autopsy! This American wants the autopsy for a deadly Pak.' Why do you not make believe?"

"I've done too much of that already."

A close-lipped smile spreads from ear to cauliflower ear. Bong Bong leans forward. Motions True close. "Okay. I tell a secret. Don't say to no bodies. They think I come down with nice." Glum silence. "We know he dies from bum in missile."

"What kind? Who manufactured it?"

"Have you not been outside the city to the country's side? Sure, sure this is tropical island para*dize*, good for tourist, yes, yes." He stretches out the final syllable. "But many kind types of soldier from the jungle here have many kind types of explosions. *And*, war bleeds creativity."

"When you were a guerilla, you saw this kind of weapon?"

Bong Bong elbow-polishes his debit machine. Puffs on it and sprays dust. "These informations are expensive."

True wonders how it could have lain around idle long enough to get dusty. Bong Bong types in an astronomical amount and True lops off a bunch of zeros. They bargain, insincerely bandying figures back and forth, Bong Bong bragging of the importance of his information, True claiming poverty, until True pulls out an Automatic Debit Card and swipes it through.

"I give you the discount because you are my friend." Bong Bong's cash-box eyes register satisfaction.

"I'm touched."

Bong Bong tells True the names of some missiles and their manufacturers. True has never heard of the companies, but that's not unusual given that companies are constantly bought, sold, downsized, and stripped.

True looks up from his wrist-top screen. "Is it possible it was an accident?"

"Then no boom."

"I mean was someone trying to kill the girl, not Aslam?"

"Who knows? She was maybe a little bit of crazy."

"She was a child."

"I tell you something. I take you Americans, stick you here for twenty years in this hot climatic condiction and you go kookie cookies too." He twirls his fingers around his ears and whistles.

"How about a blood sample and a few tests? That would help me figure out what kind of explosive killed him."

"What's up? You have police indentifications?"

True shrugs.

"I do not need your help, Mister Journalist."

True drum-rolls on Bong Bong's desk with his fingers. "Can I see Aslam's body? At least let me see him one last time."

Bong Bong glances at his Automatic Debit Machine. "Okay. Let's call it, Christian-amity. That is your religion, no?"

"Close enough."

Bong Bong sends True along with Pidge, who leads him out of the office, down the hall, and past a cop extorting a hooker—True sees the wrist barcode wrapped languidly around the undulating man's neck—up a metal staircase, betel nut spit staining it dull rust. On the second floor he hears a man's screams. Hall lights hiss, brown out, flicker on, off, on. True halts in front of a faded door. Fingerprints from hundreds of sets of grubby hands seeking entry form a concentric ring around the knob. He peeks in a jaundiced window. A torture chamber. More gurgling groans, fluttering lights.

"What did he do?" True asks.

Pidge smiles through cracked teeth. He's chewing on an indigenous root, a natural amphetamine. His eyes are bloodshot, pupils hard, and a string of spittle rappels from his lips to the floor. The steady babble of a tribal language, a confession. Interrupting Luzonian laughter soaking through the chamber's door is the sound of a lock bolt being slid back. An officer pops out, holding a pair of weather-beaten sneakers.

Pidge chews furiously on the narc, admires the shoes. True glimpses the victim strapped to a table: naked, a crescent of blood leaking from the slit of his mouth. Wires run length and breadth. His toes claw air, seek a path to freedom. Pidge pushes True into a room a few sleepy doors away—the crematorium, a low-ceilinged coffin-shaped room, gray walls of stone blanketing a furnace where piles of naked bodies lie stacked. He thinks of the touts who hang out near Nerula's deluxe hotels, charging for the privilege of filming the freshest corpses. A major cottage industry. No doubt Bong Bong's in on that action too.

True imagines movement where there should be no movement. Off to the side, sitting on the room's lone bench, a man sits, licking rice off a banana leaf, transfixed by a fizzy TV blasting a local game show. He sees True's with Pidge and goes back to his meal.

Smoke stains his lungs. True feels himself losing control, but Pidge's insipid laughter helps him focus on what needs to be done. Close up, he sees why he senses movement. Flies. Feasting on these lifeless souls. On top of a pile is an old woman, a burn mark hyphenating her face, her skin a glutinous pallor. A boy from an ethnic enclave in the country's disputed Northwest territory stares up in wonder. True scouts for Aslam.

It's Pidge who helps. Calls the man on the bench. "Mug!"

Mug breaks his TV trance, and after licking the leaf clean, steps over and around bodies. He pulls stiff corpses from the tops of piles, drags them by their ankles. True notices odd scars on the bodies, slithering gashes along their sides, gaping holes in chests, missing eyes. One with blood soaking the floor must have been alive when he was dumped here. Another with a crushed cheekbone was beaten to death. Mug topples over a heap of cadavers. Near the bottom, True sees him—not just his clothes, shoes, and shattered computer stripped away, but also his limbs. His neck and torso are clotted black and purple, stiff from rigor mortis. Rushing over, True tangles his feet in other bodies. Pulls himself free. Makes his way over, tripping, slipping.

Mug holds out his hand.

True, caught off guard, reaches into his pocket for his emergency wad of bills secreted away. Gone. Pickpocketed.

True holds out his hands as if checking for rain. "I don't have anything."

Mug insists. "Baksheesh."

Pidge weighs in. "Baksheesh. Ha ha. Baksheesh."

Mug points to the wrist-top. True covers it up. Indicates True's shoes. "No." Fingers True's shirt. True taps his socks. OK. Takes off his shoes and hands his socks over to Mug, who pockets them and saunters back to his bench.

After kneeling down, True secretly scans Aslam with his wrist-top, videos the head, neck and torso, takes an atmospheric sample so the computer can compare atmospheric contributions to Aslam's chemical state, holds the wrist-top to the gash in Aslam's neck. Through the hologram playing in front of him, invisible to others, True sees Mug sipping from a thermos, Pidge spitting streams of betel nut juice and narc root into a corner while counting dollars. His dollars, True presumes.

He turns Aslam over and scans his back, flips him back and caresses his head, brushing ringlets of hair from his eyes.

"Forgive me, Aslam." True reaches into his pocket and pulls out a few commemorative coins: *The People's Revolution for Justice and Purity.* All the money he has left. Digs the coin into Aslam's neck, extracts a tiny chunk of bomb-resistant fabric and blood, wipes the blood on the inside flap of his pocket, and hides the metallic fabric in his coat. True can scarcely see through his own tear-filled eyes. Wonders what Aslam would say if he could see this. He wants to open Aslam's eyes one last time, wants to see inside his soul, but someone stole his eyeballs.

He kisses Aslam's cheek. Another electric crackling, a brief blackout. The door opens and more naked corpses are tossed inside, one at a time, onto the messy piles of death.

The game show is zapped away, replaced by a commercial for a home chemotherapy kit. Mug, unhappy with the additional work, runs his hand through his hair and down the back of his neck. But wordlessly creaks open the furnace door and shoves bodies inside.

CHAPTER 3

True's walking through Snake Alley, the central artery of his local mall, a cluster of grouchy stores stocking home remedies, food, and oils derived from rattlesnakes; financed with Japanese money, erected after a tenuous peace was reached between Luzonia and its neighbors.

He traverses this mall practically every day, the only safe pedestrian route out of his neighborhood. Other routes lead through the surrounding shanties, with their tin and plastic box-houses crammed together, suffocating the hills on which they are tenuously anchored. A murky river serves as the sole source of water, and all along this river, locals drink, bathe, and wash dishes in factory effluvium.

True leaves the din of the mall for the din of a game arcade, washed into overlapping explosions and searing bubbles of lights. Women, a few men, are plugged into virtual reality machines, interacting with established soap opera actors and starring as queen bitch guest stars, battling holograms in hand-to-hand, severing the spines of medieval warriors, decapitating Roman gladiators, taking aim as guerilla snipers in jungle warfare, living out sexual fantasies in fantastical worlds. He heads to the back.

Sitting behind a coffee bar counter, framed by a dazzling display of lottery tickets, is a woman perched on a stool, counting loose money. Her eyes are the color of *dhal*, her hair imprisoned in a messy ponytail. True leans over the bar. She's built like a Greek statue that's fallen victim to vandals.

"Hey!" Her harsh-bud voice is muffled by a dangling cigarette yet carries easily over the arcade noise. "What do you want today?"

"Coffee." True takes a stool. "Since when does Pinatubo work the counter?"

"Like, Piña runs her business hands-on? Besides, three girls in for cancer treatments. Fucking melanoma? Fourth time this year."

"And Piña?"

"No problem." Raps on the counter with her knuckles. "Know why?"

"No."

"Piña stays inside and works out." She flexes biceps, squeezes her arms until veins pop blue and ridges of muscle ride up her forearms. A butterfly-shaped tricep asserts itself when she straightens her arms. Shy pride. "These days, girl's gotta work out."

True reruns his amazement every time he sees Piña. Her angelic face, olive skin, worsted hair that, when she allows it, cascades to her shoulders, superimposed over iron—etched with scars, painted with tattoos, pierced with rings and studs. But it's not just her tree trunk torso, thick wrists and forearms, breasts layered over tiled muscle (they almost seem an after-thought), and that she achieved this without steroids or synthetic muscle surgery. It is that she has no legs.

Piña spins, plants coffee in a microzap, and seconds after hands True a cup, steam wisping into air-conned air. He blows on the coffee, sips; the sting makes him feel alive.

Piña massages her bicep. "Piña heard you down at the cops."

"I had a little problem."

"No. A little problem's when you gotta go in for a melanoma treatment and there's no one around to watch your shit. Or you come down with AIDS and gotta pay a fuckload for black market drugs. When you gotta deal with the cops, that's more than a little problem."

"I had a big problem."

"You're learning. Some guy got popped, right?"

"Yeah."

"Who?"

"A friend."

"Drag." She flicks ashes. "Need some FREEze to get you through the day?"

"No."

"Some meth? Ganja? Girl to keep you warm?"

"I'm all right."

"Bong Bong try any shit? Piña hates that motherfucker. Always trying to slice in on her action."

"Does he?"

"Sometimes." She blows on her nicotine ash, watches it glow. "Since Bong Bong started bizzing with the yakuza, you want to connect with Japan, you gotta go through him."

"How much business is the yakuza involved in?"

"Lots."

"Who do they work with?"

Piña flutters her hand as if she just touched something hot. "Shit. They're into everything. It's not like there's a difference between the yakuza and Japanese gov. They're doing the same shit. Running factories, cutting down trees, shipping whores back and forth, organ trading."

"Organ trading, as in musical instruments?"

"Yeah, right."

Medical technology lags when it comes to transplants. So many variables: chemical, biological, mathematical, that artificial organs require significantly more maintenance— something that doesn't sit well with a society addicted to fast food, instant cash, and home shopping. "People make a living selling their own body parts? Sounds like a short career."

"Sell an organ, you don't have to work no more. No jobs anyway, so you gotta do what you gotta do. Practically Luzonia's only export."

"How else can you get organs? From corpses?"

"That too."

That explains the zipper marks and scars on the corpses at the police station. Aslam's missing eyes, too, as if True can't rely on Aslam as a witness to help solve his own murder. Bong Bong must be doing a thriving business. Between cancer and debilitating illnesses caused by pollution and pesticides creating demand, and Bong Bong's world of torture creating supply, it's an almost perfect model of capitalism.

True back on track. "What do the Japanese get from Bong Bong, besides unfettered access to delicacies like pancreas, alveoli, and islets of Langerhans?"

"Huh?"

"Why do the Js need Bong Bong?"

"Bong Bong keeps the factories open. Keeps order. You know how the Js love order. They fucking live for it. You ever hear of any strikes here?"

"No."

"Bong Bong tells them what's going down."

"Kind of like an outpost."

"Yeah, kind of."

True takes a long swallow of coffee. "How does Piña know Bong Bong's working with the Js?"

"Like she knows everything. The word."

The word on the street. A strictly low-tech response to the preponderance of high-tech. True may be able to float through reams and RAMS of data, access billions of bytes of information, and hold virtual statistics in his hot little hand, but Piña can surpass all of that by checking with her contacts.

"What else does Piña know?"

She cups her hands behind her neck and makes her biceps dance. "The Js're also bizzing with the ethnics. Word is, they gonna help the ethnics end the insurgency."

True didn't know this, but now that he thinks about it, it makes sense. Right after Luzonia's independence, Japan promised all sorts of aid packages. Now, if Piña's to be believed, Japan's government and the yakuza are throwing their weight behind the small ethnic enclaves. By supporting instability, they promote Japanese power in the region.

"Why would the Js end the insurgency? And how? They don't have an army."

"Why's easy. Some fucking Japanese tire company came out with a new tread design, and I shit you not, it spelled out *Allah*. Can you believe that? You peal out in your car and leave the mark of God. This pissed off some insurgency commandos, who started fucking with some J holdings here. You know how J corps stick together—wound up real tight—so they got together and started stoking the ethnics."

"With what?"

She lowers her voice. "You won't believe this. Piña heard the insurgency almost wiped out because of the Js."

"What?" News to True.

"In one battle."

"How?"

"Some new weapon. The insurgents had like ten times as many soldiers."

"What kind of weapon?"

Piña shrugs and True watches her deltoids dimple. "Fuck knows. All Piña knows is the insurgents are here one day, almost gone the next. If it's true it's some serious, serious shit. That means there's a technology window, a gap some corporation could step into, then nab control of the Global Fortune 1000. That'd be bad for bizzing everywhere. Bad for the black market. Bad for Piña."

"You know any insurgents I could talk to?"

"Don't last in town here, you know? Your friend was of the faith, no?"

"Yeah. What else did Piña hear about the murder?"

"Had to be an outside job. DNA bomb, right? Piña'd know if somebody local had one. If you want, though, she can check around town, do some four-one-one action."

"Thanks."

Piña spins, tears down a Jackpot card. "Try your luck."

"I don't play."

"Come on. Somebody's gotta win."

True taps on the card twice and watches the wheels inside the slot machine: *gram* spin, a jack, a queen, a king—True holds his breath—an ace. But then the last card is a three. A loser. "Been that kind of day." True waves his card through her ADC machine.

She plugs in her standard info fee. "Jackpot's on the house." She squints into his face. "You look like shit. Want a ride home?"

"It's not far."

"Piña will drive."

She grabs a skateboard propped up in the corner and pushes herself along with her hands. At a cybersex game she stops to jam her thumb into the key lock. The game shuts down and a breathless woman, a smile smeared on her face, emerges. Piña indicates the bar with her thumb and the games-woman stumbles over. True follows Piña out of the arcade.

"Get on." She points to the glitter-sprinkled board, which is measeled with stickers advertising batteries, tires, sex toys.

"On this thing? Where?"

"Behind Piña, asshole."

She plants his hands on her shoulders. He can feel her muscles work to pull them through the mall, straining at the extra weight. Wonders why she doesn't buy an electric board, or simply hire a chauffeur; suspects the answer is that Piña takes pride in doing things on her own. She slides them through a side exit and onto the sidewalk, bellows a warning at which people scatter, then jumps the curb. True struggles to stay upright. She cuts off an electric limo and grabs the bumper of an ancient gas guzzler with a grapple hook.

Grappling is ubiquitous in Luzonia, endorsed by a government intent on conserving energy but without the means to convert from gas to solar-powered cars. At all hours Nerula's streets are crisscrossed with elastic cords connecting auto and truck to skateboarder, in-line skater, bicyclist. Weaving through traffic, Piña maneuvers over gravel, around pot holes and roadkill. When the car pulls them into the left lane, Piña springs them free and they're thrown toward a jeepney. She latches on and they roll down the boulevard.

Piña shouts back to True. "This jeepney isn't right. Piña wants the 707"—a city bus.

True hangs on as Piña swerves around a gravelly section of road. Poking up through the smog are twin 10-story towers. Almost home. Piña reels them close to the 707, the bus so laden with people hanging out of doors and windows it lists drunkenly. True can see how worn the tires are, how worn out the riders look. How soon will it be before the bus topples over? If not from weight, from sorrow?

One last burst of speed and Piña releases the grapple hook. They coast down a narrow stretch, past the edge of the shanties and into a one-way tunnel, through the echoing darkness to True's apartment complex, where she leans hard left and they skid to a halt. True's building is constructed in prefabricated mall-like architecture motif—the foreigners' ghetto. But since few *guarangs* call Luzonia home, True lives in relative isolation.

True, his eyes watery from leaded exhaust, steps off the board. "Thanks for the ride." Wobbles slightly.

Piña grins until she notices a boy slumbering in a doorway a few steps away. "Fuck. He thinks he's going to earn money sleeping off the FREEze?"

"One of Piña's boys?"

"He's one of Piña's. He gets fucked up, now he doesn't

want to work. That little bitchy boy wouldn't be doing shit if it wasn't for Piña."

Or wouldn't be whoring for her if she didn't pump him full of drugs. But life, True decides, is full of these cycles of dependency. Piña depends on the boy. The boy depends on Piña. True depends on Piña who depends on the boy who depends on Piña. But Piña doesn't depend on True. That's one way the cycle is broken. And it worries him.

"Tell me if Piña finds out more. I want to know what happened to my friend."

"Yeah, yeah. Listen. Word don't like insurgents, so don't wait up for me, daddy."

True walks into the lobby. Looking through the window, he sees Piña beat the boy, but can't hear anything through the thick glass. But he can see the boy crying, curled up on the ground, trying to protect his face from her blows. She burns him with a cigarette.

True's in his apartment, studying the piece of Aslam's collar and the bloodstained coins. He uses scissors to cut out his pocket, stuffs the whole mess into a plastic bag, scribbles a note, puts it all into an airfreight envelope and calls a courier. Then he checks into the bomb information Bong Bong sold him. Gubbish. Well, Bong Bong *did* call them "bums." True fingers Aslam's debit card, which he'd palmed before the police arrived. As soon as Aslam's death is logged—and that depends on Bong Bong's efficiency—all transactions would be voided retroactively. Then Bong Bong would piss ammonia, maybe bust a kidney. But he'd just scare up a replacement anyway, maybe one of True's.

He pulls up Aslam's dossier. Nothing regarding his latest job, just his life as an insurgent and Pakistani military officer, college transcript, credit rating, the usual personal data; no links to defense contractors. As if Aslam had started a new life but hadn't told anyone. He expands his search. Nothing. True codes his wrist-top to link with his computer and plays back the explosion, trying to isolate the missile on screen. He replays the section, watches Aslam's eyes round in terror. Slows the scene down. The missile shoots through the air, under a parked car, over a street stall, through a vendor's legs. True freezes it. He orders the computer to identify the weapon based on aerodynamic tendencies, velocity, size, suspected outer-shell materials, but the computer keeps repeating *Insufficient Information.*

He lets the video play out again, sees Aslam pull the young girl down with him, and at the point of impact, True instructs his computer to ID the type of explosion. The missile struck Aslam and the girl simultaneously, and as the blast grows into a fiery sunflower, the computer flashes: *Compressed TNT. Genetic-seeking guidance system. Manufacturer unknown.*

The sight of Aslam and the girl breaking apart makes True uneasy. He paces, summons his courage, and gets back to it. *List possible manufacturers.*

The computer lists corporations with the know-how to manufacture a weapon of such complexity. 47, blinking at screen's bottom.

True drums on the side of his keyboard. Then an idea. The computer is listing corporations with access to the technology. This technology—specifically, genetic identification—could have other uses: *Delete all corporations that do not engage in weapons manufacture.*

Twelve corporations are erased; now *35-35-35-35*. "A lot of help that was." He types: *Missile guidance must be programmed with DNA of victim?*

The computer responds, *Correct.*

Access DNA sequence of victim, Aslam Qadar Aziz.

Victim's DNA not listed in standard medical records.

How did they access Aslam's DNA? Types: *Expand search to all known data banks regarding victim's DNA sequence.*

The computer covers trillions of files in seconds. Burps an answer: *No reference to victim's DNA sequence in any accessible data bank.*

Is it possible his new company erased all references of his DNA sequence? But that means Aslam lap-linked with one powerful corporation. So how, then, did the murderer learn his genetic code sequence? True tries a new tack.

Is missile a new type of technology?

Affirmative.

He doesn't know where to go from here. Takes a stab. *Is this weapon manufactured by a Japanese defense contractor?*

Insufficient information.

The whole thing could have been an accident. Or maybe someone wanted to kill the girl; although why waste expensive tech on a job like that... unless someone's debugging it, perhaps.

Judging from present data, is it possible victim's death was accidental?

Insufficient information.

Could missile have struck incorrect target?

Unlikely.

The more likely explanation is Aslam was the target. True zooms in on the figure of the girl and runs an ID check, but there's no sight of her anywhere in the datasphere. He himself headed to 24-7 before going to Piña's arcade to find traces of her DNA, but it was already washed away by a thrust of late-morning rain. His intercom blisters. True lets in an expressmail courier and hands him the envelope and his ADC. The courier debits the cost of expressmail and True adds a healthy tip. Figures on a day to get to New York; after that, a relatively simple analysis—two days max before he hears.

True checks his online messages. There are a dozen, all from WWTV's local anchor—and his boss—Rush Gelding. True deletes the messages sight unseen.

The sound of the telelink. True picks up, knowing who.

"About freaking time. The reason the company gives you a wrist-top is so I can communicate with you when I need to. Why didn't you tell me you were meeting a Muslim? I mean, Ailey, an insurgent? Nobody told you they don't like insurgents here?"

"Aren't you going to ask how I am?"

"You're in shit up to your neck. Check out the local news, you're on it. The network's not going to like this."

"Thanks for asking."

"I won't let you fuck up my career like you did yours. I had the editorial board e-post your in-house dossier. I didn't know you were some weird beaker baby, hatched à la carte from some DNA mail-order catalog. Nobody told me what a troublemaker you are, either. Sure you got results, some awards, some solid scoop action. Back when, though. You haven't made the adjustment to the new corporate order. *And* you're old. Fuck up again and after I'm through, the only media-related work you'll get will be as a DJ at a Singaporean wedding."

"I'll be OK after a night's sleep."

"We need to talk. Now."

"About?"

"What do you think?"

"I need to sleep. Goodbye, Rush."

"Ailey. I mean—"

True flicks off the telelink and Rush is sucked from sight. He doesn't fear his boss's pungent mood of late. Before True arrived in Luzonia, Aslam canceled an exclusive interview with Rush. Aslam's excuse was he didn't like the promos. Perhaps he was merely twisting an old Arab maxim: *The enemy of my friend is my enemy.* But cancellation after a blitz of promos is one mondo media sin. It's been sagging Rush's career since. The network declined to renegotiate his contract. Plans for a *Talk to Rush* show were buried. And he's not getting the perks he did when he was WWTV's rising star.

Couch-relaxed, True pulls up the news menu. He's already programmed his system to provide unedited coverage, doesn't opt for pasteurized news. Even so, he's asked to choose between news with varying levels of reported violence, news that leans heavily on the sensational or sexy, with or without sports, international, business. True's fingers skitter over the remote. Fast-forwards through the first few local stories for foreign residents on the government-sponsored TV network. A woman in revolutionary khakis, surrounded by an unfocused backdrop of Nerula at night, reads. All those iron monuments dedicated to revolution, ethnic cleansing, the peace treaties du jour. Practically every time he turns on the local news there's a segment on ribbon-cutting at a new monument.

He slices through the commercials for ceiling fans (*the latest technology*), solar-powered air conditioners (*a new approach* in air-con technology), software (technology answering your needs), car alarms (protecting your investment in technology), impregnable locks (technology protecting your investment), weapons (the latest, greatest technology), and betel nut (tradition takes on technology and wins the battle for your pleasure).

Finally, Bong Bong's spiky face. True backs up slightly, turns up the sound.

"Aslam Aziz, a Muslim insurgent, was"—Bong Bong makes a throat-slitting noise while running a finger across his Adam's apple—"trying the escape. He try to pass the secrets of an American journalist, but we are too smart." Taps his temple, scrunches up his forehead as if thought physically taxes him. "We make instigation of relationship between this Aziz and"—he reads from the oil-stained buffalo burger wrapper—"True Ailey. A journalist of WWTV. We think he makes the trouble with Aziz. Start a war or something."

Bong Bong exacting revenge for Aslam's debit card. "Luzonia will not tolerate bad things. Ethnics, Muslims, enemies of the state are not allowed." Bong Bong mugs for the lens, then titters. "Not allowed. Maybe we deport this journalist. Yes, yes, I think a good idea. Or maybe incarcinate him. Put him in the jail."

As True's cheesy passport hologram is flashed under a screaming yellow headline (Enemy of the State), he hears Bong Bong and Pidge's harmonious giggles.

Why is it, True wonders, I can't stay out of trouble?

CHAPTER 4

It's True's belief that the wars that led to the establishment of Luzonia as an independent nation were a result of Mother Nature's wrath. She was tired of being battered by business, her resources robbed, her land raped, her bounty carted off as booty by the earth's only creature outfitted with a thumb. In a fit of pique over global warming she melted the polar ice caps, raised water tables, flooded coasts, submerged low-lying areas, suffocated crops, washed away cities and towns without a trace, drowned people, animals, and insects. Cities like New York and Tokyo exist precariously, a single disaster from extinction. Other lands, other peoples—Bangladesh, Sri Lanka—accepted their fates stoically, fading into the blue. Land stripped of trees became stripped of soil, which washed down mountainsides, rubbing away more soil, leaving hillsides bare. Rainclouds floating over nouveau-desert land couldn't replenish.

Man-made flooding. Man-made drought. Man-made wars. Man-made natural disasters. Because of man-made materialism.

But, as in a marriage that turns sour when one partner cannot tolerate the other's abuse, the earth turned on them. She spat out the man-made toxins that trickled into her, poisoning those who poisoned her; convulsed whenever faced with greater man-made contamination, grinding man-made cities to powder; offered sanctuary to a new array of insects, impregnable to man-made pesticides.

Luzonia's tale is set before a similar backdrop. Before sun and cold fusion stoked the global industrial juggernaut, the Nihon Oil Company set up exploratory rigs in the peninsula's largely uncharted interior, where the Tembuocs, a primitive coastal tribe, lived off and with the land. Noise from the rigs drove the fish from shore and the animals into the interior. At first the Tembuocs sabotaged the rigs, but the company immediately repaired them. A few skirmishes later, the company's representative agreed to restitution: $61—plus free sneakers for all. The company guaranteed the animals and fish would be brought back through the miracle of modern technology. The company would spare no expense, would contact the greatest scientific minds, gain access to the most dazzling technology, airlift prey in by the kiloton if need be.

Now, the Tembuocs, thanks to their satellite dish, knew of the power of Western technology, of wrist-tops and Rice Krispies, hydrogen cars, microzap ovens, massively multiplayer games, and splendor. The Tembuocs were convinced bringing the animals back would be simple. Besides, they wanted those sneakers.

The Tembuocs waited for their prey's return well beyond the point their shoes were shredded. With starvation clawing and their restitution dwindling to mere copper coins, they lashed out. At the same time Muslims were fleeing flood waters in the north, Catholics in the south were dodging drought. Trees were hacked down for settlements. The degrading environment led to trespassing on tribal land. The Tembuocs attacked: a massacre at a Catholic settlement, a rampage through a Muslim town, leading to swift and bloody reprisals. The Muslims turned to Arab countries for arms, the Catholics to Europe, and other tribes suffering from encroachment by the so-called environmental refugees joined the fight. Soon, calls for separate homelands. Peace initiatives were proposed by the U.N. More arms streamed in.

The result: another post-millennium land cracked into tiny ethnic and cultural granules.

Bzzz bz bz bzzz bzzz. Bzz bzz.

True wakes, his face caked with sleep. Beads of sunlight fleck the room, filter through pinholes and rips in his curtains as if they can't wait to prod him awake. True groans. *What time is it?* Seems like he slipped into dreamland moments before.

He rolls off his futon and pulls on stale pants and a shirt. Puts them on as he goes to squelch the sound. Looks through the hallway monitor and opens the door. "What are you doing here, Rush?"

Rush ducks under True's arm. "I've never seen your place before." Rush, to True, is little more than a human replica. Plastic pectorals, silicon calf inserts, synthetic biceps, plaster of paris shoulders. The skin on his face is tightened twice a year, pasted with color-inhibitors to produce a glowing visage. His teeth are perfect, white; his gums rosy. And when he turns his head, his whole body moves with it. Literally a sculpted physique.

True rarely meets Rush in person since most of their business is conducted via telelink. It's disconcerting to see Rush without artifice. Without a backdrop, he's less self-assured, less real than his TV persona. His eye and skin are lightly blemished, lacking broadcast allure.

Rush looks around, notes the dirty plates slopped by the sink, the unmade futon, clothes strewn-about. "This is a dump. Strictly old tech, Ailey. Mine's much bigger. New too. Even got a Jacuzzi. You should move to my side of the complex. Lots of empty apartments. Cheap, too."

True doesn't tell him the reason he lives here is because Rush lives there. Closes the door.

"It's after ten. What are you doing in bed? Don't you have work to do?" Rush doesn't wait for a response before gravitating to the home entertainment center. "Look at this dinosaur. Must be three, four years old."

"It came with the place."

"Yeah, but that doesn't mean you can't upgrade. Like total sheesh-kay-bob. Stick a fork in it, it's done. You should compost this puppy. Mine's got twice, three times the megs. I bet there's a lot of software you can't run."

"Undoubtedly."

Since there's no couch, Rush sits on the edge of True's futon. "I just came from a meeting with Bong Bong. Did you know he doesn't like you?"

"I had an inkling."

"Usually when he's not happy with our coverage, he gives me the old applesauce enema. You know, lets me know he's not happy but doesn't threaten to kill off my manhood. But this time he reamed me. Said if I couldn't control you, he'd do it for me. And he didn't forget to mention that neither you nor me would—is it me, or I?"

"I."

"I would enjoy it. I mean, what the hell is this about you meeting up with a Muslim at 24-7? I was here two years before you got here, and Bong Bong and I got along just swimmingly. No problemas amigo. Now you get here and undermine everything I accomplished."

"What did you accomplish?" True really wants to know.

"I get along with the locals. I don't make waves, they don't cause me trouble. It's a healthy relationship, and I won't have you messing it up."

"Spoken like a true reporter."

"A true reporter gets ratings. This is now, and today's motto for the press is cooperation."

"Maybe you mean the motto is *corporation*."

"Shut up, Ailey. *Cooperation*. I know what I'm saying. Either you work with me, or you're out of here. Cooperate or you don't operate."

"Catchy."

"Look, Ailey, I've come here to tell you, nobody knows more than me what a journo stud you used to be. You were my hero, the way you, uh, you know, all that great stuff you did. But you're slacking now, and on my beat that's not copacetic." Rush picks at his cuticles. "I don't know what happened with you in New York. Heard you went mental. Got a new hard drive installed. But that doesn't mean you shouldn't do your job."

True thinks of electric snow.

Rush rages on. "Got to tell you. I was not looking forward to you coming over here. Told the home office same-same. I could do more with someone young, hungry. But they sent you. Either you upgrade your job performance or I'm aborting you." Rush stands, ankles crossed. True's seen him do the same thing on a newscast—*canned concern*, he calls it. Luzonians think it's a sign of decreased fertility. "So, you histoire or you going to get real?"

True shrugs. "Real enough."

"Your dossier says you were born in a test tube."

Not exactly a test tube, but True was more planned than born, one of the first to spring from a movement of retirees opting for parenthood past 50. The stigma follows him like a misbehaving shadow. True's parents ordered him (piece by piece, code by code) from a DNA catalog, scanned electropages for donors with primo characteristics, paid a lab in Italy to mix and match until an embryo was produced and left to grow in an incubator until developed enough to post home.

What they ended up with was something, or someone, far different. A random access, but this did not stop American red-bloodeds from torturing True throughout his childhood, blaming him for... what? he wonders. Their shortcomings? True's shortcomings? Society's?

Rush rushes on. "What's it like, growing up a beaker baby?"

True looks out the window to the yellowing sky. Briefly wonders how he can clean the windows, then realizes they are clean. It's the pollution. True recites: "*In the Bottling Room all was harmonious bustle and ordered activity. Whizz and then, click! the lift-hatches flew open; the bottle-liner had only to reach out a hand, take the flap, insert, smooth-side down, and before the lined bottle had had time to travel out of reach along the endless band, whizz, click! another flap of peritoneum had shot up from the depths.*"

Rush asks, "What's that?"

"Huxley. *Brave New World.*"

"A book?"

"A book."

"Thought so. Sounds old. When did you memorize that?"

"Seems like I've always known it."

Skeeeee! True's console alarm. The message, from WWTV: a news emergency in Japan. He tunes in to hear a woman he recognizes as Reiner Jacobi, one of WWTV's top news anchors, as she heli-floats over Tokyo. The viewing audience is offered flattened neighborhoods, bodies strewn in wreckage, fires screaming toward the heart of the city.

"...at five fifty-five this afternoon a massive earthquake struck Tokyo, a city with fifty million people living within a hundred-mile radius." Reiner has to shout over the rotor's soft *rat-a-tat-tat.* "Information is sketchy, but already estimates put the number dead at more than one million and climbing. Millions more, it's impossible to say just yet, are homeless. Hospitals report massive casualties. Whole sections have been destroyed."

Reiner soars over the damaged shoreline as a tidal wave smacks the shore, further decimating Japan's capital. With a telestrater, she replays the tidal wave, again as a reverse-angle replay. The helicam pans the cockpit, shows Reiner, a pilot, and a large black Labrador, barking and panting. Reiner shoves a biscuit into the dog's mouth. The shore is shredded, coastal buildings hammered into chunks and washed out to sea along with cars, couches, futons, clothes. True feels he's a voyeur, peeping into lives he has no right peeping into. The screen breaks into grids displaying different close-up views of the damage.

Rush's murmurings. "Wish I was there. Reiner's one lucky bitch."

True's fascinated by nature's wrath, knows he'll face his sadness later, in private. For now it's reporter-mode. He switches off most of the grid sequences and enlarges a shot of the downtown business district, which is relatively untouched, built as it is on solid rock. People stream into the area, awaiting guidance, searching for refuge from the inevitable aftershocks. True pulls up the next option: bed towns, the suburban towns that serve as home to salarymen and their families, a two-, three-hour commute from their jobs on packed trains and buses, have been eradicated as well.

Reiner ends her report by focusing beyond the crumbling embers of what was one of the great cities, beyond the skyline to the sun, the color of the inside of a roasted sweet potato, taunting the city by dripping below the horizon. The Rising Sun is setting.

A request for more options: *Repeat telecast? More news from around the globe? Local news? Sports? Weather?* True buttons it closed and the earthquake is tucked from sight.

Rush speaks first. "I hope they call me to Tokyo. That could really help me upgrade my career. Great anchors get their breaks covering wars and disasters."

True focuses on the here and now. "There's a lot we can do here."

"Like what?"

"Many J-corps have set up shop here, so there are bound to be refugees. We can interview them, especially given the context."

"What context?"

"The bad blood that exists between the governments of Luzonia and Japan, since Japan is supporting some of the ethnic groups fighting for independence."

"I didn't know that."

"These refugees will be bringing stories of their escape. Victim profiles make for interesting viewing and solid ratings."

"I'm glad you're getting the idea how we do things at the new WWTV."

"And you know what else? After a major ecological disaster, what happens next?"

"What?"

"Rebuilding."

"So?"

"There will be tremendous incentive to begin construction in Tokyo, which means great demand for labor. With imported workers come prostitution and a thriving black market."

"How do you know all this?"

"Check your history. And where do you think many of these prostitutes will come from?"

Rush furrows. "Luzonia?"

"Luzonia."

"Ailey, you're showing me something. Maybe you haven't used up all your processors, after all. What's the plan?"

"We find out where the refugees are and interview them. Human interest stuff, too. Tap into the black market here and see how they plan to play in Tokyo."

"Do it. Lots of pain and suffering. Find an outbreak of cholera or plague, too, if you can. You know, the usual ratings grabbers." Rush slides through the door. "Ratings call."

CHAPTER 5

Outside a makeshift refugee camp at the Nerula's port. Black marketeers have vined wood and plastic together for makeshift electric currency conversion booths. To express its displeasure over Japan's support of autonomous ethnic regions, Luzonia's Parliament banned yen. Currency pirates extort the nouveau-refugees, proffering ridiculous rates for the conversion of yen into Luzonian currency into American electric dollars, tacking on a 50 percent surcharge; or they trade wads of Luzonian toilet paper money for Japanese heirlooms, electronics, jewelry, liquor. And with each stolen minute, the rates change; Luzonia suffers such severe hyperinflation that traders have to weigh the money. This day, 800 grams of Luzonian 100-peseta paper notes fetches one electric dollar. In an hour or two, a greenback could bring as much as a kilogram.

True lolls to a section squeezed by scriggly wire. Through fence coils he sees luggage—suitcases, plastic bags, cloth coats tied up to hold the salvageable—and next to that are heaps of foreign aid: sacks of Indonesian dried noodles; Polish canned hams; squeeze bottles of Vietnamese fermented fish sauce; corn; wheat; boxes of stale pancake mix. Food no one wants. It's True's experience that food passed off as foreign aid usually couldn't pass muster as pet food. He aims his wrist-top at the pile and his Geiger counter squirts off the scale. Enough ambient radiation to power a space launch.

Not looking, True bumps into Maxi Khoompootla, anchor of *Aussie Beat*, a popular TV tabloid show, at the press entrance.

"G'day, mate. *GDAYGDAY* you here, too?" Maxi mock-salutes True.

It usually takes True a moment to adapt to Maxi's heavily accented English. He's broad, hulking, with a beard framing a face frozen in perpetual sneer—as if, True thinks, he's about to sneeze. Claims he originates from the outback, but True knows he's Sydney born and bred. "What, miss this?" True says.

They flash press passes at a rheumy guard, who sits in the sun with his feet up on a plastic table, and cross inside.

"*GDAYGDAY* downtown with the coppers. Trouble, Ailey?" Maxi once told him he refuses to call any journalist "True."

"Yes and no."

"Could be worse."

"How so?"

"You could bloody well be Japanese. Say, Ailey, look at these." Maxi taps wrist-top keys, and a 3-D hologram of backdrops mushrooms into view. Parodies of Luzonian monuments. The statue commemorating the ethnic cleansing of Nerula sporting a decal: Sudzy—a popular Aussie detergent.

Nerula's Revolutionary hero doing the hula. Liberty, the country's dog mascot, proudly flexing—if, True thinks, that's the right word—an erection. Maxi elbows his ribs. "Phony backdrops for all occasions." Maxi zips up his screen, the backdrops zapped to infinity. "Time to have meself a Captain Cook. Ratings call, mate."

"Right."

Maxi's words echo off wood- and urine-colored sea. "Good afternoon, ladies and gents. I know you've suffered, you're scared, and all that, so let's not waste your time or mine, shall we? Anybody here been raped or tortured? Speak up now, you get an exclusive." No answer, so he says to True, "They'll be here a while. Gonna check out the UND camp first. Need some updated footage. Wanna come?"

UND: undesirables. Besides taking in garbage from other nations, for a price, Luzonia accepts UNDS, locking them away in camps like these, lets them claw and kill one another. A nation within a nation. Drug addicts, political prisoners, rapists, child molesters. Garbage and undesirables make up a significant percentage of the nation's GDP.

"No. I've got things to do here." Besides, at Rush's behest, True came by a few weeks before, gathered enough UND footage to get them through "Sweeps Week" times three.

True turns his attention to the Japanese refugee camp, a hastily assembled plot of land and dock reclaimed from the sea with Japanese technology. Notices an old man, alone, lying on the dock, his head propped on a small bag. He sees True, motions for him. Approaching, True reads the motto stitched on the bag: *Tomorrow's Fashion Today.*

"*Mizu onegaishimasu.*" The man whispers while True kneels.

True turns on his wrist-top, accesses the Japanese translation program while surreptitiously filming. He says, "What did you ask?" and the old man watches Japanese characters dance before his eyes. If the man couldn't read, True could change the program to repeat whatever English sentence he utters in Japanese, but this often leads to an uncomfortable, confusing, time lag.

The words *I asked for water, please,* float before True's eyes, accompanying the Japanese babble. True gives him a squeeze bottle.

Reporter? The man has a tear-shaped face and coin-slot eyes.

"Yes."

He licks his lips. *Tell them it was bad, very bad. My wife is dead. My children, I do not know where they are.*

"How were you able to survive?" True hopes the man can pick up on his gentle tone.

Tears soak into the dock's hot wood. *It was late afternoon. I was shopping for my wife, who has been ill. As I was preparing to enter my home there was a tremendous sound. The ground shook and large cracks in the earth opened up nearby. There was a terrible explosion. Someone had left gas on and immediately other houses caught fire. I don't know how long it lasted. When it was over, I saw my home collapsed. My wife was inside.*

He sobs. True places a comforting hand on his shoulder, knows that although he can erase his presence from the footage later, he can't erase the man's sorrow. When the man calms, he says, *I have lived through many earthquakes and tremors. I have been awakened by a grumbling floor, shaking my futon like an electric massage. But I have never experienced such an earthquake before. My wife, my house, they're gone.*

The man shudders again. True asks his name.

Endo, he says, sniffling. *Hiroyuki Endo.*

"Mr. Endo, soon you'll be able to return to your home. And Japan will be rebuilt. Your country has always rebounded from adversity. After Admiral Perry, after World War Two, after the Tohoku tsunami—"

Deep sobs. *No. No. It will not be possible. I sold my land so I might have money to survive here, but these Luzonians are cruel. They do not accept electric yen. They make us pay two commissions. Now I can never return to my home.*

"Why did you sell your land?"

There was no way I could go west from Tokyo. Only people with relatives had anywhere to go.

"Who bought your land?"

I don't know. At the airport, a man offered me money. My house and property was split in half. I saw it with mayonnaise. What else could I do?

"Mayonnaise?"

Mayonnaise. He says this with conviction. *And I trust mayonnaise.*

A software glitch. It's happened before. True plugs "mayonnaise" into the dictionary and the Anglicized phonetic "my own eyes" pops up.

He offered cash. I had no choice. Bank records were wiped out. I knew that to survive, I would need money.

"How much did he pay?"

I received very little, a fraction of its value just yesterday. Now the land is ruined. Endo shakes. True mops his forehead with his shirt tail. *You know, I was an insurance claims adjuster.*

"Yes?"

That is so. I know a few things. I know the insurance industry can survive such destruction, since so little of Tokyo was insured. But I would not wish to be American or European now.

"Japanese foreign assets will flow back to Japan?"

Perhaps it was irresponsible to place Japan's capital on four fault plates.

"And the majority of the vast majority of the nation's wealth as well."

Yes. The man slips into heaves, covers his eyes with his arm.

"Great, mate, ya got him to cry." Maxi's filming the scene. "I owe you one." Later, True knows, Maxi will erase him from the scene and frame the old man alone, wallowing in sadness. Probably patch in his own questions as well. True wonders why Maxi bothers to film at all when he can fabricate any footage he wants.

True interviews other refugees—salarymen and their families, young Japanese *cyberjinrui* and *otaku*, the latest generation of cyberjunkies, elderly, hunched-over women called *obaasans*—takes some standard background footage, edits it on his wrist-top, and files it with Rush.

Rush is a domino-sized cube lodged in True's screen. "I got the footage. But I have a collagen appointment. I'll look it over later."

"Whatever."

"Hey, Ailey. You think we need a hacker?"

A question without a context. "Why?"

"Reiner got the network to sign on for one. A guy with a mix of numbers and letters in his name. She gets one, I think I should too. Got to run."

Numbers and letters? Could be True knows WWTV's most recent acquisition. The electric datasphere is indeed an intimate place.

Back in Bar 24-7, True's shouting through barbed wire at the club's bartender while filming the bizotic events on stage.

"About yea high." True's holding his hand chest high. "Eleven years old, maybe. Squatter kid."

The bartender's response is drowned out by the crowd, an emcee shouting, "She is beautiful, yes? Young. Drug, disease free."

The center of attention is a pre-teen girl with hair hanging to her tailbone, standing sadly amid the hubbub. She wears a yellow floral-print dress, hoop earrings, and her face is smeared with makeup: deeply rouged cheeks, thickly painted lips, nails bright red. Tears well in her eyes, adding to her vulnerability, and, True assumes, her price. He turns his attention back to the bartender. "I couldn't hear you."

"I have not seen her."

"Know anyone who might know?" True slides a sheath of money through the cage vent.

The bartender, eyes holding True, covers the bills with his hand, reels them in, counts them and shrugs. "If you have the money you can have any woman. They're all the same, if you ask me."

On stage the emcee fans his face with the girl's skirt. "Look! No hair. Fresh, young. Tits like buds on trees." Holds up a piece of paper. "A doctor's report. She's a certified virgin. See?"

"Three thousand!"

"Four thousand!"

"Four thousand five hundred!"

True forks over more bills.

"Wait." The bartender confers with a bouncer with knuckles of calloused corduroy. A kickboxer, a necessary prerequisite for Nerulan bouncers. Just in case there's a cache of weapons nearby.

Applause and table-thumps. The price is escalating. Virgins are at a premium.

The emcee shrieks, "Ten thousand. Do I hear ten thousand?"

A chainsaw buzz. But no bid.

The girl tries to run, is slapped by a thick matron, who forces her into modeling positions. The girl shrieks, kicks. And the men laugh in that way that men who go to whores do. So does the bartender.

"Where's her mother?" True asks.

The bartender's smile carved in wood. "Her mother is with her. There." Points to the stage. The matron.

"Ten thousand! I bid ten thousand!" A tourist with a physique that reminds True of gnocchi—sticky pink skin, pudgy knees.

Over the sound system. "The bid stands at ten thousand. Once ten thousand."

The bartender whistles. "Talk to the Rajput."

"The Raj-what?"

The emcee shouts, "Twice ten thousand."

"The Rajput is a rounder. She knows the ways of the street." Rounder: a hustler.

"Sold for ten thousand! Collect your prize!"

The tourist lumbers to score his winnings.

True asks where he can find the Rajput. The bartender points to the door.

Outside, True sees only one rounder—an Indian woman

wrapped in a sari. She stands beneath a sign radiating waves of red neon. True studies her: black and gray strings of unkempt hair, twisting and tangled in a bun. Her skin is loose around her bones, a size eight epidermis draped over a size six frame.

She hisses. "Pssst. Surveillance Sentry?"

"What?"

"You are searching for Surveillance Sentry?" Her voice is sing-songy, staccato, rising from deep in her throat.

"No. Are you the Rajput?"

She draws coated software cards from the myriad folds and ties of her tattered sari, displays them as a fan. "Maybe you are lonely. If that's the case, let me help." She inches a pink and gold card out of the deck with her thumbs. "With this you can invent the lover of your dreams. And what is more important than being loved? You are limited only by your imagination. It can do *any*thing, any *thing* you want."

"Did you see a shanty girl begging here night before last?"

"Dose on some FREEze, plug in the program, and *life* may even be worth living."

He's out of practice, too easily sidetracked, his interviewing skills rusty. The first order of business is to control the tempo, to be the one asking questions. "She was about eleven years—"

"—you cannot find it anywhere else."

"Find what?"

"This software. It is scarce. Very valuable."

"I don't need it."

"And if I were to lower the price?"

"You haven't given me a price. But whatever it is, I'm not interested."

"Baba," she sighs. "Life is hard. I lost my family, my husband, parents, sisters, brothers, uncles and aunts, cousins, everybody, *yaar*. You know how it is to lose your whole family, to wake up in the night, to see their faces, to hear them talk, but only in dreams? Do you know how empty life is without them?"

Not as empty as life would have been if she'd never known them, True thinks. Or maybe having and losing is worse than never having. For some reason, images of Crick and Watson wind through his mind. But the Rajput's words unsnag him from these thoughts.

"My brother was a parliamentarian. I wonder what he is now. Perhaps a goat. After all, he must bear some responsibility for the war. Or a bull. He *was* a stubborn man." She stops. "At least sample some technology."

An opening. "Answer some questions, then I'll look at what you have."

The Rajput studies him. True waits patiently but feels impatient inside.

"Come." She motions for True to follow. Leads him down the street, her sandals sticking to mud.

"Did you see a little girl, squattering outside night before last?"

The Rajput doesn't look back, calls over her shoulder. "She is now dead, is that correct?"

"Yes, it is."

"Why do you care?"

They pass People Protectors, and True peeks in the window to see lightweight armor plating on hangers, laser and bullet pistols lined up in a wall display, genetic-coded bombs that lock onto a target's DNA, force fields, torture devices, an assassination's hotline, souvenir t-shirts, sneakers. The store, like the bar whose patrons it serves, never closes: grudges, vendettas, and contracts to kill don't always jibe with normal business hours.

True tries again. "Did you talk with her?"

"Yes."

"Was she a regular around here?"

"No. Of that I am sure. I hadn't seen her around this club before. She did so at perilous risk to herself. This area is protected."

"Protected?"

"She was interfering with legitimate beggars who pay to work this territory."

"Like you?"

"Like I."

"Do you think she was killed because of this?"

She walks on, past the crumbling shell of the church. "No." She lowers her voice when an in-line skater, grappled to an electric limo, rolls by. "But I warned her about bizzing here."

"What else did you talk about?"

"I said if she continued to vex these beggars she'd soon be dead. But she wouldn't listen. I heard later she died begging from a filthy Muslim. I would not wish to die in that manner."

"She mention her name?"

"No."

"Where she came from?"

"No."

"Who she was waiting for?"

She shakes her head.

"Where she was staying?"

"No. It didn't come up."

"You don't have any idea how I could reach her family, do you?"

She slips into an open doorway and part way up a set of steps, many of them broken or missing, the wood decayed and decaying, names and curses carved, painted, and penned in myriad tongues, no space untouched.

"No. And if you search the shanties, you may not get out alive." The Rajput stoops to brush away crumbs, mud, dirt, packets of disposable air syringes and empty vials, then sits. True joins her on the stairs.

"Now, it's your turn." She hands True a program card to insert into his wrist-top.

She types in initial commands. In response to the computer's query, *Is this game program in English?* She taps *y*, yes. The computer analyzes the card, and then the screen carries another question: *This program takes up a great amount of memory. Shall I compress your other files to make room?* She pecks another *y*. When the computer requests a password to prevent illicit copying, the woman shields True's eyes with her free hand and punches it in. Five taps.

"I will tell you the code after you buy it." She unblocks True's sight.

"I'm not going to buy it."

"What is your name?"

"True."

"What kind of name is that?"

"The name I was given."

She types it in. "Only someone who could live up to such a name would possess it, or someone who flaunts his dishonesty."

"What's your name?"

"I do not have one anymore."

"What was it before?"

"It does not matter."

"Well, where in India did you come from? Rajasthan?"

"Yes. I was born in Rajasthan and am directly related to

Rajput kings. We were known for our courage. If my ancestors lost a battle and all the men were killed, the women and children would march into a funeral pyre to their death. That is called *jauhar*."

True notices cancer acne on her forehead masked with mud. She'll need money for treatment, a simple technique, but probably prohibitively expensive for her. Without treatment, she has five months to live, seven tops.

"Why did you come to this country, baba? It's laden with miscreants."

"Why did you?"

"I was here on business when the war with Pakistan started." She flicks at one of her sandals with a toe. "Where else could I go? And anyway, this capital city—Nerula—reminds me of a great leader, Nehru. This offers some comfort."

With a flourish she taps a key and moves aside. Immediately, tie-dye mists—orange, purple, turquoise, pink, gold—swirl. Then the opening credits, a list of software researchers, writers, producers, composers, the caterer, copyright date, and a warning that unauthorized copying of the enclosed program is expressly forbidden. Even the pirates are trying to cut down on piracy. A menu appears in front of True under the program name *Building Love*. The first options have to do with historical settings. The categories are *Primitive Womyn/Man, Romyn, Greek, the Middle Ages, the Renaissance, 17th c., 18th c., 19th c., 20th c., 21st c.,* and *the Future*. True points a finger, locks onto the 21st c. Then new listings appear: Ethnicity (*choose 1 or more of the following*, it says). Subheadings are *European extraction, Asian extraction, African extraction*. True chooses Asian and European. Further listings narrow his choices to the relatively simple mix of Japanese and English.

He navigates through the program easily, knowing what he's looking for. For height (in both metric and American measurements), he chooses 5'6", for weight (in kilograms, pounds, or stones), 125 lbs. The waist size he opts for is 26", the chest size 38", probably a little on the big side; but this is, he tells himself, *virtual* reality.

Hair color? Dark brown bordering on black, hair length medium, ending at the shoulders. Eyes more green than brown. Skin tone: *Sticky Olive Oil Fashion*, which he loved in contrast to his own whole wheat toast hue.

A woman's naked figure appears, slowly rotating so he's able to get a full circular view. Slightly slanted eyes of green and brown, shoulder-length brown hair, rounded breasts, a taut abdomen. True checks the further options catalog, widens the space between the breasts two, three, four percent, shrinks the nipples, lightens them from brown to brick red. He further tightens the figure's abs, darkens its skin tone. Also widens the shoulders, rounds the rear. The hair is wrong—too shiny and straight—so he adds flaws, some split ends, a matte finish, an almost invisible streak of red in each strand.

Satisfied thus, True goes to work on the face, first adding some strategically placed freckles and choosing a nice aristocratic nose with the touch of a flare. Next come eyebrows, ears, the strong hands and slender fingers, wide feet, angular toes.

He stops to rest. It's her. Or just about. Goes back and waves his finger at the pubic hair category, chooses to make it fuller; and for the naval he digs an innie. Admires his handiwork, realizes what he's created isn't just as beautiful as what he remembers. It's more beautiful.

The program compliments him on his taste, asks if he'd like to save the figure he's created, store it in the database for convenience. When he indicates yes, it asks for his secret code.

"As I said, unless you purchase the program I cannot tell you the code." The Rajput's voice from outside True's world and inside his head at the same time. "But keep going, there is more of interest, I think, to you."

It's uncanny how perfect it is, how memories of love can be relived with just the sight of her. True moves to attribute a personality to the blank expression (*choose one or more of the following: soft, angelic, happy, perky, flirtatious, masochistic, sultry, nymphomanic, intellectual, bimbo, distant, cold, tough, angry, sadistic, evil—press this space for more options*).

But before he can choose, a whirring noise emanates from his wrist-top; the program locks, lightning bolts of pastel colors frozen vertically in space.

Turning his head, True sees the Rajput through the jagged beams. "What did you do? You broke it."

True hits the escape option. Is returned to the damp hall-way.

She steps toward him. "Now you *must* buy it."

"It's software. It can't break. There must be a program glitch."

Sighing, she yanks the card out of the computer. "Yes. You are correct. I have worked on this many times, but I cannot seem to overcome certain one-offs."

A one-off: that one in a million chance combination that can cause a system to stall, break, crash—like hitting a lottery jackpot, True thinks, or ending up a serial killer's victim.

True rises, produces the stash of dollars he uses to get things done in a country that doesn't have sufficient numbers of automatic debit machines. He hands her a crumpled hand-ful of notes.

She holds out the program card, but he waves it away.

"You're from America?" She tucks away the money and card.

True cocks his head, eyes her thoughtfully, says nothing.

She insists. "You are. I know because American tourists believe in charity."

"You're wrong about one thing."

"You are not an American?"

"I'm not a tourist."

The Rajput's laughs slip into parched coughs that fade as True skips out the door.

CHAPTER 6

True's tired and the weather's all sideways, ocean wind pinning rain clouds against Nerula's surrounding hills. He flags down the first taxi he sees—an old diesel job, more rust than paint. There's a bullet-proof partition separating the driver from the passenger. The taxi looks like True feels. He gets in.

After telling the driver his address, True leans back, rubs bits of foam padding from his pant leg, and watches the city stream by through the window. The driver, a squat woman squeezing a pistol between pudgy thighs, takes the expressway along the river, and True sees the crispy shells of buildings painted with pictures of cartoon-like windows with drawn shades, families sitting around dinner tables, flower pots and plants, ivy winding up the sides, a lone man reclining in an easy chair, reading a book. Swedish foreign aid, a plan to raise commercial property values, accomplished by literally painting over Luzonia's problems.

Packs of shanty children, skin spray-painted over skeletons, are wilding; police chase them with tasers, clubs, and water cannons. The war left a generation of street orphans to fend for themselves, and this they do by forming gangs, stealing and murdering together. Wolf packs, except wolves never prey on their own.

The driver looks back, spitting out her window carefully so as not to spray her passenger. Just that's worth a tip. Past the national broadcast corporation where the day's major stories are neoned as headlines. Today: *Muslim Insurgents Murder 472 Luzonians in Terrorist Attack.* Tomorrow only the number will change. True checks the time, realizes he has to call New York before the lab closes. He types in *Slovo de Bris,* and after the usual run of four or five 15-second advertisements in deadtime, a 3-D image of his friend floats before his eyes.

"Hello, True," de Bris says brusquely, his lab coat starched and stiffly white, his face puffy from constant weight fluctuations. De Bris is in one of his thin phases. When True was just a collection of sperm cells and ovum in a test tube, did he look through the glass and see someone like de Bris?

"How are you, de Bris?"

"You didn't follow proper safety precautions. I opened up your package and was faced with blood and bits of skin and some unbreakable plastic shards. Thanks a lot."

The driver rolls down her window to scream at a grappler. She jiggles the steering wheel, tries to shake the extra weight to conserve fuel.

"Where are you calling from?"

"A taxi."

"I almost had to pass up dinner: a hormone-free roast leg of lamb, homemade mint jelly, organic oven-roasted yams, and, for dessert, a lovely forest berry tart made with pesticide-free fruit. It cost a fortune." De Bris is addicted to food, his seasonal obesity testing his wife's loyalty. Three times a year he has fat cells drained from his body in what True always thought of as a bulimia program for the rich. True wonders what he does with all that leftover lipid. Make soup stock?

"I presume business is, as usual, booming." Since the government moved toward privatization in grand fashion, farming out work to the private sector, de Bris's lab has been thriving. It doesn't hurt that forensics is the fastest growing medical field in the U.S., or that murder and terrorism top the crime stats.

"I have my days." De Bris puffs out his cheeks.

"What were your findings, maestro?"

"Let me pull them up on screen. Can you see?"

"Yeah." As the cab jumps up and down over the rough, potholed street, angular models, enzymes, ions, protons, and chemical formulae air-dance frantically, matching True's wrist movements. "I see them. What do they mean?"

"I found particles of a highly durable material embedded in the traces of skin you supplied that had the same properties as the swatch of material you sent along. I also found powder— TNT powder, which leads me to believe that, at least from the evidence you've supplied thus far, at least two people were struck by an explosive device. I identified two sources of blood, type A and O negative."

"Go on."

"The A blood originated from a male, approximately 35 years old. Blood analysis shows he spent a great deal of time in tropical climates. There were traces of malaria, giardia, bilharzia, and dysentery, along with scads of other Southeast Asian microbes. In fact, the subject was recently exposed to Japanese encephalitis."

"How recently?"

"One and a half, two weeks before he died. I can't be any more precise than that."

"Anything else about the male subject?"

"Well, nothing groundbreaking. What are you looking for?"

"Anything that will help me find out who killed him."

"Well, first, let me tell you about the other subject. A girl, aged ten or eleven, I'd say. She suffered from a cornucopia of illnesses. Her growth was stunted from lack of food, and she carried traces of bubonic plague, dysentery, malaria, elevated white cell count—probably lived near sources of radiation."

"What kind of radiation?"

"Toxic waste would be my guess. Not the same ions as a nuclear plant or blast. I'm afraid running a trace and superimposing pockets of residences on a map of potential toxic waste site areas wouldn't be of much help. I already thought of that."

"Because it's so common. So there's no way of pinpointing where she lived?"

"Not from this evidence."

"Given the medical data, there's no chance they were in contact before the explosion?"

"Probably not. Lots of microbes and afflictions, but from different sources."

"Tell me about the explosion."

"The explosive was your run-of-the-mill but highly effective TNT charge, carried in plastic explosive casing, the type you'd find at construction sites, mines, and in many weapons."

"How would I find the manufacturers of this explosive?"

"I could walk outside my office and pick up enough of this explosive to blow up the White House. Might not be a bad idea either."

"The bomb was carried in a sophisticated missile, guided by software able to key in on a person's DNA. Why equip a sophisticated piece of hardware like that with TNT?"

"For the very reason we're scratching our asses wondering why. Compressed TNT works: It's reliable, so widespread that it's impossible to trace, and cheap."

"What else did you find? Any traces of the missile?"

"Well, the outer shell was probably plastic, but I can't be sure."

True spots crumbs on de Bris's shirt. His weight is going to yo-yo back up again soon. "Why not? Can't you trace plastic?"

"Not in this case. My guess is that it was a type of plastic designed to disintegrate in an explosion."

"Wouldn't that make it unstable?"

"Not unless the targeted DNA makes contact with it."

"What do you mean?" True leans hard into the door as the cab veers left.

"I mean, this device was sophisticated in the sense of guidance system and trigger mechanisms. It wouldn't go off, I assume, unless the DNA it's programmed to come in contact with makes actual contact."

"So in other words, this missile could have collided with a house and wouldn't have gone off."

"Or a car. Or another human, although the guidance system seems to have been sophisticated enough that the missile was able to miss everything except the intended target. I accessed your video file and mapped out its flight path. Smart little fucker. It bobbed and weaved like a heavyweight fighter."

"Or a Luzonian taxi," True says, his head skimming roof. They skid to a pause, stall, then run Nerula's lone traffic light, which nobody heeds anyway. Right of way goes to the biggest vehicle. "You see the missile on screen. Why can't you tell me who made it?"

De Bris scoffs. "Do you think somebody who has the resources and technology to commit a hit like this is going to leave a calling card? The shell doesn't mean shit: It isn't as if you'll find a decal. You can't judge a missile by its cover. As for the flight path, it could have been preprogrammed, could have been fired from twenty feet away or two thousand miles. Best way to avoid getting wiped out by one of these babies is to stay inside a well-fortified bunker. Better yet, don't let anyone in on your DNA sequence."

"No idea as to its range?"

"No."

True looks out the window, watches bruised clouds collide against the mountains. A single drop of rain on the windshield, but no others. "Shit."

"Who bought it?" de Bris asks.

"A friend."

"Tough luck."

"A shanty girl too."

"Even the most sophisticated bomb guidance system doesn't care who gets in the way at the moment it makes contact with the intended DNA sequence. One of them was just in the wrong place at the wrong time."

"That's what I was thinking."

De Bris clears his throat. "Sorry. I hear about tragedies like this every day. You're lucky you're not here in New York. Things have really gone toxic. This morning four corporations boycotted their trial on conducting drug, virtual reality, and psychological experiments on unsuspecting citizens. Some of these people were driven to suicide. Others ended up in psych wards. Ugly shit. But you'd know all about that."

"Thanks, de Bris." A twinge, that's how True would describe it, in addition to his hospital-stay memories. There is something familiar about what de Bris is saying, something that stimulates True's memory neurons, but he can't place it. Isn't sure he wants to know. Says, "You think they'll get away with it?"

Sputtering, de Bris accidently spits on his screen. "Sorry." He rubs away the spittle with his sleeve. "I'm sure these corporate gods will get off. Hell, they'll probably fine the victims. Already affiliated companies are threatening to relocate their operations abroad and take their technology with them, if there's a guilty verdict. The government is divided on whether to prosecute."

"Corps rule. I can imagine the electronic town hall is overloading its circuits with constituents' calls to Congress."

"Mostly in favor of dropping the charges. I mean, fuck! Unemployment is at twenty-five percent. No one wants to see corps pack up and leave. America doesn't need the vote anymore, now that we live in a *corpocracy*."

De Bris falls silent, as if everything that needs to be said has been said.

True says, "Let's get back to the plastic. Have you come across anything like it before?"

"In a murder victim?"

"Anytime. Read anything about it? See it? Experience it?"

"No, not unless—wait—yeah. There's a new microcamera used for diagnostic medical tests. Shoot it into a patient and you get clear pictures of arteries, veins, organs. Kind of like *Fantastic Voyage*."

"And these cameras are made from plastic?"

"Yes. They disintegrate after 24 hours or so."

"Do a lot of companies manufacture this camera?"

"Only one, far as I know. A Japanese firm. I can't recall the name."

True starts. "Can you find out?"

"Hold on a sec."

True watches de Bris type in commands on his console. The taxi slows, squeezing into traffic, then is cut off by a city bus spewing grapplers. The taxi rams into a bicycle rickshaw, running it onto the sidewalk. But then they're stuck in traffic. The driver punches the horn, yelling along with it. Like a sing-along, True thinks. As the car idles, True watches an auto-sprayer painting road lines. Another UN development project: more traffic symbols to be ignored. A dead body lies on the road and the robotic sprayer engulfs it, then flattens it into a pancake with a yellow line bisecting it. No other cars are coming on that side of the street to mush it down, although True doesn't know why.

"Hmmm. I was wrong," de Bris says. "It's an American company: MedTekton. Based here in New York."

True snaps back to attention. "Not one of the corps on trial?"

"No. Nice try."

"Anything else I should know?"

De Bris reflects a moment. "No, except that by the look of it, this missile could have been fired by any number of hostile groups in—what's that capital city again?"

"Nerula."

"Nerula. There are so many damn countries I can't keep track. Fifty years ago, there were 180. Today, more than 250.

Where is Luzonia anyway?"

"Next to Malayanalaya."

"And where the hell is that?"

"Next to Luzonia. They're both young Southeast Asian republics." True's trying to be helpful.

"Well, be careful. I don't relish analyzing your skin cells, DNA, and blood with my lab's computerscope."

The taxi yodels through the tunnel hugging the shanty's edge. True sees his building. "Thanks for the help, de Bris. I'm home now."

"But not home free."

The sky bursts with ash-colored droplets falling hard as pigeon shit, staining windows. True pays the driver and steps out. His intuition is telling him something is up. Even though MedTekton isn't a Japanese company, Edo is still emerging as a major theme. Is there some connection he's missing? Blinking from the falling gobs, he watches the taxi soak into the distance, sees it stop at a long line of vehicles cramped this side of the tunnel. A traffic jam, maybe an accident. Since the tunnels are the only safe vehicular route through the shanties, odds are most of the drivers will wait.

True doesn't feel like home yet. He's frustrated by his slow thought process, feels like sponging up the city through the rain, searching for inspiration. He's a shadow of what he was. Like a physicist who burns out at twenty, an athlete at thirty, a fighter who's gone too many rounds, a pitcher who's thrown too many pitches, he's a journalist who's raked too much muck.

"Don't make moves or I shoot." A voice True recognizes in an instant.

True turns to face Bong Bong and Pidge, armed to the

gums. He looks around for help or witnesses, but even in nice weather, True's is a neighborhood with few people out and about. "Saw you on TV, Bong Bong."

Bong Bong steps closer. "How you think of me?"

"Good presence, but your grammar needs work."

"But no presents for you, American." Bong Bong shakes water from his cap. Even in the dim light cast by his building True can see new splotches. Bong Bong will have to go in for more melanoma treatments. "Why you break your words?"

"I paid you what your information was worth."

"I give good informations. I give you good informations and you break your words."

A Wagnerian symphony of horns. Drivers impatient with the traffic. "What's with the traffic backed up from the tunnel?"

Bong Bong spits. "Big garbage truck and not-so-big tunnel. It's stuck. No one knows how to fix. Ha ha. Ha ha."

"To fix. Ha ha. Ha ha," Pidge echoes.

The driver was probably afraid to drive the road to the incinerator because shanty dwellers are notorious for stripping trucks; and since he's paid by the metric ton of imported garbage, he chose the tunnel. Bad move. Before True can react, Bong Bong laces into him with his pistol's slab-side. Shock. True falls, touches his cheek to feel for blood, but there isn't any. He knows it'll hurt later, though.

Bong Bong standing over True. "You break your words and I break you." The rain stings True's eyes. A boot drives oxygen from his lungs. True rolls around, feeling ridiculous and hurt at the same time. "Goodbye Yellow Brick Road," Bong Bong says, taking aim.

True reacts to the tempest with calm. What would it like to be dead, to not have to deal with life's vicissitudes and the accompanying pain, to breathe just one last breath? Death to love, to fear, to pain.

"Bong Bong," True hears himself say, "if you kill me, you'll never get the money."

"This is not about money, Mr. American."

"Someone's hired you to kill me? Who?"

Bong Bong steadies his aim with his other hand. "Such informations is not peritent to you."

"Pertinent, Bong Bong, pertinent."

"OK OK OK. Pertinent." Bong Bong itches his nose with the butt of his gun. "I mispoke."

"You know, you kill me, and this place will be crawling with journos. Is that what you want—what your government wants? It's bad PR. Plus it'll draw attention to you and to those who hired you to snuff me."

"Tsk tsk. Not good enough."

"But look, Bong Bong, I've taped and transmitted this whole conversation. If I disappear, this video will implicate you." True holds up his wrist-top, a sapphire glinting light into the mist.

He screeches. "You lie!"

"Look!"

There's silence, the sole sound is rain skittering on pavement. Peaceful. In the hurricane's eye. Then Bong Bong kicks True, the dull thud inside his head undoubtedly less impressive than the satisfying smack Bong Bong hears. True weighs kicking Bong Bong's legs out from under him, taking his gun away, firing on Pidge before he can react. But he's braver in his fantasies than in reality. Bong Bong clutches a hunk of True's hair, jerks his head back. Wet plastic rubs raw ear.

"You're lucky, American. Today. But not so lucky I think."

Bong Bong falls on his knee, cracking into True's ribs, punches madly in a windmill motion. Pidge then hands Bong Bong a taser and he jolts True with it, sending him into spasmodic fits, zapping his organs, noogie-ing his bones. He pants into True's wrist-top: "I mistook this American for other criminals. Yes, I mistook. I am sorry to American government. Please excuse."

The weight from True's back is lifted; he watches Bong Bong and Pidge skulk off. "Bong Bong!"

"Goodnight, John Boy."

Pidge's hee-hees mix with traffic noises. A siren.

True lies there, the rain dripping into his eyes, nose, mouth. The big difference between real and make-believe? The pain. He calls, "You want to know how to get the truck out of the tunnel?"

It takes time for the message to travel to Bong Bong and for Bong Bong's to get back.

"OK. You tell."

"Let the air out."

"What?"

"Let the air out of the tires. The truck will sink lower and you can tow it through."

Bong Bong looks at True with a big McBuffalo Burger grin. "Good idea. But you are only lucky today, American. Tomorrow or tomorrow's tomorrow, dead men tell no tells."

Bong Bong is right. True is lucky. He looks at his wrist-top, which is and was off the entire beating.

CHAPTER 7

After soaking in the shower, swabbing his body with anti-septic and bruise relief gel, focusing ultrasound repair waves on his organs, and injecting liquid bone into his frac-tured ribs, True's feeling better. But when his medkit, factory-synched with his DNA (to discourage piracy), malfunctioned, he had to spend a torturous hour telelinked with global tech support.

He strips off his clothes and hangs them to air, thanking technology for producing clothes that never need washing or ironing. Really, he can't imagine how people did it in the past—they must have spent half their time in laundromats, mesmerized by spinning shirts and towels, sniffing soap and softener fumes. But True's clothes are paved with chemicals that repel dirt, stains, and odor. A few minutes of airing and the clothes are factory fresh.

True sits at his computer, elbows leaning on his desk. He knows he's safe only until Bong Bong risks murder, or subcontracts the job to another hired gun. Either way, True may not be long for this earth. He lifts his eyes to the screen, types in commands for information on MedTekton. As he waits to funnel onto the infonet, True bites into a lemon and his mouth is flooded by tartness. For the first time in ages, his tastebuds are not merely an afterthought. He wonders if in some way Aslam's murder has resurrected him, given him a purpose—something in short supply in Luzonia.

On screen, True reads the computer's summary: *MedTekton, a New York-based medical technology company, is a small company dealing with high technology in the medical marketplace.* True plugs in the command for more specific information and enters the word *phaseplast.* The computer displays: *100% degradable plastic and circuits.* Within hours, the material in this camera—which is capable of producing sharp images from the interiors of veins, arteries and organs—dissolves, then is flushed from the body along with liquid waste.

All those data banks, with all those trillions of bytes of information, and this is the sum on phaseplast?

He types: *Who invented phaseplast?*

Phaseplast was patented by MedTekton. No credit given to a single inventor.

True searches for past stories on phaseplast but the only two he finds are inadequate: one announced Food and Drug Administration approval, the other from a medical trade TV journal, which discussed the merits of internal camera work. Since the company doesn't cultivate the media, blitzing on-line dailies, zines, and TV news ops with press releases and freebies, the media doesn't bother to publicize the company. When True cross-references phaseplast for military uses, zippo. Requests a chemical breakdown. Still comes up empty. It's secreted away. The Environmental Protection Agency has authorized unconditional approval based on the company's confidential medical tests, which indicate the material to be nontoxic and fully degradable.

True queries: *Could there be military uses for phaseplast?*

Affirmative.

Types: *List possible uses.*

The response: *Specify.*

True bites into the lemon, puckers his lips. Wide awake now. *Can phaseplast be used as missile casing?*

Affirmative.

Could such a missile have a range of twenty miles?

Insufficient information.

What causes plastic to dissolve?

Insufficient information.

Can certain biological chemicals dissolve phaseplast?

Affirmative. Phaseplast dissolves inside the human body.

Can TNT cause phaseplast to disintegrate without a trace?

The computer weighs all chemical data on phaseplast, its behavior in the human body, and after taking a moment to correlate and calculate, responds: *Affirmative.*

Access file on Aslam Q. Aziz. Compare video data of Aziz's death with data on phaseplast.

Accessed.

Can this missile's shell be constructed from phaseplast?

Affirmative.

Check all data banks. Are there any other materials exhibiting similar properties that could be used for missile skin?

The computer stays silent. True pops the last of the lemon, skin and all, into his mouth, silently rejoicing in the citrus burst.

Negative.

True's famished now. In the fridge, limp lettuce hangs over airplane scotch bottles, along with some eggs that were here when True moved in, olives, month-old bread, and more lemons. He picks at the olives and bread, is surprised by the salty, smoky olive flavor. Later, he promises himself, he'll stock up on candy and fruit, maybe pick up some fish; not the local mercury-laced fish, but trout or tuna flown in from America, raised on organic fish farms. It'll be expensive but worth it, if it ends up his last meal.

He's under no delusions. Even though there's a good chance he's found the composition of the shell casing, it's taken too long and too much effort. Why didn't he discover it earlier? He pulls up the keyboard conversation he held with his computer after Aslam's murder, and after scrolling it, realizes he asked the wrong questions. His reporting skills are shit. True rubs his forehead, feels a sandpapery gash over his eye— an injury he forgot to fix. He feels like shit, too.

Wrist-top peeps. De Bris calling.

"Hello, True." True sees his friend's eyes widen. "What happened to your face? You look like hell."

"Somebody didn't like what I reported."

"If you're covering the theater, you might consider giving more favorable reviews. You look awful."

"Thanks."

"Why don't you alter your image through the telelink? That way no one will know you've been beaten up."

"Why should I?"

De Bris is flummoxed. "I don't know. Just a habit, I guess. Look. I've some information for you."

"I'd say shoot, but given where I live, just tell me."

"Right after we got off the phone, I was performing an autopsy on a guy who died on the operating table."

"So?"

De Bris plunks himself in the forehead with his palm, as if True's brain is denser than rush-hour traffic. "You used to be a lot sharper."

"Spare me the critique."

"Okay, okay. These days, it's standard OR procedure to use microcameras, so I was actually able to pull one out before it could dissolve."

True's interest is piqued.

"And sure enough," de Bris continues, "it was beginning to degrade, but I extracted enough to run some tests. It's some pretty amazing stuff, True. Durable as all hell. I mean, you couldn't crush it with a twenty-ton reactor or melt it with a supernova. Fuck. Even a nuclear explosion might not do it. But like Sampson being vulnerable to scissors, phaseplast has an Achilles' heel."

"Historical figures, mixed metaphors, what's next?"

De Bris ignores him. "I analyzed the molecular structure. Know what I found?"

"That TNT dissolves phaseplast?"

"No, uh, well, yeah. That, and certain elements in blood. How did you know?"

"Educated guess. I'm pretty sure the shell of that missile was phaseplast. Nothing else fits."

"I agree."

"This helps narrow the search. But I'd imagine there's a lot of this stuff lying around."

"No. I called MedTekton. Turns out an old medical school friend of mine works for them. She told me some stuff, strictly confidential, so it's on background. Okay?"

"Go ahead."

"This company's jonesing for secrecy, keeps tracks of every device it sends out. Employees sign secrecy oaths. Hospitals failing to keep track of every single microcamera are cut off. Can't get them. Since insurance companies demand they be used, and MedTekton is the sole manufacturer, they get away with it. As far as she knows, the company's lost track of maybe ten of these cameras in five years."

"Not enough to construct a missile shell with."

"Right."

"Is it possible someone reverse-engineered one of them, figured out how to make phaseplast that way?"

"Nope."

"Really? Why's that?"

"Whoever designed this stuff attached an extra molecule to it. Makes analysis impossible. As soon as I started to reverse-engineer, the molecule ran wild and the plastic disintegrated."

"I take it there's no more phaseplast."

"All gone."

"That means MedTekton must be supplying phaseplast directly to some weapons manufacturer. But to whom?"

De Bris blows his nose. "Damn allergies. Did you know that all those genetically altered fruits and vegetables they've cultivated have spawned whole new viruses and microbes? Everybody I know is sick. The government says its tests don't show any correlation. Bureaucratic fuckers!" He sniffles. "I've got to go. I've already done enough work for you for one day."

True's absorbed in thought. There's only one way to find out where phaseplast is ending up, and that means tripping through Cyberia. There are many risks, none more so than tipping off MedTekton. Why is he subjecting himself to this?

It's suicide, and there are waves of ways of accomplishing that. Heroes—the ultimate sacrificials; unrequited lovers, loners too, passing notes soaked in self-pity; the condemned, their free will eradicated by illness or internal strife, who orchestrate their own destruction. True's moons are aligned with theirs. When he admitted to Aslam he wasn't the person he once was, it was the last time, perhaps, he was honest with himself.

No. Nothing is worth going back there. Aslam never believed in justice anyway. Whatever that computer model calculated is wrong. True's staying put in reality, where things are as they seem. No way he'll risk dying in the limitless expanse of virtual worlds. If he has to die, he wants it to be a tangible death. A searing laser wound, an explosion, a missile, a knife slicing skin.

True lets his home entertainment system carry him away. He lies down on his couch and program surfs—game shows, talk shows, dramas, re-runs, re-reruns, news, sports, commercials, commercials, commercials, more re-runs, re-runs, re-runs—never settling on one show long enough to get hooked. The evening is husked away. Now it's 1 a.m. And True's able to pull away from entertainment's grasp. He switches on the news, skims international, American national, Luzonian local. But he doesn't see any of the stories he filmed earlier. Nothing on the refugee camp or raffling virginity.

True checks his messages. One from Rush beeped in hours ago.

"Why don't you ever pick up, dammit? You're really in deep shit now. Get over here ten sharp in the a.m. This order's not just coming from me, but from the network board. I should have never listened to you. You fucked up—*again*—and I bet you don't even know how. You're a disgrace, Ailey, a disgrace to fucking test tube technology."

True's screen turns to icy static.

What *did* he do? The last few days have sucked precious moments from his life—Aslam's death, the afternoon at the morgue, Bong Bong's assault and battery, and now he's about to lose his job, left to face an idle life at home, living off government largesse, plugged into the virtual void to stem the tide of boredom.

He decides to act professional to the end. Turns on the latest earthquake news. "Live from what's left of Tokyo." Reiner's image and voice clear and strong. But True detects exhaustion, which even phony backdrops and digitized enhancements can't cover. Reiner announces she's going to interview an aid worker: Eden Sakura.

True watches the interview, and when it's over, cues it up, watches it again. And again. Over and over until her words are etched into his memory.

He freeze-frames her, staring, studying Sakura. Her aqua-emerald eyes, tiger's eye hair. Age sits well, only rounds out her features, imbuing her with wisdom and magic.

True sits by the screen, touching it, tracing her face with his fingers, reaching out to her, his wife.

CHAPTER 8

Seeing Eden has disconcerted True, brought him back to the good old bad days of commitment. It was Eden who introduced him to the most interpersonal of virtual reality worlds. She was a researcher for an American R & D firm and True was a known samurai of hyperspace. It was logical for Eden to seek him out as a technical consultant.

True once knew a woman whose sense of direction was so keen she could, in a city she'd never before visited, effortlessly find her way, using buildings as reference points, made possible by a mere glance at an aerial postcard. This was how True functioned in the narrow void separating life and information. He couldn't explain his sharp sense of virtual-direction: it was innate—you might as well have asked him how he breathes. Instinct, body chemistry, luck of the DNA draw?

Eden's software programs overwhelmed him, and as he floated though these virtual worlds, pedaling through software designed to react with mere words, nuances of speech or thoughts, the program extrapolated from these clues a whole universe. The software learned from him, produced tailor-made worlds that, in time, grew more vivid.

True remembers flipping through aching beauty, skies layered with crystalline stars, his body touched by wisps of energy, his eyes filled with brilliant colors, patterns. Able to interact with fantastical people, shoot up strands of a virtual net, skim along with the notes from Charlie Parker's saxophone, negotiate chord changes, his hair whipped by wind, scream up a melodic mountaintop, glide to the bottom on a flurry of notes. In space, inside time, flowing through a cerebral vortex of melody.

Flashback. Blink. *Flashback.* He's working with Eden, the neutral blue walls of her lab suffocating.

"Intense, huh?" She's seen it all, sees it all, watches True's virtual activities through a monitor. "The most intense trip."

"Ever. Ever." True's gasping, grasping.

"I've never seen one so intense. True. You are intense."

"True."

"Your pulse is too quick. Your body temperature is forty-one centigrade. You have to come down."

"No body. Nobody." True remembers now.

"What do you remember?"

"You read my mind."

"I listened to your words. You want to make love to me."

"Yes."

Then Eden's voice, far away this time, calling to him from somewhere inside. "True, you have to let go, you have to come back to reality. You'll burn out. I'm unhooking you."

"No! No!"

"You're going supernova!"

"N-o—"

True

lies

in a puddle of his own body water, hyperventi-
lating, a helmet squeezing his ears against his head. The room
is dark, the floors coated with crumbs and dirt, the air stale. He
rips off the VR helmet, flings it violently to the side.

Eden's holding a plastic drinking straw. "This is the last
straw, True. I mean it." She curves over him and True glimpses
a nipple, or a birthmark, can't take his eyes off her breasts. Soft,
pillowy, pure and white and fragrant like freshly scented
sheets.

"See something you like, mister?"

"This, this here is the last straw?" He grasps it in his hand.
"Meaning you won't stand for any more of this? Or is this just
the last straw in the apartment?"

"It's a game." She straddles his chest as if it were the most
natural thing in the world for her to be doing. "And I love
games." Takes his hand, kisses his fingers, rubs them along
supple lips. "You dreamed of this, of me. I saw it."

Her body heats when they kiss, her skin bathwater rosy.
Peels her dress away, revealing Eden, the side not her intellect.
Sensuous. Magnetic. Electric, eclectic. They love into tomor-
row's morning.

After he's not sure it wasn't a virtual adventure in reality.
Soon their limbs, minds, and hearts intertwined. They shared
residence. Married. Carried on with careers. But True began to
spend more time in the witches' brew Eden concocted, and
their marriage fragmented. He could not give up floating freely
through paradise, even when Eden threatened to leave him,
then did. And as True's mind and creativity withered, he found

himself even less able to separate reality from synthetic reality.

One moment he was lazing through space, rolling in freshly mowed grass, the next he was being suspended by the network for absenteeism. Eden slammed the door, leaving the shambles of his life in shambles. True was walking through a tangy-scented garden. Surfing a killer wave in Hawaii. Making love to Eden, lips brushing, but Eden was gone now, had left him, and now it was not Eden but another woman, her skin creamy chocolate. He pulled her hair, and beads and bangles splattered rain on a tin shanty roof and he was in bed under that roof with her, thrusting, driving his pelvis into her, trying to hurt her, to inflict pain because she left him.

But it wasn't her.

True was lucky he was found, wallowing in his own shit, nude, dehydrated, brain cells baked, and carted off to the hospital. Eden had indeed left him, that much was true. And all that is left of this time of True's life is a stream of virtual memories and dreams, melted and indistinguishable from one another like possessions after a fire.

But now there's Eden in disaster relief. Somehow it was fitting she left one disaster—him—and found another.

Reiner asks, "Is it true your agency has never dealt with a disaster of this magnitude?"

Eden's mystical smile. "It's true. It's true, but we're hoping to make a difference nevertheless."

Each time he replays the interview and hears her say *true*, he shakes.

Now he knows where to find her. And when he's ready?

He'll have to wait until he's ready.

CHAPTER 9

True notices her upon leaving his apartment. She's there when he stoops under the breeze and crosses into Snake Alley, shadows him as he rises to the second floor walkways spreading as metal tentacles over and through the mall. When he slips down to ground level she's still there. He thinks he may have lost her when he slithers through the crowds staring raptly at snake oil demonstrations. Circles back, but there she is again.

She's quick through a crowd, as if she knows where he's going before he does. A shimmering sight. True's not even one hundred percent sure he's being tailed, but his brush with Bong Bong has unnerved him. It's possible she's a razor assassin, concealing an array of weapons under her robe. True wants a closer look, but she's covered head-to-sandals, wrapped in a saffron-colored robe.

Even by zooming in with his wrist-top camera, True can't key in on her face. No DNA identification, no weapons check, no way of determining her motives. His wrist-top, he notes ruefully, isn't up to the task of saving his hide. All True can see of her are blackpool eyes peeking out from under her hood. They look inquisitive but not judgmental, as if they're saying she has a job to do and that's it.

He sprints down an alley, and after crisscrossing a maze of connecting passageways, he's back at his apartment complex. She can't see him, but he can't see her either, and this, in many ways, is more unnerving. Carefully sneaking toward Rush's, sidling against the building's façade, True keeps a wary eye. He slips up to Rush's apartment.

"Look, Ailey," Rush says after True's inside, "I've been on the phone all morning with New York and Reiner. I've been ordered to Japan to help with the quake coverage."

True looks around the expansive one-room apartment, taking in the brash tint, the mammoth entertainment system particular to bachelor life. He grimaces at the TV posters of Rush hawking shampoo, aftershave, a worldwide chain of plastic surgery salons. Commercials that are memorable because they're so forgettable. True turns down Rush's offers of vitamin shakes, protein drinks, the carbo-replacement fluid system, free-radical enhancement beverage technology, and mineral water. Then says, "Congratulations. I know that's what you wanted."

"Yeah, well, I have to tell you. Reiner doesn't sound happy I'm getting in the closing credits. She told me she'd rather you came."

"Oh?"

"But I told her your meatware's defecto."

"What'd she say?"

"What could she say? Orders are orders, although she's

got some kind of clout with the Board. I mean, they did free up enough bucks in her budget so she could hire that hacker."

"An elegant solution. Whatever computer systems haven't crashed there are vulnerable. Others that have been rebooted will be fair game. A good hacker could navigate through these systems, help her to set up one mammoth database from stuff you couldn't touch a week ago."

"Ailey, you're deftly in the upside of yo-yo mode. That's what she said, exacto. I'd never heard of him, but he's a real bagbiter. Cut in on Reiner's and my conversation. Reiner didn't even tell him to. Said he could tress whenever he wanted. Attitude problem, but Reiner says he's one of the best. His name is 16ea3e."

"Or just Peace. It's cyberspeak. P is the sixteenth letter of the alphabet, C is the third, so 16ea3e is Peace."

But 16ea3e was only his moniker, the hackers' lexicon of cool. His real name, True discovered in the days he warped through mirror worlds, was Odessa Flashfire, yet this too seems more moniker than real name. Once, while jacked into the infonet retrieving data on a candidate running for political office, True was smoked by Odessa, who locked him inside the candidate's speeches, imprisoned him inside an electronic force field of halcyon promises—a balanced budget, better schools, more prisons, lower taxes, a return to family values. It seemed it lasted years; probably just minutes. But Odessa was only sending the message that he was the world's hippest cyberjockey. True felt he could have tracked him if he'd been spliced with more genes of vengeance.

Rush says, "Tomorrow, two WWTV reps are coming to this DMZ."

"Two?"

"You're reassigned. To New York."

True's lips fade. "I'm flatlined?"

"That's up to the Board in New York. All I know is it's not working out here. Let's face it: It's been total bogosity, Ailey."

True's in another place, another time.

"I told you if you got in trouble, you'd get zapped."

"You held my stories last night."

"Bong Bong told me he'd turn me into particularly piss-poor protoplasm. Your stories reflect badly on his country."

"A true patriot. He actually said 'particularly piss-poor protoplasm?'"

"That was the gist. You want to talk to him? He's liquid nitrogen, Ailey, an ice man in broken syntax. What could I do?"

"He denies the Luzonian government is ripping off refugees? He denies foreign aid food is glowing with radioactive isotopes?" True scarcely believes the naiveté of his own defense.

"He claims there are positive aspects to life in Luzonia, so why don't we ever do stories on that? Book a plane ticket and submit your invoice to accounting. Don't make this harder than it already is. Maybe the network will give you another chance."

But True knows he's soaked up all his chances and wrung them out. He's overwhelmed by the injustice. Anger springs him into worthless action, and, before he can stop himself, he slams his fist into the edge of Rush's table. Ruby-jewel drops trickle down his wrist onto the rug. But it doesn't hurt; just a dull, electric sensation, as if his body can't believe he'd sabotage himself.

Rush returns with a wad of toilet paper, tears off some squares. True wraps them around his hand, then drops to one knee.

"Go, Ailey. Get out of here. I'll clean up your blood."

True stands, waving toilet paper like parade streamers. Pathetic, he thinks. Rah, rah.

He trudges down the stale hallway to the elevator, and as he pushes the down button there's a sound of smashing glass and a tremendous explosion. As True covers his face with his arms, the walls and ceiling crack into kaleidoscopes. True is heaved to the floor by a gush of blistering air. Heavy debris rains down. When his eyes blink open, he barely manages to avoid a girder knifing through the floor.

His ears buzz and ring in different pitches. He pulls himself out of the rubble and is, as far as he can tell, unscarred. Wades over to Rush's, leaping through what was once his doorway. The wind spits inside—there's no exterior wall. Seared to wall plaster is what's left of Rush. True stares. A blood-red hologram appears in a swish of air, of True twisting in agony, screaming silently, disintegrating.

He knows he has to get away. He stumbles through the rubble.

CHAPTER 10

True contemplates vanishing into the countryside, or better yet, fleeing the country altogether. He doesn't dare return home—nothing there worth the risk. Heads to the most crowded section of town, the mall, to lose himself in the throng. At a boutique he buys clothes, a baseball cap, sunglasses. He grabs reflections whenever possible to ensure no one's following.

It's also useless. He's probably under electronic surveillance at this very moment. True ducks into an alley and flips open his wrist-top to monitor communications. As he quickly makes his way through the mall, changing directions, dodging bodies, winding his way through the crowds, he periodically checks it. But can't isolate any communication patterns.

But this doesn't add to his security because in the reflective front glass of a store selling artificial eyeballs he spots his tail again. True zoom-scans her image, then runs through the minions, glances back, only to see her follow. She's talking into her hand. But when he checks his wrist-top, it records no con-versation, no radio or any other communication waves. Just the perfect time for a malfunction.

He loses her when he joins a crowd of knotted-kneed tourists. The tourguide: "This, ladies and gentlemen, is Nerula's Liberation Monument. Constructed out of coral mined from the surrounding sea." True thinks he should men-tion that the removal of the coral reefs increased flooding, wreaked havoc with the local fishing industry, and increased soil erosion. He opens the maintenance door and tucks inside. It's dark, probably the coolest non-air-conned place in Nerula, although True's still sweating rivulets. He doesn't think his shadow saw him, but can feel her move inexorably toward him nonetheless. He peers through a tiny porthole. Right outside she stops, standing guard. Or waiting for reinforcements.

True weighs climbing to the top, to maybe jump from the steeple top to the building across the way. Far, but maybe, just maybe. But the trap door leading skywards is blocked. Tries hit-ting it with all his might, but it's sealed tight. Only one way out and she's blocking it. Up higher, a window. He might just be able to squeeze through, but it's too high. Looks for something to stand on, but the inside walls are slippery and there's nothing to grip. If only he were on the outside looking in, he'd be able to climb up the beveled edges easily enough. Looks for a weapon. Nothing. Scuffling outside. Nowhere to hide, so True reaches for the door. Maybe take the assassin by surprise. Maybe she'll lose her balance, afford a narrow avenue of escape.

The handle turns and True notices a shadow over the brass knob glint. Odd, True thinks. His legs are wrenched vio-lently from under him. He tastes cold concrete.

"Don't say a fucking word if you want to live."

The door creaks open and the robed woman steps inside. Closes the door.

"Okay." The Rajput pulls down her hood.

"Okay," Piña says.

"She working with Piña?" True's sitting up now.

"Duh."

"Hello, baba," the Rajput says. "As always, a pleasure."

Piña nudges True in the ribs. "You're lucky Piña found you. Word says you into mountains of shit. You look like you landed in it already. Bong Bong really fucked you up, huh? Then that bomb. Piña thought you were dead, but the Rajput saw you leave the building alive."

The Rajput peers out the porthole. "Some men are difficult to kill. They live their lives while those around perish. It is their karma. Perhaps it is your karma, baba."

Piña shakes her head. "Don't get all mystical. He's just lucky his fucking karma wasn't blown into the Pacific. You the target? Or that other guy?"

"Me."

"How you know?"

"There was a hologram of me at the scene."

"You *are* fucking lucky. That kind of missile doesn't make many mistakes."

"Any ideas who it is?" True asks.

"No. But if they go to that apartment and don't find any of your DNA dripping down the walls, they'll come after you again."

"Or they'll assume I'm dead already."

Piña pats True on his head. "Would you?"

"Assume I'm dead?" True holds the thought. Turns to the Rajput. "No. How did you stay in contact with Piña? I scanned you and didn't pick up anything."

"There are many forms of communication, baba. There are the tribes that speak through clicks. There are those who speak through their lovemaking. Others speak through art and music. We use sign language, since I do not trust portable transmitters."

Chalk up a victory for low-tech, True thinks.

"Piña's got people around. That's how she knew Bong Bong was waiting for you last night." She takes True's hand, her own calloused from years of pavement propulsion and iron hoisting. "Most people just take, but you treat Piña straight up." She produces a package.

True takes it. Stuffed into a synthetic paper bag, almost weightless. "What's this?"

"Since you're not a mindreader..."

He tears it open to reveal a black designer protecto-vest with an ornate tattoo on the back. A snake chewing its own tail, weaving in and out of a fiery wreath. A name on it: Ramos.

"What happened to Ramos?"

"Eh, he don't need it. Put it on. A boy's gotta protect himself." Pina absently plays with her eyebrow ring. "You could stay. Be Piña's assistant. No one's going to fuck with you then. And Piña needs someone smart. The bizzing get so big sometimes."

But True has a better plan. Piña says, "It's fucking perfect to hide out in. A guy could get lost there for a while."

"That's what I was thinking."

Pinatubo takes True's hand and jerks him down to her level. Eye to eye, nose to nose, she kisses him, playfully nips his lower lip. Whispers: "The hologram means it was a professional hit.

PART TWO

THE VIRTUALOSO

CHAPTER 11

Narita airport is redolent with the scent of a desperate people on the move but getting nowhere. The terminal buildings are in jigsaw pieces: glass shards, cement crumbs, twisted sticks of steel laying in hastily swept piles, support beams wrapped in gauze to increase their tensile strength. True studies the gauze, stops to touch it, feel the rough fibers with his thumb and fingers, is tempted to bandage himself.

Japanese wander—some aimlessly, others with purpose—in search of food, water, or medical aid. They wait in lines that tail out of the videophone bank, the government aid center, the food bank for twice-a-day rations; they suffer sleep fever, bodies draped over plastic fast-food-colored chairs and couches, and then bad dreams, negative karma prodding them into a quasi-waking state.

They've been waiting days, not hours, their lives crammed into shopping bags or stuffed into wilting rice sacks or water-logged boxes. And that smell, the odor of malaise, hopelessness, overcrowding, stagnation. True knows it threatens to trap him, too, if he lets it.

He has to step over an old man lying flat-boarded, his back brushing the floor.

"*Mizu. Mizu.*" The man is trembling, administered to in rusted whispers by a woman.

The woman: "Shhhh." She's old, too—his wife?—stoop-backed and haggard.

True's sure the man's voice is of another. But it's not, couldn't be, the old refugee he interviewed on Nerula's pier. Just another ancient man not yet ready to take leave from this life but being shown the door nonetheless. True offers a bottle of water. Leaves before he can be thanked.

The quake split and spat out gobs of airport, formed one-of-a-kind architectural wonders, wonders that ceased, ending in jagged lines and crumpled walls. The second floor lacks confidence, teeters uneasily; glass not shattered is taped dull brown. Departing flights quintupled in recent days. A diaspora ensued, is ensuing, to McSingapore, McBangkok, McSeoul, places known for fast food and technology, already Eden to clusters of Japanese expatriate salary-*tachi*.

True searches for a means to town, but service centers are unwomanned and unmanned, as if these once banally smiling figures had cut and run, leaving counters spread with dust. Through holes punched out behind the counters, he peers out to the parking lot, where crunched cars and buses are piled in heaps. He knows not to rent a car, even if any are available; that would render him traceable.

"I knew you'd get your ass here, True Ailey." A woman's voice behind him, familiar, yet not one he recognizes in a split.

True pirouettes. "Reiner Jacobi. This *is* a coincidence."

Reiner scrunches her forehead, amused or disappointed, it's hard to tell. She looks every bit and byte as good as her broadcast image: long, spiraling strands of cordovan hair, buff physique, skin moist and thick, as if in her line of work she requires more than the usual seven layers. "Yeah, right, a coincidence." Surrounds her words with a drafty sigh. "Perhaps I could interest you in some prime pieces of Tokyo real estate. At bargain-basement prices? Oh, shit." Spits the final t. "Basements are all we have left in quake-ee-yo. Give me your wrist-top."

"What?"

"Believe me, I'm doing you a favor." She snatches his wrist-top and transfers the data to another miniature computer. Seconds later, the light pulses green, transference complete. "I can't decide whether you have a death wish or you're just *molto retardo*. I did a story once on a dude on the run from the yakuza? Innocent kind of guy, a lot like you? Lasted about a fucking week before they found him skewered, charred like *yakitori*." She smiles sweetly. "Be right back, darling."

Reiner taps keys percussively while striding to a family waiting for transit to Luzonia, a post-quake launch pad to other lands. She talks with the boy, maybe eight, takes his hands into hers, wraps them around the wrist-top. And as he watches this, True realizes he can actually smell Reiner's perfume— flowers: roses, marigolds, lilacs, petals ground to powder and stirred in alcohol, misting down, a dab behind the knee, a smudge behind the ear. And this is remarkable; extraordinary, really, because True hasn't been able to smell anything in a year-plus, 400 days of silent odors, smell-less scents, conducting his life in a world he could see, feel, hear, but not smell or taste.

The child accesses the wrist-top video games and is instantly enmeshed in a 3-D graphic net, spaceships firing salvos as he ducks and fires back. True gives the family the once-over, guesses middle-class with nothing now save for tattered clothes, tattered boxes, tattered lives.

Reiner hands True another wrist-top. A newer model. More RAM, more memory, more power, more features than his own. Someone else had the same type. Seconds later, the answer: Aslam.

True snaps it on. "Will the kid have access to all my files, too, or just games?"

"Unh-uh. I erased everything except the games. It's all he wants anyway."

True's files are in order. "What was wrong with mine? It doesn't have all these features, but it was getting the job done."

"You mean setting you up for the kill. It's amazing you're not toast already. I heard about Rush on Aussie Beat. When I heard you were missing, I figured you'd pull some *Fugitive* shit. Judging by the pizza stains on the wall, Rush isn't going to be irritating viewers with his formica personality anymore."

"How'd you know I was coming to Tokyo?"

"I tracked you."

"How?"

She taps on his wrist-top. "You've been leaving a beeping trail of electronic breadcrumbs since you fled."

Every WWTV wrist-top is equipped with a location key, for use in kidnappings or other emergencies. He's sure his wasn't activated, though.

"It's not like you'd left your location beam on," she says, almost reading his thoughts. "I accessed your code through the WWTV data guide and homed in that way. When I discovered the signal was moving this way, I knew you were coming. I mean, it made sense, right? Where else could you hide? I simply checked the air scheds. And—what the hell?—there was a flight from Nerula arriving right about now."

No wonder she ditched his wrist-top. The thought occurs he shouldn't let the kid have it, but fear—fear of dying, fear of pissing off Reiner (he hates to admit)—crams these misgivings back. "Thanks." What else can he say?

"For meeting your plane? Don't mention it. It's not like I have a lot to do around here."

"No. Listen—" True searches for a soft spot, anywhere. "I should have ditched the wrist-top before I left Nerula. It was—"

"—stupid."

"OK."

"You know what the definition of a good journo is?"

"Tell me."

"Someone who comes down from the hills after the battle is over and courageously shoots the wounded. That's how you get stories. And the story is that Rush is now two all-beef patties, special sauce, lettuce, cheese. I want to know why the fuck."

True isn't sure he wants to work with her.

"I *know* shit's going down, and you and me, we're going to hash it out." Then Reiner, as quickly as she heats up, ices cool. "True, we're pros. I'm not doing this just because you're WWTV and it's part of my responsibility to save your ass. Frankly, I could use your help." She tugs him toward the exit. "I need you. There's too much here for one reporter. What do you say? We need to work together on this."

Spelunking through a hole in the terminal, over to an abandoned runway where vehicles are parked. To prevent theft, armed hoods sprawl lazily on car hoods; except in one case, a big, clunking electric Ford, all hood, a jet-black Labrador leashed to the front bumper. True remembers the dog from Reiner's hovercraft broadcast, the day the earthquake jiffy-popped Tokyo.

"Don't worry Rue—uh, True—well now that's a slip," Reiner says. She reaches into her pocket for a dog biscuit. "No, it wasn't a slip, True. I was acting like an asshole. Don't mind the bitch."

"Which one?"

Reiner ignores the insult and turns her attention to the dog, which is straining against the leash. True is amused by the puffs of fur floating into the air. "Sit. Shed. Breathe. Breathe. Drool. Good girl." Reiner says this in a monotone, cramming the biscuit into the gaping maw, squeezing it shut, and pats the dog on the head. "It's not that she's dumb, I figure, it's just that expectations of her abilities may have been inflated."

"Is she going to pull us into town?"

"The car works. But there's so much shit in the atmosphere the solar panels on the roof are useless for energy storage. But I have my ways for recharging it. At least the car won't get stolen with the dog here."

"What's her name?" True tentatively pats its snout.

"Just 'Dog.' I found her wandering around outside my condo on my way to grab a hovercraft to cover the quake. I figure she came from a nearby pet store. I was going to bring her back but there was no pet store anymore. She has good karma. Some animals are hard to kill."

"Some people, too." True remembering the Rajput's words.

Reiner punches wrist-top buttons and the car doors chatter spasmodically, like plastic novelty teeth. "I didn't say the car was without its charms." She unleashes Dog. After a brief but energetic struggle, she crams the animal into the back seat. Shuts the door. "One good thing about the quake is that navigation systems don't work. All the roads are fucked up. God knows how many detours we'll have to take, so you'll have to trust my driving."

She peels out of the parking lot, swerves right then left, past a pile of wrecked cars; then, flooring it, shoots out onto what True assumes is an expressway, empty except for abandoned hunks of metal along the shoulders.

Sweat dribbles into True's eye. "The A/C doesn't work?"

"Cuts down on mileage. I can't rely on getting a charge, so I conserve."

"Fair enough." True hits the switch to roll down the window.

Reiner, clipping along at ninety-five, dodging potholes, fissures, and other obstacles, takes her eyes off the road. "You have to pull the thing down manually. I turned off all the electrical gadgets except the engine."

True tries to pull down the window down. It stays stubborn, shut. "How?"

"I rigged it. Hold the switch down and pull on the window at the same time, it'll open."

True does, and dank air hums in, clouded in burnt rubber, chemicals, and singed earth. There's fire in the sky, pockets of blood on the horizon mixed with darker hues—brown, deep purple, sticky sickly green, mauve.

"See that?" Reiner points through the front glass. "There's a cult here that sees that kind of atmospheric disturbance as proof there's a new world order. Old Tokyo, old Edo, is dead. Long live Tokyo. These Hari-Krishna Rajaneeshy Sun Myung

Meow Bows think the quake was more than a quake. Like God's way of wiping out the old and foisting upon this world the new."

"Maybe they're right."

"Maybe." Reiner offers this doubtfully.

The night's not dark. Fires lick spastically at buildings and rubble. The car's lights wash out tracts of road as Reiner slaloms around potholes, turns hard to the left, to the right. Dog skitters and slides in the back. True can tell Reiner enjoys playing race car driver. They exit onto another expressway, the *Kosoku Dori*, and after swerving around a ramshackle shack constructed on a tiny island separating the Tokyo's two main road arteries, they're surrounded by a motorcycle gang, matching Reiner's frantic speed. Rising Sun flags parachute behind the dozen or so bikes, engines rattling. Gas engines. No electric whirrs here. No helmets either, just pompadours.

Reiner looks back. "Shit. *Bosozoku*."

"What?"

"Speed Tribes. Nipponese Hell's Angels."

Reiner drops an anvil on the accelerator and the car leaps over a gaping pothole, hits the ground skidding, and maneuvers around a snaking fissure that takes up most of the highway's six lanes. When she straightens out the car, True hears a knock on his door. There: a bosozoku, close enough to touch, his hair crafted to his head, frozen in gel even as wind rages around him. Even his ponytail stays stiff. The biker reaches into his jacket.

True paws at the window.

Reiner screams, "Pull up the fucking window!"

As True's about to seal them safe, the biker pulls a pistol. Reiner veers; there's a crunching thud and the bosozoku's sent sprawling. There's a moment where the wheels turn on the flipped-over bike, and True thinks he sees a leg twitch through the rear view mirror. Then an explosion.

Other speed tribesmen pull up behind, slowing to fire old-style rifles, machine guns, grenades. An explosion rattles the car. But since they can't ride and shoot at the same time, and with the windows closed, the car is bullet- and laser-resistant, True and Reiner, for now, are safe. The last of the bikers recede into the distance.

Reiner says, "You don't have much of a survival instinct, do you? How did you get by in a DMZ like Luzonia? Here are Reiner's Rules of Order for a successful holiday in post-quake Japan. Take notes. Rule one: Do exactly as I say. I do not want to have my head blown off because you cannot roll up a fucking window. Rule two: Do exactly as I say. Tell me everything you know about what happened to Rush. Rule three: Do exactly as I say. I call the shots here. It's my turf."

She checks the rear mirror, then enters a code in the car's keyboard. "Hate to waste the power, but this should tell us if anyone else is packing weapons nearby. Finding charges ain't easy." Almost as an afterthought: "So, tell me. *Was* Rush the target, or were you?"

"What makes you think I was?"

"You're here twenty minutes and already there's trouble. Besides, Rush couldn't stir up trouble if he was the lone man in a women's prison. Figure you were on to something but the hit went awry."

True lets his eyes mist, his vision blur around a pachinko parlor, shiny chrome and electric lights dazzling, an elongated blur. Reiner's words catch his attention.

"Rush is like a cat I once had. Whenever I'd come home,

he'd race out, jump in front of me while I walked down the path to my door. It was funny. He'd be looking back at me as I walked, slowed to a crawl, until I stepped on him."

"You sound like an ASPCA poster girl, Reiner. What other fun things have you done? Changed channels on Alzheimer patients to see if they'd notice?" True senses Reiner's feelings can't be hurt. Rumpled perhaps, but never hurt.

"C'mon. What were you on to?" Her voice drips insistence.

True stares through the window again. Another glassed-in pachinko parlor. The only lighted buildings around. "How come pinball parlors get power while the rest of Tokyo is dark?"

"They're run by yakuza. Practically the only places open for business are run by organized crime. Don't change the subject."

"I'm not sure what I was on to yet."

"Fill me in."

True blows heavy air. "No."

Reiner swivels her head. "No? No? You're telling me 'no'? After I saved your ass? You owe me. Quid pro fucking quo."

"You don't know those bikers wanted me."

She pounds the brake and the car screeches still. "If you won't come clean, get out, get the fuck out of my car."

True elbows the door open. Dog leans forward, frantically prods the earthy-smelling air with her nose. Something is burning. Still, True feels alive, all five senses accounted for. He doesn't trust Reiner, can't trust anyone he can't read, is spooked how she found him. The need to escape, to get on his own until he can make sense of things, overwhelms.

He gets out without closing the door, heads toward a distant patch of undulating lights. The thud of a car door, rubber squealing on asphalt. Instinct commands him to turn, to face the oncoming headlights, and his heart flutters as the light grows, two eyes in barely camouflaged terror. He stands unmoving, knows he can't outrun or dodge a hurtling car, and as the distance between him and Reiner shrinks—to 50 meters, then 20, 10, the hood now taking up most of his field of vision—he's suffused with a sense of serenity, knowing Reiner can never stop in time. He criss-crosses his arms in front, feels the protecto-vest under them.

A rush of air brushes past. She's gone around him, and in the process, with the accompaniment of a sickening, crunching noise, heaved over a gasping pothole. She sacrificed her car's undercarriage to make a point.

The car rumbles away until it's a tiny speck in the distance, the size of a grain of sand, then a micro-microchip, finally a particle of light. Then infinity, or nothing.

CHAPTER 12

True's been walking for hours, his legs and lower back throbbing. The remnants of Tokyo are eerily still. Still, he's surprised he's seen so few people about. No traffic, no apartment complexes, only lonely roadside restaurants gutted like trout and burned charcoal black. Empty. Nowhere to rest or eat, just an arrow-straight stretch of road leading to faraway, ebullient lights. The scenery is of a land ransacked by war, where anything of value has been stripped bare. What remains are the shells. The devastation. The memories. 'Before' and 'After' pics, an example of how far Tokyo has plummeted, how far it would need to go to bounce back. A painful lesson, a reminder of what happened and what would undoubtedly happen again.

True passes some makeshift shanties heaped together from scraps of plastic gleaned from appliance boxes, wood, sheet rock, and glass. Clothes are stretched over sticks, scraps of metal, plastic, wound like a web and covered with blankets and comforters. The lights dim then brim, alternate between ivory gasps and beige flickers, not magnetic like the blinding white lights that get closer with each step. True studies the prefab materials used to construct the post-quake ghetto. Silent children play in the debris. Adults prepare meager meals or reinforce their new homes. But they are ill-equipped to deal, unprepared to build lives and homes from scratch, to hunt, scavenge, or fish for food, to deal with the lack of imposed structure on their lives. Technology removed them from the land; the death of technology is as much to blame for their malaise as the quake.

Behind him, gas engines grumbling. He tenses, ribs rubbing against the flak jacket. The bosos are back and there's going to be trouble. He keys in on the wrist-top, struggles to make sense of the "new and improved" hardware, and after agonizing confusion (in which he accidently accesses a telesex line and a portable shopping network), he runs a weapons check on the approaching bikes.

Correction: bike. A lone rider packing what the wrist-top refers to as *light arms*. A 20th century-style rifle, a laser pistol critically low on power, and a nine-inch steel knife, Japanese-made, with a footnote explaining that in Japanese the word for "nine" is the homonym for "suffering." As the varooming nears, True crosses the line from walking to running. Closes on the electrical oasis, hopes it offers something he can use. He's on the ramp that feeds into the lights, a long, unfurled yarn of road-ramp leading to a high stone fence. About 100 meters up the road, he figures, is the entrance. The bosozoku blows closer. Cursing himself for being out of shape, True sprints to the lights. His limbs turn to gelatin, like in the dreams he sometimes has, the ones where he's running to Eden, searching for her, and all of a sudden he's running *from* something, as if something in his dreams draws life from him; and he runs, getting weaker, and just before he's about to fall to oblivion, he awakens, sweating and cold, less alive, he's sure, than when he went to sleep.

A motorcycle beam catches True and he sees his shadow become elongated. Surrounding revs. A boot clanks against the backside of True's protecto-vest. He stumbles and stops. Glances at the fence, but knows he can't fly. The biker is filthy, his hair stiff with road grit. It's fitting, True thinks, that he's parked on a pile of rubble. He waves True over, palm-side down, and when True inches closer he notes his eyes, bloodshot, red lines spoking crazily from the center like two Japanese Imperial battle flags superimposed over one another.

"Money." A voice all edge.

True checks the rubble under and around the bike: bits of glass, plastic, a metal rod. He moves closer, reaches into his pocket, and as he does the bosozoku grabs his rifle. True's fingers caress sky. The boso nods and True slowly extracts Piña's cash card.

The biker's broken smile. Greed.

"You can't access the card without me." Even though True's assailant isn't versed in English, True doesn't show the wrist-top obscured under his sleeve. But his leathery adversary understands the magic of a gold and onyx-gilded card. Only the keyed-in user, conscious and alive, can access money.

The biker produces a debit machine from his saddlebags, and, the rifle slung under an arm, enters an amount, holds it up. True deletes it and types in a lower sum. They go back and forth, quibbling over the amount, and True casually nudges the steel rod with his foot, inserts it between spokes. When the biker hands the machine back, True jams it in his face and grabs the rifle. He takes the chance because he knows death or injury will ruin the extortion hunt.

True wrests the rifle away, sprints away, and javelins it over the wall, watches it disintegrate in a crackling wisp. The engine grouses, and True looks in time to see the bosozoku lurch forward, then flip, the steel rod lodged securely between his fork and spokes.

The entrance is near. As True turns, the ground gives way and he trips. He rolls off the road, down the embankment, whirling, spinning. When he stops, he's looking into the dizzying symbol of the Ouroboros propped up on two pairs of boots. Around, men in various degrees of undress are showing off a rainstorm of tattoos; the Ouroboros, the biggest and best, belongs to the apparent leader. Beyond, a fake medieval castle etched with nuclear neon and halogen. True hears the bosozoku's bike, knows he must have gotten back on to finish the pursuit. But before he can scream down into the parking lot, he's fired on. The bosozoku crashes, his bike tumbling over him. When he's able to get up, he has to dodge laser spizzes from a roof-mounted rifle. Really only warning shots, but he retreats anyway.

The roar of 20th century technology drives True, a 21st century man, to seek refuge in a 16th-century motel, to bury himself in the past in order to survive the now. True sits up. The parking lot is clovered in electric cars, a few gassers, too. The burning air stings his nose, and even this close to Tokyo's nucleus lights are muffled—power hasn't been restored in most sections yet. An oasis of gaudy, tawdry bulbs in the midst of the cracked, angry earth, kept in the dark, except for this, a yakuza tailgate party.

True serves first. "*Konbanwa.*"

A splash of grunts.

"Water?" True looks to the leader, the Ouroboros, greasy eyes, his body all tendon and gristle.

"*Mizu?*" More like a grunt.

True nods.

They volley suggestions among themselves. The Ouroboros says, "Money?"

The international word. In Japan just a few hours, True thinks, and already—

"Money?"

Reluctantly, True produces the debit card.

"Gold and onyx. OK." The Ouroboros indicates the club with a sweeping hand.

"Go in?"

The Ouroboros, his sweaty arm necklacing True, walks him to the door. "Gold and onyx good at Ko Ko's." He speaks slowly, carefully.

"What?"

"Ko Ko's Karaoke Kafé." The Ouroboros hums a scratchy tune and points to the 3-D kanji sign over the door. The club teeters on the edge of an abyss; behind it is nothing except a sheer drop, lights washing away a meter over the edge. True hears a posse of chainsaw bike engines. True's nemesis bringing reinforcements. The Ouroboros leaves to deal with them.

True doesn't hesitate.

CHAPTER 13

Crinkly styrofoam music. Polka-dot lights pock True like some exotic disease. The walls are experiencing a serene sunset. And a virtual hostess—a 3-D hologram geisha—greets True. He recognizes the "Theme from Shaft," the retro-70's classic, but it's not Isaac Hayes. The voice is tinged with too much reverb, modulating when there shouldn't be modulations. More like Charles Ives than Isaac Hayes.

"Welcome to Ko Ko's Karaoke Kafé. Come this way, please." Parts of the hostess keep cutting out. Reception, it seems, is bad.

"Water. I just need some water and some food."

"This"—the voice cuts mid-word—"this way." The virtual geisha sashays into the main room, invisibility streaks creasing her kimono. Somehow the image manages to ride out the flickers. True wades through the club's glitter. Onstage, a Japanese business-samurai sings, backed by an all black band. Their clothes are retro-70s, pink talc shoes and polyester shirts, and their hair is styled in sitcom-style afros. Patrons eye True, but he's used to it. It's a yakuza hangout, but most here don't look yakuza, don't sport the oily hair or gruff exteriors. He helixes around table after table, the room seeming to roll along with him. He's brought to a table far from the stage.

"What a coincidence." A smile creases Reiner's lips. She holds True's eyes with her own and toasts him with a sake cup.

Billions of pulses and impulses fire through True. Leave. Stay. Upend the table. Scald her with sake. Ask for another table. How could she have known he'd end up here? She'd sped on ahead after almost flattening him into roadkill. And yet, she ended up here, knew he'd appear, instructed the club software programmer to lead True here. He looks at the wrist-top, then at Reiner, knows he's been tracked.

"You see that table over there?" Reiner indicates a table in the balcony radiating wealth. "Those are the mega-shakers of post-quake Japan."

True's not prepared for her calm demeanor. She acts as if their conversation had been interrupted and now they're back to where they left off.

She kicks out a black velour-covered chair. "Sit down."

True resists.

Her voice, softer now. "C'mon, True, I get a little abrasive sometimes. It's my nature. Sit. Please."

True wrestles with his urges. He sits, grabs a glass of ice water, downs it in percussive gulps, and stabs at a block of fried tofu with Reiner's chopsticks.

"Your eyes got about this big"—Reiner pantomimes a cantaloupe—"when I drove at you."

True pushes a button on the virtual menu. Although the writing is Japanese, there are pictures for the literacy-impaired.

He pokes at a thimble-sized cup and vial icon framed in blue.

Reiner cancels his order. "Get the *atsukan*—the hot sake. It's better than the cold stuff, and it's on me." Which means it's on WWTV. She pokes at the atsukan icon, gilded in red.

"Cold is fine."

"Trust me."

"Trust you? It'll probably be spiked with xylene. I'll stick to my instincts."

"Your instincts led you here, to me."

"You tracked me."

"I didn't have to."

"This is the only place around to get food and water. You knew I'd end up here."

"If you survived."

More retro-tunes. A waiter places the sake on the table. True scrolls the electric menu, selects assorted Japanese snacks—a few *maki*, raw soybeans, miso soup. When his order arrives, he eats quickly, efficiently. His taste buds burst in fireworks. Is it Reiner who brings out this change? Should he be so hasty to get away from her?

"For a weedy-looking guy, you certainly can munch. You know how many liposuction treatments or Fat Away tabs I'd need to be able eat like you?" Reiner's way of bridging gaps.

"Here are the rules," True says, after swallowing a sticky tuna roll. "Number one: You give me info, I'll give you info. Tit for tat. Two: Don't order me around. Three: I'll check into Rush's murder—with or without your help. It's my piece, so I call the shots."

"Okay."

No telling when she'll be this amenable again. "I noticed construction workers on the plane over here. Prostitutes, too.

And drug dealers."

"Oh?" Reiner in mock shock.

"What kind of construction's been going on since the quake?"

"What do you think? Outside of patching up the city's power plants and the usual attempt to get the hospitals up and running again, it's been karaoke bars and whorehouses. Been a huge influx of construction workers—the yakuza are in black market heaven."

"Who's buying land now?" True asks.

Reiner snorts. "Who'd be that stupid?"

"Someone is buying up everything in sight. People are desperate to sell and somerichbody is grabbing their land."

"Is this somehow related to Rush?"

"What's the latest news from the States?"

"Geopolitical? Economic? Sports? Gossip?"

"Foreign aid."

"No aid, not from Europe, not from the States. Governments are screaming about foreign investment draining to Japan."

"Real estate markets, stocks and bonds are reeling?"

"That's right."

"Who here would have the muscle to buy land now?"

"You think someone's selling their assets overseas and using the proceeds to buy here?"

True pauses. "I don't know."

Reiner shakes her head. "Unh-uh. The land's worthless. That would mean someone's planning long-term, but basing projections on mega-fucked up data."

"What makes you say that? You yourself said that there would be massive rebuilding."

"There will be, but not here. We're talking about government plans to shift the population to other cities in Japan, to more evenly distribute resources. The only reason land was so dear was due to its scarcity. Japan is an island, dear, and the reason fifty million poor motherfuckers lived in this sitcom living room known as Old Edo was because it was the political and business capital. They're not going to rebuild the capital here."

"How do you know?"

"Because they know they shouldn't have plopped it here in the first place. They've been expecting the big one for forty years. It finally came. Now they'll move it. Before they couldn't. Now that they're starting at—pardon the pun—ground zero, they'll move it."

"You're never wrong?"

"Not this time."

"Where'll they move the capital?"

"To Osaka. Kyoto—that's the ancient capital. Nagoya. Some place like that. Not Sendai, though, after the tsunami and nuclear meltdown of 2011."

"Indulge me. Who'd have the means to land grab now?"

"Before I tell you, let me ask you something. Did you come here to hide or to find out what happened to Rush?"

"Both." Even he's not convinced by the uneasiness clinging to his voice.

Reiner shakes her head, almost sadly. "You're lying."

True studies the swirly-curly Japanese neon blanketing the walls and cutting through the sludgy darkness. "What's the deal with this place?"

"It's a karaoke bar."

"I *know* that. I mean, why's it still open?"

"The rich need entertainment in times of crisis. Take away people's food and jobs, they get pissed off. Take away their home entertainment systems and booze, they revolt."

The band plays on. The lead singer is not from the audience but is a regular band member. She wears—no, she exudes red leather. Her mascara is visible from across the cavernous dining hall, hair spiked, neon tattoos affixed to her shoulders, arms, even her neck. She's licorice-thin, sinewy, has a catlike face. Sings gruffly and tunelessly: "Killing me softly." True thinks if Piña were to sing, she'd sound this way.

"You want to know who has the bucks to buy all the land? There." Reiner indicates a table up in the balcony where a quartet of salary-execs play mahjongg. "Japan's most powerful business leaders. Add up their combined wealth and you're talking ten, twenty percent of Japan's GDP."

"Before the quake."

"Right. Who the fuck knows now, right? The fat one in the gray houndstooth?"

"The pattern's like taste buds."

"That's the one." Reiner laughs. A first since they met. "Never known for sartorial splendor. That's Hideaki Kyono. He was practically ruined by the quake; most of his money was in real estate, and you know what that's worth now. Look at him sweat. Probably just dropped a pant load. The lady next to him, that's Keiko Kibayashi. From Osaka. Rumors say she sexes with the Korean mob."

"You think it's true?"

"No question. They're all dirty scum, although I've got to admit to a sneaking admiration for any woman who can make it in this place. The one in black—it's his trademark—is Tsuyoshi Sato."

True looks him over. Can sense fury in Sato, barely restrained by layers of wealth and power. It gives True's intuition a kick.

Reiner leans closer. She talks softly, barely audible over the music. "They say he's so smooth he could rip your liver out and make you pay him for the privilege. A martial arts sensei. You want to be the man in the corp, you gotta pass tests in weapons and hand-to-hand. Cra-a-zy?"

"Yeah?"

"A couple years ago there was a scandal? One of his initiation rites got out of hand. They tested out some new technology on some would-be corp chieftains, and they went lalalala." She harmonizes with *Killing Me Softly*. Not badly either, True thinks.

"Dead?"

"If only those sad fucks had been so lucky."

"Where'd you hear this?"

"Grapevine, gossip teleshows—you know, like *Celebrity Stalker*, and there was another piece on *Weekly Global Newsmaker*. You know what shit those raggy shows are. We'll access the stories when we get back to my apartment. The legit press would have nothing to do with them."

"They afraid?"

"That—and the story was impossible to substantiate. Run a piece like that without at least double confirmation, you're not just looking at a mega-lawsuit, you're looking at corp torpedo hits on your network. Global Fortune boycotts. Even the big media outlets wilt when faced with lost ad rev. Producers undoubtedly asked themselves, Who needs that shit?"

True looks back over. "Who's the last guy? He looks harmless."

"Kodera. Came up the hard way. Ex-yakuza."

"Is there such thing as ex-yakuza?"

"Usually no. In his case: possibly. He was part of the Yamakita gang—started out as a kid money runner, depositing pachinko parlor profits. Apparently he was a natural computer stud. Showed gang members how to steal without leaving their homes. One of the gang's lieutenants recruited him and they made a play for control of the gang's finances. When the boss found out, war broke out. But no one could believe a kid could have been the culprit. The lieutenant was never found— Kodera turned him in, then covered his tracks. He covered them so well, the boss rewarded him for his loyalty. Two years later, Kodera wrestled away full control. Been on top ever since. Publicly he leads the political fight against them, too. Most yakuza hate him but can't touch him. They know if they attack his holdings, he'll sabotage their computer systems and bankrupt them. He's done it before."

"Isn't he worried about getting blown away here?"

"Not here. Never here. The whole place is rigged for surveillance. It's an agreed-upon neutral territory. Come near the place armed, you get smoked. They have missile defense systems, anti-aircraft, a force field, lasers, the place is a fucking fortified bunker."

"A fortified karaoke bar."

"You're safer here than practically anywhere else in the country."

"Unless Rush's killers are playing mahjongg."

Reiner pushes a button and the 3-D geisha flickers before them. "Thought we might splurge on the deluxe service. The easy-to-read menu bores me."

"*Konbanwa.*" The image bows.

True reaches for his wrist-top translator but the virtua-geisha, recognizing English, says, "Good evening, sir. Would you care for a drink? We are proud to present the most extensive bar in Japan."

"Sake, please. Atsukan."

"We Japanese have a variety of different types of Japanese traditional rice wines. Perhaps I can recommend a dry, light rice wine. Many of our foreign guests find it most satisfying."

"You see? That's not an option with the literacy-impaired menu." Reiner elbows True with a smile.

"I'll take your recommendation."

"Ditto," Reiner says.

The plug is pulled; the virtua-geisha turns to static.

True pushes his hand into the TV snow. "Why are the holograms cutting out?"

"The yakuza might have access to power when others don't, but that doesn't mean everything works. You saw how it is outside."

"Aren't you worried about being bugged? If this place is so sophisticated, how can we talk? I mean, I'm so careful I type instead of verbalizing commands to my home computer. You know there's technology that can pick up conversations from thousands of miles away."

"There are two results of everyone being equally vulnerable. Prison, or labor camps, for example, where everybody's belongings are accessible to everybody else. What happens there is that usually the meanest, toughest, ball-breakingest motherfucker wins. On a ship, however, where there's a modicum of discipline, theft is almost unheard of—and for that same reason. Everyone is equally vulnerable."

"You're saying since everyone is equally vulnerable, no one would dream of bugging anyone else?"

"Yup."

True stays pat at skeptical, reminds himself to watch what he says. He's about to pick up his sake vial when Reiner stops him. He thinks he feels her thumb trace a light circle on the crook of his thumb. Continents away from the screaming fight on the expressway.

"Now that you're here and going to stay a while, I hope, it's time you learned a little about Japanese etiquette." Pulls her hand away. "Pour your friend's drink first, then your own. It forces you to be aware of the needs of whomever you're with."

"Now you're concerned with my needs. Before you almost pounded me into roadkill."

The moment the song ends so do a thousand conversations at once. People look around, don't want to be the ones to break the spell. Then a virtua-geisha takes an order and the din rolls on. Like there was a glitch, a tear in the psychosocial behavioral matrix.

True swears Reiner's appearance is changing; she's softer, warmer. His own feelings toward her are metamorphosing as well. He may have been wrong.

"I fucked up, True. I was expecting an awesome journo. I know what you've accomplished in your life. But when I could trace you so easily, I said, 'Who the fuck is this guy? He's shit.' I'm beginning to see I was wrong."

Something not right, though. True's guard's still up.

She continues. "I know I can be a real solid platinum circuit-buster sometimes. I'm sorry. OK? Happy? So let me help. Tell me what you know of Rush's death."

"What do you get?"

"To be on the inside of a fucking juicy story."

True picks up his sake. "Ouch!" He drops the vial on the table, dribbles a few drops.

"Traditional sake cups. And tradition can be a real killer."

True sticks his thumb in his mouth. Cools the sting. "Not much to tell. I went to Rush's apartment, cut my hand, then left. Then the place blew."

"So *you* were the target."

True doesn't think it necessary to tell Reiner about the blood hologram, a vision he'd just as soon forget. "The missile must have keyed in on the DNA in my blood. Rush got in the way."

"Why'd you cut your hand?"

"You make it sound like it wasn't an accident."

"Rush dying instead of you is an accident. Unless you purposely left your DNA lying around."

"Why would I do that? Because he was sending me back to New York and I was pissed off? I didn't even know before I got there."

"What a coincidence."

"You said you don't believe in coincidences."

"Why were you axed?"

"For doing my job."

"Knowing Rush, if you really were doing your job, he would be anxious to get rid of you. He was not one to thrive on trouble."

"Unlike you."

"Unlike us. What were you on to?"

True shrugs. Uneasiness.

She clones his shrug. "Who's Aslam Aziz?"

The sake coats True's throat in dazzling lights. Aslam's murder made it on the local newscast, so he's not surprised.

"What do you know about Aslam?"

"That he was killed and that you were with him when it happened. I know it was a genetic-coded missile that did him in. Coincidently—there's that word again—the same kind of weapon that nuked our boy Rush."

"You talked to Rush."

"A couple hours before he died."

"You saw Bong Bong's interview?"

"Rush ran it for me."

"And…?"

"…and said you couldn't be trusted."

"He told me you'd rather I came over here to work with you."

"He felt threatened by you. And here you are."

True glimpses Reiner holding her hands in a teepee. Out of the corner of his eye: the bass player, charred wood skin and haloing afro, answering her.

Back to Reiner, who's sipping sake. "I'm going to order a beer chaser—you want one?"

"Sure."

She pulls up the virtua-geisha and orders. "All I want is the chance to help, True. I want to get in on the scoop. We split the glory. You need me."

"I *don't* need you."

"You *do* need me. And you know what? I should be the one who's bug-eyed and shit. Your last partner ended up Jackson Pollocking a condo wall. Your friend, Mr. Aziz, fell apart after meeting with you. So, like, what's your fucking problem?"

True weighs what he knows, accesses his intuition, but gets no read. "Let me think about it. If I think we can biz, I'll fill you in. On an NTK basis."

"On a need-to-know basis. Agreed."

The band breaks. The bass player is making his way toward True's table, with Sato at the mahjongg table tracking his strides. When Sato notices True, he turns away. The bassist becomes more familiar, and a few meters away, True places him.

Reiner doesn't stand. Instead she yawns and stretches in her chair. "I have someone for you to meet. He'll be working closely with us. His name's Odessa. My hacker."

Odessa pulls a lanky, insolent leg over a chair and squats. "What the fuck? I know you." Odessa grasps True's thumb with his hand, saws back and forth. "Finally get to hang in real-time. Last time I saw you, you were doing time in some cracker's bullshit."

"You've met?" Reiner's turn to be surprised.

"Not officially." True wonders why he didn't recognize Odessa immediately. "Awesome spell you pulled."

Reiner brushes hair from her eyes. "Another coincidence? You encounter a lot of them, True."

"It's a talent."

"Yo, sorry about that. It was fucking immature. Though that shit was funny, watching you varoom around inside that corrupt pol's speeches. But I found out it's better to keep a low profile in this biz."

The beer arrives, in a frosty mug gilded with liquid crystal ads. *Taste The Rising Sun*, it says. Odessa slides it away from Reiner, toward himself. Sculls a half-mug's worth, which leaves a hops and barley moustache. Reiner shrugs. Orders another.

"What's he here for?" Odessa asks Reiner.

"Same as you."

"Saint Fu, man!"

Slang new to True. "What?"

"Means shut the fuck up. Who you running from?"

True's eyebrows move almost imperceptibly.

"She-e-et. The world's best hacker and a fucking idiot sa-vant cyberoid both end up in this glitter hell. If the shit wasn't so tragic, it'd be fucking funny." Odessa lowers his voice. "I hacked the wrong motherfuckers. Leave it at that. You?"

"Similar." Odessa could be a major asset. True hopes when it comes time to go data shoplifting—and that time, he knows, fast approaches—Odessa will be the one to go. A game of one-upsmanship True's happy to lose.

"Safe here for a while, until computer systems are back on line. Then trouble may come in many forms."

"How much time?"

"SWAG?" Hackerspeak for *shitty wild-assed guess.*

"Sure."

"A month, maybe two." Odessa drains the rest of the beer. "Then somebody's going to try and get like the fucking Mar-quis de Sade on my ass."

Reiner says, "Marquis de Sahd, not Shar-day."

"What the fuck? I've only read the moniker myself."

True sips ice water. "Why are you playing at a karaoke bar?"

Odessa's shoulders graze his ears.

Reiner answers. "It's a great cover."

"Playing cover tunes *is* a great cover. 'Sides, I have a thing for retro-seventies. My daddy produced blaxploitation films back then. Collected residuals the rest of his Motown life, just like the white man." Odessa peers at the stage, then shoots mo-bile in a huff. "No time for a break. One of them corp gangsta motherfuckers wants to sing. So I got to play. Before the quake they had themselves a virtual band. Now they got themselves the real deal. Later." He clips True on the side of the head on his way to the stage.

Reiner looks almost sad. "He's running out of time. I don't think even he believes he's going to be able to hide here, get himself an ID that can't be traced. There are a lot of people looking for him—govs, corps, mafiosos. He fucked a lot of the wrong people."

"There a bounty?"

"Big big big fucking bounty. Metahackers, CyberCops the globe over are tracking him, all for that one lotto pay day. I pay him shit next to what he used to get, but he can trust me."

On the stage. Odessa plucks at his bass strings, the notes resonating less than they plod. Yet Odessa in most respects is as True pictured him: Someone who, though jalapeño-headed, is someone with whom he can biz. But he and Reiner will have to hurry. Neither Odessa nor True has much time before Tokyo is back online. Then he and Odessa will be like a virus under attack from corp hacker antigens.

Sato, meters away, closing fast. The kind of man who can frighten daylight. Reiner looks concerned. The first time he's seen her thrown off guard. Sato places a hand on her shoulder and True notes the scarred knuckles. His suit fits snugly, tailored to bend to his will. He whispers into Reiner's ear. At first, she denies what Sato says, then nods, holding out her hands as if trying to slow him down. Finally says, "OK. Fine. You win."

"And who is this?" Sato's sleet-y voice. A pursed smile.

Reiner switches to Japanese, but Sato cuts her off. "It is rude to speak Japanese in front of someone who is not familiar with the language."

"How do you know he doesn't speak Japanese?"

Sato to True. "*Nihongo ga dekiru?*"

True swallows. Guesses. "I don't speak well. I'm learning, though."

"Good." Sato holds out his hand and True shakes it. Can't get over how damp and hard Sato's hand is. "Japanese is not so difficult, I think, to learn to speak well enough to express oneself. But it is difficult to read."

"I'm aware of that," True says.

"What with all those kanji," Reiner adds.

Sato's measuring them. "Reading requires some two thousand characters. It is much simpler to read English. It's also simpler to read Americans. Can you say the same about Japanese?"

True volleys back. "The inscrutable Japanese?"

"Precisely. We do not wear out hearts on our wrists like you." Sato taps a finger on True's wrist-top. Uneasy silence. Then, "I didn't get your name."

True can't afford to lie, can't afford to tell the truth. "The name, Mr. Sato, is True."

Flashing gold molars. "How do you know my name?"

"Reiner pointed you out. I was curious as to the game you were playing."

"Mahjongg. And what game is it that you are playing?"

"Cut the intrigue. He's my assistant." Reiner blurts this too quickly, True thinks. "He's here to help me work on some stories. You know how messed up things are these days."

Sato cracks his knuckles. "Well, we all can use help in these trying times. I must see to my guests." To Reiner: "Please reflect on what I said."

"Reflecting now, Sato."

"That is all I ask." Sato, mahjongg-bound.

True's amazed at his own calm. "What'd he say to you?"

Reiner napkins away sweat. "He's PO'd about my quake coverage. Says I paint a negative picture, exaggerating the extent of the damage."

"Why does he care?"

"Think about it. He says if I tell people Japan is ruined, no investment will flow in. He told me I have a responsibility to put a positive spin on things because it'll make people's lives better. Now you know the major difference between a free press and a Japanese press."

"What are you going to do?"

"What I've been doing. The real question is, What are *you* going to do?"

Sato is patting Kodera. True averts his eyes when Sato looks over; studies his cup, runs his fingers over the black kanji painted on the side, wondering what they symbolize. "I don't know. You think he's going to check up on me?"

Reiner can't stop laughing.

CHAPTER 14

Reiner's apartment is framed by a dead sign over the door that when pumped with ions and electrons glows *WWTV Tokyo Bureau*. Reiner lights gas lanterns that color the walls newsprint-gray. Marijuana plants near the window stand two meters tall, the tops coated with cinnamon dust, the buds bursting. Female plants, because male plants don't flower. To cultivate, Reiner must have pursued the strategy Death To All Males. Reiner's creed in a nut graph. True pretends not to notice the indoor forest of contraband under 300-watt sulfur light, nor the skunky odor.

Reiner at her computer console. "I don't sell it, you know. I smoke it, sometimes entice sources with it."

"It's been decriminalized, so I don't know why you're bothering to explain."

"Not here. The Js treat all contraband the same."

True collapses on the couch, cornflower blue linen, delicate. No wonder Reiner left Dog outside.

Reiner's home office is a study in contradictions. Although it's well-ordered, it's an order that masks the disorder percolating underneath: Everything is categorized, compartmentalized, stored and filed, put, placed, and parked in its proper niche; but True's positive—just positive—that if he opens a kitchen drawer or closet door he'll get bopped on his head, as if Reiner's more concerned with appearance than substance. A lack of detail where it counts most. A dangerous trait for an investigative reporter.

Reiner's typing, confusion prickling her forehead. "This is some weird shit."

"What?"

"I can't access *Celebrity Stalker* or *Weekly Global Newsmaker.*"

"Are you sure they ran stories on Sato?"

"Y-e-e-s." She's annoyed True'd question her.

"Could there be a security block?"

"No. I just can't access them." Reiner pounds the console with her fist. "C'mon, you piece of shit. What's the matter with you? Let's try this instead. I'll run a check on all video-published material on Sato, then cross-reference it. That ought to do it." She types, cackles concomitantly. Then her smile bleaches out as her fingers slack over the keyboard.

"It won't work. They've deleted these references from all the databases, right?" True's seen it before.

"No way. I mean, no fucking way." Reiner swivels the console so True can see the blank screen. "Nothing. It's like the computer accessed the information and is displaying it on screen, but it's like it's been written in invisible ink."

"It might be a virus. You'd better code in your virus prevention system."

"Believe me. If there was even the hint of a virus in my system, I got enough bells and whistles in there to notify me."

"It's not you being notified that worries me."

"What are you worried about?"

"Shut it down."

Reiner shrugs.

True is shouting now. "Reiner! Disengage!"

Reiner in smug contempt as her finger remains poised. "Say *please.*"

And True sees the console light up in an audience of crackling colors, a hand reaching through, reaching for Reiner. But this is impossible, he knows, because digital media can't suddenly transform into physical reality. Sensing True's panic, Reiner jumps back. A muffled implosion as the console, like a condemned building, collapses in on itself. True and Reiner stand over the melted remnants.

"It can't be," True says. "It defies the laws of physics."

Reiner's face is ashen. She clears her throat. "Yet there it is."

A quick check and True says, "Looks like the database and keyboard are fine. The console is another matter."

"Could the computer house a poison pill to self-destruct if it receives the proper commands?"

"Maybe. I wonder if someone's rigged a warning system. Access info on Sato, and this is a little taste of what's to come."

"But it's clumsy." Reiner rubs her elbows. Carpet burns. "Why go to all this trouble if you're not going to go all the way?"

"Maybe Sato's protected all his files this way. It could be innocent."

"This? Innocent?"

"He might be protecting himself from the collapse of the Japanese info net. If so, this is only a deterrent. If someone died, it might raise a lot of questions—questions perhaps Sato doesn't want answered. But if he puts in a system that merely intimidates, it's less risky but probably equally effective."

Reiner kicks at the techno-corpse, throws up her hands. "Where am I going to get another console?"

"I'm sure there are a lot of people who'd be willing to sell you one to stay alive." He points through her window, to the street, to the mayhem below. "Anyway, we have a much bigger problem on our hands."

"What's that?"

"What if someone commanded the system to notify them when people try to access information about Sato? They could be on to us now."

"I doubt it. They'll probably assume whoever was poking around has learned the rules of this game."

"We can't be sure."

"I'll get Odessa to run a systems check in the morning. He'll know if anyone's on to us."

"What about tonight?"

She waves him off. "We'll be fine. The question I have is, Why booby trap the *Celebrity Stalker* and *Weekly Global Newsmaker* files? No one believes them anyway."

True scratches his arm. "Perhaps he's thin-skinned. Maybe he doesn't like bad press."

"Sato's secretive. His people are next to impossible to glean info from. Must be the martial arts background." Reiner heads over to a marijuana plant, pulls off a juicy bud. "I'm not nearly as disciplined."

With a practiced hand, Reiner pulls the bud apart, crumbles

ADAM L. PENENBERG

it, grinds it into a gentle blanket, and, holding a sheet of rolling paper with her free hand, sprinkles it in. She licks the paper's edge, rolls a one-handed joint, wets her fingertips and twists the end. Something about the way Reiner rolls a joint is ritualistic.

She studies her handiwork. "It's a little moist, but it'll still smoke. The seeds are a cross between Afghani and Hawaiian."

True eyes the J, hungers for it. "So it fights for the right to lie around and do nothing?"

Reiner's smile. "Something like that." She reaches into a drawer, pulls out a lighter.

Reality ripples through True. Sato could be sending out a hit team any moment. "Shouldn't we be keeping our heads clear? Aren't you supposed to be the careful one?"

"Yeah, but that's before you brought your wrist-top signal here and pulled me into your woes. Trouble's looking for you back in Nerula—with your wrist-top—and all they'll find is a Japanese kid playing *Cyborg Missile Command Central.*"

"And Sato?"

"Don't worry about him. He only moves when he has to."

"You know what I think? You think when I fuck up, we're fucked. When you fuck up, it means no big deal. I might be better off on my own."

"Where are you going to go? How long you think you'll last out there? C'mon. Stay here."

"But?"

"No 'but.' 'And.' As in *And* stay alive."

True's feet glued to the floor. Reiner sits on the couch, cups a hand, and takes a long drag. The joint's ash glows orange, and sweet incense filters into the air. One toke, he tells himself, just one drag, to take the edge off. Then the hell with it. The hell with her. He'll be off.

She passes it to him. True takes a deep hit, coughs as the smoke stings his lungs, but then warmth, happiness, a sense of well being oozes inside. "What were you signaling Odessa in the club?" His nose is clogged. Allergies to smoke.

"What do you mean?"

"I mean the hand signals." He gestures. "I saw them."

Reiner leans forward for the joint. "He likes to communicate that way. Too many spy shows, maybe. He's always changing the signs. Says it's the only truly safe way to communicate. Actually, what he said was, 'This way we won't get our mother-fucking asses fricasseed.'" Her imitation, complete with lisp, is dead on. "Look, before you go, let's have a late supper." She goes out back.

True follows and sees something he hasn't in a long time: rows of clear plastic curling over vegetables. Reiner has constructed a miniature greenhouse, with hoses that drip water onto a small pocket of land. The plot is fenced in, cloistered from the street. True watches as she unfurls the plastic cover, and after squeezing a few tomatoes, pulls two deep maroon ones off the vine. She rehooks the plastic, moves down the row, pulls up a cucumber, a small patch of basil, checks over what True recognizes as carrots, but they aren't ready. Without a word she returns to the kitchen, washes what she harvested, cuts the tomatoes and cucumbers, deals them onto fresh rolls, salt, pepper, a drizzle of olive oil, tops it with sprigs of basil, scrunches it down with a slab of mozzarella.

True can't remember the last time he ate a fresh tomato, not one of those genetically engineered jobs with the ten-year shelf life. The flavor squeezes the hinges of his jaw. He tells himself he'll be leaving in a minute, that after finishing this meal, and maybe after a few more tokes, he'll head into Tokyo's underbelly, check out the scene from below via the barflies, assassins, drug dealers, and other sundry lowlifes.

Halfway through her sandwich, Reiner lights up the joint again, jams it between fingers, cups her hands together, inhales. This to cool the smoke and cut harshness.

"Tell me about Odessa." True accepts the joint from Reiner. His mind trembles with the satisfaction of yet again evading reality.

"What do you want to know? You seem to know him as well as I do."

"How'd you find him?"

"He found me. My computer system died right after the quake, and he happened to be nearby. I suspect he was monitoring my calls and knew what shape I was in, so he just showed up." She leans back, arms outstretched. "It's too bad. You can't hide forever. Maybe he'll board a plane that goes down or step into an elevator that turns into a gas chamber. And unless we solve why Aslam and Rush were killed, you may be joining him. But this is your lucky day, because I smell scoop." She passes him the joint. "I'm willing to give you a hand. Of course, even if we manage to get whatever it is on the air, no guarantee you'll live to enjoy it."

True's zoned, almost doesn't care whether he lives or dies. Has a vague recollection of Reiner talking to him, telling him a story about sweet potato vendors in Japan, how they play the traditional song through loudspeakers instead of singing it, how translated it goes: "Roasted sweet potatoes. Roasted on bricks. Yeah, they're tasty."

She laughs a laugh, 100 percent unadulterated Reiner. Opens the door to a side room True hasn't noticed. "You can stay here. You're in no condition to go out anyway. No need to thank me." She kicks a futon, turns the direction. "Wouldn't want your head facing north. It's bad luck."

"Bad luck?" True feels pink. "Now that's funny."

True doesn't remember having fallen asleep. Dreamless, he REMed straight to late morning. Still stoned, detached. The dull thud in his brain a nagging reminder to steer clear of ganja madness.

"MedTekton, huh?" Reiner is spooning scrambled eggs flecked with tomato, onion, and parmesan cheese onto True's plate. Her camp stove flame flickers out.

"Could be."

"The name is familiar."

"You do a piece on medical technology recently?"

"Nope. Not that." Reiner holds a wooden pepper mill over her plate and dusts her breakfast. An antique. "But I'll remember eventually." She taps the side of the pepper mill. "Want some?"

True holds out his plate. "How do you manage fresh food when everyone else is practically starving?" True blows, cools the eggs.

"From my garden. I traded for the eggs. See the new console? I bartered tomatoes, cucumbers, and *daikon* for it. The guy threw in some eggs into the deal. He and his family were taking off for western Japan anyway, so they needed food that travels well."

True savors another bite. "How can you keep your computer system running without electricity?"

"Odessa took care of that. He increased its electrical efficiency like a thousand percent, then rigged up some solar cells."

"But there isn't enough sun, is there? The quake dust blocks out the rays."

"Yeah, but he set them up to suck light out of the air. At least enough to keep my computer up. It doesn't take much. Of course, I don't have enough power to send stories via satellite to the States, so I have to go to the public phone banks and bribe my way to the front of the line."

"Where are the phone banks located?"

"You're not thinking of going, are you? My advice is to lie low."

True hugs silence.

Reiner stops chewing. "You want to catch some news?"

"Can you pull up news from Luzonia?"

Reiner taps in commands. Secs later True's watching the lead story, gagging on his breakfast.

Bong Bong's making an announcement. "We the Peoples of Nerula regret that flight"—he quibbles in Luzonian—"ah, flight 003 from Tokyo was shot down—Boom!— by our defense systems. There will be much investigations, but we think it was some Millivanilli—Wow, that's hard to speak. Malalayamama. No wait. Malayanalayan. OK—spy plane. As you know well, we been fighting a insurgency at there. No survivors. Sorry. Bye bye." Reporters heave questions, but Bong Bong will only say, "That's all folks."

Reiner and True's eyes lock.

True gasps. "Oh, no."

"Shit! Shit! Shit! Shit! We killed that kid."

"And everyone else on board."

"It's our fault."

"Yes."

"This shit is serious."

"I know."

"Get out."

"OK." True's still sitting.

"No, wait. Stay. They must think you're dead now. You're OK."

True slides his plate away. "It's sad."

"It's a damn shame is what it is, True."

CHAPTER 15

He jumps off a grumpy shuttle bus at Shibuya. It's Luzonia-hot, so damp that True's shoes practically sprouted moss overnight. He passes Hachiko, the landmark loyal dog. Reiner told True that Hachiko met his master at the station every night after work. Even after his master died, Hachiko waited. Now the statue's cracked, one paw crumpled to dust, which someone repaired with solder and a blowtorch, imbuing patches of the dog with a Stalin-gray pallor. True winds through beggars on blankets selling shoes, bicycles, car parts, clothes, misc junk like an antique key ring with the name of a hotel on it, as if the key could somehow lead the buyer to greater riches.

His nerves are jangling. He ducks out of the rain and into a building, follows the signs for Japan Aid Inc., into the lobby, down a coily staircase to the basement. The stairs' grade is steep, like falling in love with Eden: a vertiginous descent. He's shaking now, tries not to show it. Remembers his wife's software programs, clearer the closer he gets to her, artfully beautiful. They were too good. True fell ill, streams of images, childhood memories, reality music, flights of fancy, all blended into orgasmic joy. At the time he didn't know where he was or what he was doing. He remembers he hurt Eden and she hurt him. Tit-for-tat tragedy.

A spacious, open area, all aid workers equal: no cubby holes or offices, just hundreds of tables and chairs. True stands four steps from the basement, listening to shuffling feet and echoing voices, watching as food is served to the hungry, counseling to the frightened, clothes to the weary, medicine to the sick. He's about to inquire at the information desk when he sees her.

She's more radiant than ever. Her hair catches the light, her movements fluid and graceful, her skin lustrous. He watches as she bounces her head and shoulders when agreeing, a mannerism he loved, still loves. She smiles at an old woman and True's blindsided by a sickly, churning sensation inside. When Eden's gaze brushes his, he bolts up the steps, almost collides with a woman on her way down and a man waddling up.

He runs out to the street and stops for breath near Hachiko. When True and Eden announced their engagement he met her Japanese grandmother, an earthy woman fascinated by crystals, faith healing, feng shui—"wind" and "water" in Chinese—a blend of astrology, design, and Eastern philosophy aimed at harmonizing man, woman, and good fortune. She painted a sign for them, the kanji for "Double Happiness." But the kanji—he still has it buried in his possessions somewhere— was drawn incorrectly. One of the matching characters was mangled, the top smeared, a stroke off line.

True knows it was his happiness that was ruined.

He never recovered.

Eden did.

That simple.

True and Reiner spread on tatami, flanked by shoji, sipping green tea. True dips raw fish, translucent white in the air, cloudy blue on the plate, in soy sauce.

Reiner snaps her bamboo chopsticks in half. She's done. "You sure do eat. You've eaten half a plate of that stuff."

"I've never tasted anything like it."

"Well, *fugu*'s unique to Japan."

"Blowfish, right?"

"Yeah. Flirt with your chef, distract him, you croak." Reiner's cheeks rinsed in rosé. "Feel like I snorted coke."

"It's the poison."

"You're not careful, you're going to get fat." She scrolls True's physique. "Well, you still have a ways to go. Like ten kilos."

True's appetite since coming to Japan has been out of control. All he wants to do is send cascades of drink over and around his tongue, rockslides of food down his gullet, vaporous clouds of smoke to his brain. It takes a full complement of will power not to palm another piece. "Tell me more about this guy Hatanaka we're waiting to see."

"As you can see, he's rich. Très rich. And he likes to be called Hot. He's like a million years old and bed-ridden now. But he's had an incredible life, and there's no better source if you want to know what's really happening in Japan."

"How'd he get so inside?"

"His family's story goes back a ways. His father was a POW guard in World War II in what was once the Philippines, so he knows your stomping ground pretty good. Digging graves, one of the prisoners stumbled onto some treasure."

"Yamashita's gold?"

"That's a myth. Another treasure. Hot's father commandeered it as the Allies swept in, wandered around Asia for eight years dressed up as a monk."

"And the treasure?"

"He got it in. I don't know how, but he did. When he returned to Japan, the Occupation was in full swing. He built a corporate empire from the ground up."

"With the help of some Filipino treasure."

"Things went well for his family for a while, until it became clear that Hot, the son, couldn't have a son. Impotence equals impotence here. Blood ties are everything. Not long ago, his son-in-law took over."

"Why didn't his wife go in for artificial insemination? Or DNA home-shopping?"

"They don't go for that shit here. Now here comes the soap opera. When his wife's family took over, they spread rumors he'd gone insane. Moved him here to this condominium in Chiba. Mental illness here is unforgivable, so he thrill-seeks by being my deep throat."

"Who's the son-in-law?"

"Can't say. Strictly off-the-record. Don't bother checking. Records were erased long ago."

"Sounds familiar."

The door hums open. Reiner pushes herself upright. "That's our cue."

They wind through the house, the hallways narrow and cedar-scented, and wash up in a large hospital-white room with a lonely bed in the middle. IV tubes drip drugs into a withered man, his face the color of a spent cigar-ash, his hair in splotches, like desert sagebrush. He looks up. Slow-motion blinks. "You are?"

"True." He's struck by how familiar the man looks. Since arriving he's been confusing people, faces reminding him of other faces, J-versions of friends, relatives, or cultural icons.

The man breathes slowly and shrilly. "Interesting to have a name that is an adjective."

"Hello, Hot." Reiner kisses his cheek. Even though his expression doesn't change, True sees he's delighted.

"Ah, Reiner. A pleasure. Apologies for the delay." Hot unpricks the tube from his arm and hangs it over the side of the bed. "My youth-bearing injection, a concoction of hormones, really. It's hard to believe I'm so old. But on the inside I feel as young as you. That's the greatest injustice."

"The earthquake must have been frightening." Reiner leans on the bed's edge.

"As you can see, this house is well-constructed. There was a moment when I worried, but then it was all over. Quite exciting." Another breath. "Reiner, what is it you wish with me?"

"Some weird things have been happening. First of all, a company called MedTekton has begun marketing untraceable plastic for assassinations weaponry. You know of any Japanese companies with access to this technology?"

"Phaseplast, is that correct?"

"Yes."

"But it is not possible to know which companies. I have heard many things regarding this plastic. It can't be traced, *ne*. Every weapons contractor in Japan wants the technology, not only for casing, but for other products, such as self-destruct spy tools for corporate espionage."

True steps forward. "But you can't say who has it?"

"No."

Reiner's turn. "Have you heard anything about someone buying up large tracts of Tokyo land now?"

"There is an old Chinese proverb: *A peasant would have to stand a long time on the side of a mountain before a roast duck would fly into his mouth.* What I mean to say is that if you wish to prosper in Japan, or anywhere for that matter, you must seize the initiative. Of course someone is buying land. That is forward-thinking. Buying when the price has hit bottom. That is how my family earned its fortune."

Reiner ahems. "I thought it was from some Filipino treasure."

Hot's cheeks brush the pillow. "At that time my father did not want people to know the real path to his fortune. Before he returned after the war, he had my mother purchase land right after the Tokyo fire bombing. She approached families and offered next to nothing. Then with some money our family had stashed abroad, they hired men to secure our land—they worked for practically nothing. Soon, we were the most powerful company in Occupied Japan."

"Then someone has learned the lessons of history well," True says.

"Corporations are as unique as people. Some shrink when forced to confront adversity, some faint, some hold their own, still others thrive. We thrived, and after my brother died, I thrived. Although no one, not even the mightiest corporation, can predict what is going to happen. Smart, aggressive corporations can adapt to anything."

Reiner rubs her eyes. "But this land will be worthless once they move the capital."

"Why do you feel the capital will relocate?"

"Why wouldn't they relocate?"

Hot shuts his eyes, ponders. "Politics is money. Follow the money, Reiner, and you will understand Japanese politics. On every issue there is something at stake. Winners and losers. If the capital relocates, then it is safe to assume that the persons or people who are purchasing land will not reap the rewards of their investment. And if someone is collecting land, it is also safe to assume that he or they have extraordinary assets. There are few with that kind of clout these days."

"You're saying whoever this is, they'll make sure the capital doesn't relocate."

"Politicians are also affected by this earthquake. They have their investments, their homes, their families. If someone were to offer them sufficient compensation, I am sure they would help block relocating the capital. And a vote of such major importance would require a two-thirds majority."

True cuts in. "Wouldn't other corpsters benefit if the capital moved to Osaka or Kyoto?"

Hot moves his neck. There's a good old-style camera-shutter click. "Of course. The question, then, is, who has the greater influence? Remember: To move the capital would require many more votes, and therefore a great deal more money, than doing nothing. Will those who stand to benefit have the resources to prevent the capital from remaining here?"

"But won't representatives from places where the capital could relocate bring pressure to bear?" True asks.

"It would depend on who provides the most money. I would assume representatives from Sapporo and Kagoshima, cities with little chance in the capital relocation sweepstakes, would come cheaply."

True and Reiner lock eyes.

"Uncover whoever it is that is pressuring the government to hold the capital here, and you will discover the answers to many of your questions." Hot is slipping into sleep, his voice now tinny and distant. "This I guarantee."

CHAPTER 16

Tokyo's Parliament was not spared. Although constructed on solid rock, buildings heaved and ho'd with the prevailing winds, finally sighing, but not buckling, from the quake's insistent rumblings.

Reiner rearranges the dress that hugs her as a lover. "You know, one of the reasons they didn't move the capital before was because these government bureaucrats thought they'd be safe, so who cares what happens to the masses?"

Hutches of politicians aping concern for the nation's plight. Already renovation is underway. Workers buzz, paint over cracks, reseal joints between the floor and walls, install glass panes, polish what's left, replace what isn't. Telelinks are out until power's restored city-wide.

"Morita-san!" Reiner calls after a figure clad in black, and Morita makes a face like Reiner's an ebola carrier. "He loves me. I've nailed his boss five times for corruption and the fucker's reelected every time." She tramps over while True stays put.

Seeing he can't avoid her, Morita talks in pursed pitches. "Reiner. What is it now? I am extremely busy."

Reiner answers in Japanese and True turns on his wrist-top, catching the tail of her response as displayed on his air-screen: *...it moving? And if not, why not?*

True pretends he doesn't hear. The aide answers in English. The language power play. "Really, Reiner. I can't be seen talking to the likes of you after the last story you ran on Parliamentarian Takeshita."

Reiner's head dips in an unmistakable bow, albeit a shallow one. *Was I not accurate in everything I reported? Because if I was not absolutely one hundred percent correct, then please accept my apologies and tell me where I have erred.*

True's struck by how different she acts while speaking Japanese. Reiner bows, her hands held delicately at her sides, fingers together in perfect symmetry. True imagines her facial expressions turning Oriental, as if she's taking on a whole new psyche—a cultural schizophrenic.

"Many of his constituents were extremely upset at what they heard."

I included your official statement denying the charges. Was I not objective in my approach to this video-article?

The only word True catches while listening was *bee-dee-oh.* "Video" in Japanese.

"You were not."

Then you have my deepest apologies. I will review my notes and if I can rectify the situation, I will.

After hearing this last bit, True decides somebody must be impersonating Reiner.

The man grunts. True can tell he's pleased.

Reiner dips her head a little farther, her backside brushing the hall's wall. *Now. Are there any bills that deal with the relocation of the capital?*

"I can't tell you these things in public, you know that."

Reiner lowers her voice. *Do not be concerned by other politicians or spies. Everybody has a lot of other things on their minds right now.*

Morita glances around furtively, then says something softly, in Japanese. Reiner wins that battle. True boosts the surveillance levels. *Of course this is so. I've missed you, Reiner. I haven't been able to get you out of my mind.*

What impending bills are there?

Can't you at least acknowledge the evening we spent together was special?

Is there support to move the capital to Osaka?

The man sighs, and it hits True: He's in love with Reiner. True almost pities him, even though it's difficult to muster much sympathy for a politico.

You have a heart of steel, Reiner.

Don't say such things.

And a pussy of gold.

The bills, Morita-san. The bills.

Aren't you going to say something about my cock?

Reiner with hands on hips, top lip folded behind bottom teeth. Playfully pretending she's shocked. Reiner acting coy. A side of her True wishes he'd missed.

I will tell you, Reiner, but only if you have dinner with me.

Is that so? But if you do not tell me, I will just ask someone else, dear.

Another heavy sigh. True can almost hear the man's heart beating. What power is it that Reiner has over him? Morita launches into an official response, which includes numerous asides regarding the effort Japan's politicians are undertaking to improve quality of life, the usual effluvium of pols the world over. Finally he rolls out a nugget True and Reiner can use.

There have been bills introduced to move the capital to Nagoya, another bill to relocate to Kyoto, another to Osaka and one more that would eliminate the concept of a capital all together. This is the bill sponsored by Takeshita-san. It is his feeling the country would benefit from the country's representation being evenly distributed.

Is there any support to keep the capital in Tokyo?

Morita sputters. *Look around you, Reiner. That's preposterous.*

Any idea when these bills will get acted on?

There's no hurry. There is more pressing business. Morita takes Reiner's hand. *I'm taking a big risk talking with you, holding your hand here in public. No aide should be so compromised.*

Reiner pulls her hand from his and Morita's left holding air. Walking away, she says over her shoulder, *I'll call you.*

"Reiner!"

She turns and Morita says softly, desperately, *I'll be waiting.*

Outside. True sees fires still smoldering far away.

"It's not his fault." Reiner skips down the capitol's stone steps.

"What do you mean? You're so irresistible Morita can't help himself?"

"In a manner of speaking. I needed an inside governmental source, so I invited myself over and put on a hypnotic program on his home entertainment system. I slipped the suggestion in his mind that he love me." She winces. "I know, I know, but what can I say? Men are weak? At least I didn't sleep with him. He's the biggest *chikan* in government."

"What's a chikan?"

"Somebody who grabs women's asses."

"What did he say about Takeshita, his boss? He's pushing for decentralization? Why would a—I assume corrupt—pol push for that? What's in it for him?"

"Think technology. He's funded by the electronics giants, the ones who design the computers, software, and digital office work stations that would rake in the yen if decentralization took off."

"I see."

"Maybe you do, maybe you don't. Listen: The whole system is bullshit. They get their cut and then govern based on their own economic interests. The bureaucracy took control years ago, even after the Ministry of Finance almost drove the economy into the ground by subsidizing exports, manipulating the market, controlling who could have stocks by keeping stocks too high for most individual investors, the real estate fiascos, forcing banks to hold the stocks of other banks. The system was predicated on corruption, but not before manufacturers had positioned themselves in world markets. You can't take anything at face value."

"You don't believe Morita?"

"I believe him because there's money in what he says."

"What about what Hot said?"

Reiner grinds her teeth. "What he said made sense, too. Just because Morita doesn't know, doesn't mean there isn't pressure to keep the capital here. We have to keep digging."

There's a commotion by Reiner's car. Someone trying to slip inside and drive off, but Dog snaps at his leg, growling bestially.

The would-be car-jacker limps away.

Reiner races over, pulls out a biscuit. "Good girl, good girl. What a bargain!"

True stirs at first light, watches the sun stagger over the city. He suffered dreams, memories that may have been or never were; possibilities, impossibilities, and improbabilities, painful remembrances of his life separate from Eden. The skewed double-happiness kanji twists, contorts before his eyes, inky lines consumed by fire. His kanji—his character—splits, then shatters, while Eden's remains resplendent, nonpareil. He needs to talk with her. Only this can save him from TV memories supplanting prior reality. Wonders why he hungers and thirsts so these days, begs for ganja, pines for lost love.

Children scrounge outside Eden's office. Meanwhile, across the street, reconstruction in progress. Another combo dance club-hotel-casino. True, inside now, sees Eden in the flesh, lazing on the downward spiraling stairs. A familiar pose, Eden sitting on steps, her chin hammocked in her hands, her elbows in turn propped up by her knees. When she was troubled or in need of time to herself, she would sit like this, let her hair hang over her eyes to shield her.

He struggles with what to say, rejecting each thought as it arises. A few false starts, a few sideways steps, then, "I've missed you, Eden."

She doesn't move. Silence unfurls uncomfortably.

"Eden? Is that you?"

From somewhere under the hair: "Go away, True. I don't want to see you."

Watching this, not living it as if it were happening. Two actors doing their jobs, reading their lines, collecting pay credits, yearning for fame, fortune, and hot and cold running favors.

She looks up, tears magnifying her eyes' hazel color and size; deep circles are scooped underneath. "I can't, True. I wouldn't be able to go through it again. You understand, don't you?"

He does understand, just wishes he could remember what *it* is. "I'm sorry, so sorry, Eden. I fell out of this world and into another. But I'm back." He's amazed at his blubberings, aware that at some point he'd had this very same conversation with her.

Eden rubs away diamond tears. "People here have bigger problems than you."

And didn't bring them on themselves. That's what she would've said if she wanted to hurt him. He celebrates her compassion, but remembers an unstated thought is still a thought.

"I just want to talk."

"Goodbye, True. Good, goodbye."

She winds down the steps and True knows he'll see her in his mind long after she's vanished. He can't bear to remain inside. Outside, he's alone. Doesn't know what life's next step will be. Looks out over the dilapidation, the desperation.

Eden, through the revolving door and back, takes his arm. Says, "I have to think things through, then we'll talk. But no promises."

True's out of Shibuya and in Ginza, following hastily constructed signs. He's walking over a bridge that is, amazingly, still standing. Thousands of gas lanterns blot the landscape.

True watches the moon climb over vaporous clouds.

Others are on the bridge, leaping off, long, elastic bungee cords pulling taut just prior to impact. He stops to watch. There are a dozen or so jumpers, tying cords around their ankles, tipping back flasks, tripping on drugs, performing double, even triple flips. Taking risks because there's precious little else.

"Psssssst." A woman in a jacket patched together from swatches of zaggy-colored Guatemalan fabrics. "*Gaijin*. Tie my legs, OK?"

She's young, maybe 20, hair tied in scores of tight braids, her skin tanned, legs strong and lithe, her face oval and iridescent like the moon overhead.

He pulls the frayed ends of her cord. The other end is knotted around a pylon.

"Tighter." Her voice is tequila-harsh.

He pulls tighter.

"More. I don't want to end up like *okonomiyaki*, you know?"

"What's that?" True's muscles just about to give out. Ties a knot around her finger, which turns purple as he knots a second loop. She pulls it out.

"Japanese pizza. You never had it? It's good. Try it."

"I will."

She checks his handiwork. Holds her thumb, finger to her lips.

True pats his pockets as other jumpers fly, about 50, 75 meters off the ground. He finds a Reiner J and hands it over.

She pockets it in stony joy. "All right, *gaijin*." High-fives him, a message of gratitude. Then she wrists out a bowie knife lodged in her belt to trim bungee frays. True realizes the end around the pylon has to be retied after each jump, as the cord gets shorter each time she cuts herself down. She hops to the edge of the bridge, clenches the knife in her teeth, turns to face True, and jumps. He watches as she speeds to earth, her body flipping downward as the cord pulls taut. When she bounces back up, she waves, then falls. She hangs a couple of meters off the ground, pirouetting upside down, the city's lantern lights leoparding her. Finally, she cuts the cord and somersaults onto a pile of cushions.

On terra firma she celebrates, accepts a bottle from another jumper. The sky has changed color, is less moonlit-gray than quake-paint orange now. Down the other side of the bridge is the international phone bank, the only telecommunications link with the outside world. True jumps in the line for journalists and foreign diplomats. From his vantage point he sees a festival in progress. The line is long, there being only three videophones designated for diplomat and journo use, and he spends his time thinking and watching the fertility festival.

After what seems an eternity, True takes his turn, swipes his debit card into the slot and punches in the number. Since there's still too much static in the atmosphere for his wrist-top to tap into any satellite feeds, he's forced to rely on barbaric cable connections. An endless stream of advertisements fills dead time: security systems, VR sex aids, a new and improved body condom, discounts on tasers, lasers, other light armaments.

He's into WWTV's library database. Patches his wrist-top into the phone jack, keys in the names *Kibayashi, Kyono, Kodera,* and *Sato,* requests background info on Japan's business and real estate practices. The grating of a gas-powered engine. True urges on the data-transference with impatient body language. A double beep: Someone's cut access. He must have tripped the security net. True disconnects and checks the data. A blaze of pictures and digital information fires on screen. The *Celebrity Stalker* and *Weekly Global Newsmaker* video-stories are inside. He fast-forwards through them. Reiner is wrong.

It's not just any gas-powered vehicle coming for him. A motorcycle, groaning over the bridge. No time to contemplate. True sprints away from the grumbling howls of the Harley and races into the fertility festival, trying to raise Reiner on his wrist-top. But too much interference.

It's a Buddhist celebration. In front of a temple, men in white *yukatas* trimmed with blue are chanting, "*Oni wa soto, fuku wa uchi*"—"Out with the demons, in with good fortune." True heard Reiner utter these words just this morning. Part of the ritual is to eat the same number of parched beans as your age, which, Reiner said, the Japanese believe promotes good health. A sumo wrestler scatters beans over the crowd. Many swig beer from bottles and sake from casks.

Festival-goers carry a portable shrine, and True runs alongside as it bobs, supported by an inebriated foursome weaving through the mob of worshippers. The motorcycle crashes through the revelers, who are slow to clear—probably think it's part of the festivities. A gargantuan phallus, shouldered by stumbling men, snakes through the mob. Cut from gray stone, a flower attached to the tip, a face carved out of the front. A sumo wrestler, skin the color and texture of tapioca pudding, flings more beans, which people try to catch in their mouths.

True dodges the bean artillery, ducks further into the whirling crowd, hurdles a cask of sake. A man jumps True, kisses him on the lips. True slips aside, wipes his mouth, keeps searching for a way out. The bike continues to close, the bosozoku knocking people aside. The face of one of True's *Kosoku Dori* attackers.

There. A ray of an opening. A building insulted by the quake, a gaping hole cut through it leading to open air, then the bridge. Leaning against the façade, a line of people passing the time, sipping rice wine. There's a hand-painted sign, which True can't read, and a man inside practicing karate, blocking imaginary blows and striking back furiously. True fights through the bean-eaters and shoots through the hole.

He's suddenly in a field, a towering white castle in the distance. A man is scaling castle walls, eluding flying knives and crazed ninjas sprouting from dust. True looks to his right: a data grid, a list of Virtual Reality options—in Japanese. His wrist-top translator is gone. (The program doesn't allow cheating.) A ninja springs forward. True puts up his hands reflexively and blocks the kick. No pain. Out of the corner of his eye sees 20,000 added to his score. The other player is in the billions. The ninja kicks again, hits True with a series of rapid-fire karate chops, although True doesn't feel them, any of them. His point tally holds pat.

There's a commotion, but it's coming from outside the program, anger that True didn't wait his turn and amusement over his plight. Now the yowling motorcycle. True tries shutting down the program, points to the grid. First the sky changes to green, then the terrain goes from flat to mountainous to desert to urban jungle back to medieval; rivers appear, disappear, the ninjas speed up then slow down. But he can't find the fucking *off* switch.

A wizard with a cocaine-white beard drops down, waves

his wand in mesmerizing circles—into the Ouroboros. True backs away, blinded. He's been nuked. The game is over. The wizard trash talks, tells True he's toast. True jumps through the hologram and out, toward the bridge. The bosozoku shuts down the game and the Harley growls again. True picks up a plank, sidesteps the bike, and jousts. The rider strikes wood, riddling True's side with splinters. But he goes down. Hard. The bike groans on solo, lists, topples.

True limps to the bridge. The speed triber is back on his bike and gunning for him. True blurs by leaping bungee-ers, his lungs squeezed against his ribs. His nemesis is on the bridge, closing, his rifle sight jiggling with the bike, shining on an expansion joint, a bungee jumper, True's wrist.

He weaves. A rifle's smack and echo. Pandemonium on the bridge. Over there, his bungee mate waving him on, knife clenched in her teeth. No hesitation. He leaps onto her and they plummet to the ground; the bridge, the buildings, the world scream upward as True falls downward. He's vaguely aware of more gunshots as they hold each other tight. The cord groans, cranky iron joints, the ground about to swallow them. They jerk to a stop. She cuts the cord and they hurtle down an embankment, bullets kicking up dirt around them. Into a patch of woods.

"Cool, huh?" she says after they slip out of sight. She's breathing hard. Eyes shine.

"Thanks."

Waves him off like it's nothing. "Come back. We'll get high and do the inverted elevator together. Now that's, like, some shit."

She hefts his balls slightly. Her way of paying respect.

CHAPTER 17

True's back at WWTV. Opens the door and sees Reiner at work. "Where's Dog? In fact, where's your car?"

"Dog's dead, the car stolen, and I'm on deadline." Reiner says this without looking up. She's cutting footage and splicing narrative: "And in a controversial decision, the Japanese Government has voted to retain Tokyo as the nation's capital. Details are not available, but it is generally accepted that there were bills favoring a return of the capital to Kyoto, the ancient capital, and Osaka, among others. One radical suggestion was to eliminate the concept of a capital all together, proposing that governmental ministries be spread evenly throughout the nation.

"But in the end, as is usually the case in Japanese politics, it's the status quo. I'm Reiner Jacobi, WWTV Global, reporting from Tokyo." She files her story. "Finally finished. You want to get high?" She rubs her hands together. When she notices True, her eyes bubble. "Nice. I'll get the medkit."

True looks into a mirror. The splinters are ugly, but he's surprised to see his body looking better. He's put on weight recently, muscle too, looking more like he used to. Rustlings, then Reiner emerges. She cleans his wounds, lathers on cream to dissolve the splinters, and towels it off. When finished, she says, "You want to tell me what happened?"

"I ran into one of our friends from the expressway. I got away, but not without a little trouble."

"Fucking speed tribe Neanderthals. Soon, them and the yakuza are going to own the whole bowl of noodles here."

"Don't forget the corps." A memory: True wandering down 5th Avenue. A woman with a micro-boombox squeezing CyberRap ordering him out of her beat, as if she owned the rhythm. The question is, Who owns what in Tokyo today? "Hot was right about the capital."

"Never should have doubted him. I've been trying to find out who sponsored the bill to keep the capital here, or even find out who voted for it. But nothing. The gov feels vulnerable, no doubt."

"They should feel vulnerable."

"I've got something for you to see."

Reiner pulls up some video, unedited footage, panoramic scenes of a frightened city, sweeping shots of people in the days after the quake. True watches the city crumble again, buildings folding like accordions, people pinned under rubble. Then, enraged storms of fire.

The vibrations yield a tidal wave that pounds the shore and spills into the city. A train surfs by. The spectacle is awesome— nature obliterating trillions of dollars worth of property, squelching millions of lives. Then the aftermath. Dazed residents pulling themselves free from wreckage, the search for the missing. Reiner filed countless reports—on the quake, the economy, gang violence, survivalist groups, religious cults, life in temporary shelters.

Reiner freezes the video: "See this guy?"

True: "Yeah."

"I've been filtering this video chunk through a computer. Took all the possibilities, ran it through this chip-based unit, and looky here."

She accesses the phonic enhancement program. The computer answers, "Taro Tamura, aged 38, divorced, works as a vice-president for the Matsuo Real Estate Company, Ltd."

Reiner waves a finger at the screen. "After analyzing Tamura's lip movements and those of the dude he's yakking with, the computer gave me this synopsis. Check it out. This is sweet."

Subject Tamura agreeing to pay one million yen to unidentified male for rights to property, located at 5-2-11 Mitsukoshi-cho, Ikebukuro, Tokyo.

"One million yen is nothing." True plugs *Matsuo Real Estate* into his wrist-top, accesses their biz-biofile. "No land purchases in five years. Lots of sales, though. It's as if the people running the company knew to get rid of the land before the quake."

"I'll get Odessa to tap into the datasphere."

"How'll he get power for that?"

"He'll work something out. He practically put together the whole system by stealing microchips from vending machines and public phones after the quake knocked them out."

She inputs a communication's code, and almost immediately Odessa's face, grotesquely distorted, fills the screen. "Har-dee-*har*-dee-har-har." He backs up, now clear. "What the fuck you want?"

"Like, I got a job for you? You *do* want to make some money?"

"Natch, scratch be the right match for this hacker-deluxe catch."

"Sending data now."

Studying for a second, Odessa says, "Easy shit. It'll take a while, though. It ain't centralized, and if I'm going to be inside land transactions databanks, that means avoiding the mad dog. I got enough problems, you know?"

"I know. Just do it."

"Yeah, yeah."

His face dissolves.

True's awake, sweaty scared, his heart gunning. He. Is. Stoned. Extremely. Sto-o-oned. They're in his bedroom, but Reiner's on the floor, back against the wall, blowing pot rings, watching them float away like saucers.

She offers, "Hey handsome. You want some? You had a lot before you passed out."

True accepts the narc. Does the narc. Doesn't even faze his lungs now. He blows smoke through his nose and falls again into shattered worlds.

"True. I've been thinking." She leans forward, touches his arm. For a moment True thinks she may be seeking love. But no. "Sorry I treated you like shit before." She stands, legs spread in an upside down V. "Get some REM. We've got a long day tomorrow."

Reiner closes the door, and True hopes he'll dream of love. Of Eden.

"Shit. Not having wheels sucks." Reiner says this after she and True ride three buses and finally stand outside Matsuo Real Estate Company. It's a small shop held together by tape. Inside, a lone cop waving a halogen torch. True's first instinct is to run. Reiner steps in.

"Ah, Reiner-san, *Konnichiwa.*" The cop bows, his light bouncing off the walls, off True.

"*Konnichiwa.*" Reiner bows back.

Electric Translator on.

The cop notices his light is on and flicks it off. *I am impressed. There is a murder and you arrive seconds after I do. Are you monitoring my communications again?*

I would never—Why aren't there any police cars out front?

No electricity. No gas. How did you hear of this so quickly?

I thought I might get a good deal on a new WWTV office.

Matsuo Real Estate is not a landlord.

Who's dead, Captain Togo? Reiner makes a production of turning on her wrist-top.

Togo poses with a vinyl smile. *This is a strange circumstance, but the public should be assured that the police are working on it assiduously.*

Noted. Reiner at her driest. If only Togo knew how fizzle-brained Reiner is after a night of reefer madness. *So who's dead?*

Togo leans over and whispers into Reiner's ear. She looks at him and turns off her wrist-top. Off the record. But True can still pick it up.

Witnesses claim that Taro Tamura, while speaking with a customer, collapsed into air. There is no body that I've been able to locate. The witness is being truthful, so far as I can determine.

Tamura disappeared, like poof?

It appears so. And with most of my platoon either dead or with their families, I'll be working on this, and many other cases, alone.

Not much a chance to figure out what happened here, then?

I am sad to report that what you say is true.

Is it possible he was murdered? Perhaps a new type of laser. But then why would anyone murder him?

Maybe speculation.

Go ahead. Speculate. Temper, temper, Reiner.

No. land speculation. My guess is he was involved with the yakuza, or maybe a keiretsu, *and he lost a substantial amount of their money on a poor investment. The earthquake has most certainly diminished the value of assets he may have brokered. If you find out anything I would greatly appreciate it if you would contact me.*

Usually you and your boys try to squelch my curiosity.

Times have changed, Reiner-san, maybe forever.

Reiner grins, tickled by this reverse in fortune. *OK. If I find anything out, I'll call you. How's your wife?*

Togo switches on his halogen torch, and lost in thought, seeks a more elusive answer. When Reiner turns to leave, Togo calls to her. *My wife died a few hours ago. She was badly injured in the earthquake. Thank you for asking.*

Out front. True: "It could be a new technology. Cops never know the 'new and improved.'"

"Could be, rabbit. Too bad about his wife, though. I studied flower arranging with her for years. But the captain's analysis is backwards."

"Yeah. My guess is that Tamura was killed not because he lost money. He was killed because he *made* someone money—

a *lot* of it, too—but he couldn't be trusted to keep his lips fused. You think someone's on to us, decided to shore up his or her defenses?"

"Odessa checked on surveillance. Zippo."

"What if Odessa did the intrigue bit and sold us out?"

"Anybody who'd want us would want to lash that hacker's ass with a rattan cane first." The bus squeezes to a stop. True and Reiner climb aboard. She grouses, "Wish I had that fucking car."

Hours and many bus rides later. At Reiner's place.

She checks her messages. None.

True's losing himself in her plants. "When are you going to harvest?"

"Don't need to. It's a new strain. Forever budding."

"You should call Odessa."

"What I'm doing right now." She waits. Tries again.

True sniffs herbal-scented fingers. "Not there?"

The screen reads: *engaging.*

Reiner talking: "Scotty says 'Transporter malfunction, Captain.'"

She pans his room with the telelink, eventually priming on a twitchy boot, then the whole. Odessa. There's no way to revive him long distance. Off to Odessa's, a few standing buildings away. By the time they arrive, Odessa's groggy-wake, sipping coffee. He offers True and Reiner a cup of "El Exigente."

"No, no coffee," True says. "What happened?"

"Say nanu-nanu to a fuckup. I'm checking into your shit and get blind-sided."

"What shit?"

"Doing my usual leaping over tall buildings, bending steel, and what have you. I got to the recent land transactions you wanted. Then this bright light hits me, discom-fucking-bobulates my ass. I could be dead."

Reiner says, "Find out anything?"

"Yeah, yeah, didn't come away empty-handed, you know? No doubt about it. Somebodies are buying up this lunar landscape."

"A few corps?"

"Correctomundo." Odessa kisses his fingers.

True: "You should check the banks. Find out which ones are funding this."

"Did it, and no, they ain't. These corps got bread baking in a lot of ovens. Streams of foreign assets are being sucked here. Dude could get steamrolled in data like that."

Electricity has been restored in some sections, buildings are patched together or razed to earth, restaurants and stores reopening. Tokyo, bloodied, dazed, but not dead. And the news that the capital is staying brings renewed vigor.

True sits in a ramen shop, watches the shogun-old owner roll and flatten noodles by hand, take orders, fry vegetables, steam gyoza, boil noodles, and serve cavernous portions. There's still an exodus from Tokyo, people whose homes are no more, whose land is marked by gaping tiger-striped cracks. There are too many homeless now, too many have-nots, and the government at a loss on how to act. Tent cities do not match the warmth and succoring of relatives in other cities or of friends abroad. It will take years to erase the physical effects, longer to rid the mind of the memories.

Eden arrives, harried, her hair slicking down into her eyes, her sundress crumpled. She rushes to True's table and sits. She calls out her order. True orders the same, whatever that is. Eden's not looking at him. She's searching, True knows, for the right words. Looking bad. Very bad. Yet he can't take his eyes off her. Her beauty tugs at True's unfurnished soul.

Against his better judgment, he stabs the silence. "What is it?"

No words, no assurances, just tears and shakes. True reaches over, plants a hand on her shoulder. She pulls away, cries alone, in silence, and True feels wrenching emptiness inside. Their food arrives, the old ramen-ya staring, customers gawking.

Finally, Eden speaks. "Seeing you has made me question a lot of things in my life, True. And I wanted to give you another chance, really I did. But I can't. Life has to go on. *My* life has to go on. I can't turn back."

"So this is goodbye?" The words barely stumble out of his mouth.

"It is."

"Why?"

"I have to follow my own path, and it doesn't cross yours."

The lunch-hour crunch. Pans rattle. The old proprietor scoops up six gyoza, sweeps them onto a plate. Repeats. Empties tangled noodles into bowls, flicks in assorted roots, pressed fish cake, bean sprouts, corn kernels. He rushes over and places bowls in front of True and Eden.

True scissors his noodles with chopsticks, blows then sucks hard, burns his lips. Profound desperation he doesn't want to show. "Who is it?"

"What?"

"I said, 'Who is it?'"

Eden mulls denial but knows there's little reason to bend truth. "How did you know?"

"I don't know, I just know. It's been a year since I saw you, so I can't be surprised you found someone else. But since we're in the same place at the same time, let's spend some time together. Get to know each other again. Let's"—he's the one searching for words now—"see if there are feelings, feelings we should explore, a future. Together. Despite what you may feel for someone else." He drops his chopsticks in his bowl. Abandons them there.

Eden takes his chopsticks out of the bowl and places them on the table. "You're making a mistake." True's not sure if she means his table manners or his words.

"One more chance, Eden."

She pushes her ramen away, the steam winding into the air. "This is goodbye. For keeps."

He's too upset to reach out to her. All he can do is watch as she exits the restaurant and re-exits his life. Customers slurp stale noodles—one continuous giant sucking noise. True feels the life being sucked out of him, too.

Out front waiting for Eden, a suedey woman, who pulls Eden close, lips to lips. True's heart spins down as Eden hugs another as she once hugged him. Eden's lover glares through the steamy, depressed pane. At True. Then she and Eden, arm in arm, turn a corner and are out of sight.

As he eats, True stares at miso broth dripping from each glob of noodles. He finishes Eden's ramen and orders a beer, three more after.

Seems to True, though, the times you most want to get drunk, you can't.

True doesn't want to be sitting next to Odessa, watching him jack a line into *Special Systems Control,* then run it through *Japanese land transactions,* cross-reference it with *corporate holdings,* thread it through two dozen other files, bits of info that could congeal into a coherent whole or come crashing down, showering them with electro-feedback, fuzz balls and jolts, energy that can kill.

It's a risk, and the more True thinks about, not one he wants to take. Eden shattered his heart this time; the first time was just a dry run. The taste is formaldehyde in his mouth, old age suddenly around the corner. No amount of reconstructive surgery or steroid therapy could turn it back. True weighs death. Erupting into a fireball. Let those cyber-assassins or bosozoku, yakuza, ninjas, and Bong Bong have their way, let them collect their cut, because what the use of running? What's the use in fighting?

He struggles against the tears that push at his eyes, but can't even get that right. Soon, a droplet splatters the console, and more tears blaze a trail down his cheek. The loss of Eden overwhelms. He isn't prepared for this intense feeling of unmet need and desire. She's all he wants. She's all he can't have.

Odessa daubs a finger on the keyboard. "What the fuck is this? Water?" He surveys the ceiling, walls, gets to True, who turns away. The instinct: *No male, no cry.*

"That you?"

"Something in my eye." True manages a whisper.

Odessa won't accept that answer. True prepares for getting the hell out. He needs to reason this through.

But Odessa changes the flow. "Reiner ever tell you why I'm here?"

True clears his throat. "She just said you hacked the wrong people, like you said."

"That all?"

True nods.

"Bitch can keep her lips krazy glued. Then you'll appreciate what I'm going to tell you." Odessa leans back in his chair. "I'd done this gig for the U.S. gov, one of the three-letter agencies. Can you imagine? Me working for the CyberCops? Now that's some ironic shit."

"What did they hire you for?"

"To play James Bond and get the goods on the Global Fortune 1000." Odessa says this cool, like, no biggie.

"You hacked the Global Fortune 1000?" This rustles True awake, pulls him from his problems. Images of twisted steel and glaring lights, flooding walls of danger, cruel despair. Sneaking around Fortune 1000 databases is slightly less dangerous than chewing radioactive grit.

"That's right. The data told me they were going to pull this corporate America shit, that they were going to form their own corporate nation, a business without borders. It was wild being in the inside of that ice, man. I was flying. I know you know what I'm saying. You've been inside. You come on to some motherfucking enemy troops and there's a fire fight and you got to rely on your intuition and think fast or you're meat. Now speed up the game a hundred times and that's what it was like in there.

"I found out about an internal power struggle and they'd set up this tribunal to solve these disputes. So I go back to the CyberCops and they said it wasn't enough. I told them to fuck off, cause that was all they were going to get, and those motherfuckers with their brass balls gave me some coordinates and said copy this shit. I said 'Hell no.' Chief said he'd tell the corps I'd hacked them; let it slip, like, accidently. So they had me by my balls. I mean, I guess I could have taken on every single CyberCop in the country, and lasted maybe a week before one of them shorted my brain. Or I could use the element of surprise, hope those corp bastards weren't on my tail."

True sees it now. "They marked you?"

"Yeah, the CyberCops set me up. I went in there, copied the info. It was hell getting in and worse getting out. But I did it."

"What was the info?"

"Fuck if I know. I didn't have time to study it while I was inside. I did make a personal copy, but the CyberFucks took it. All I know is that it has to do with some weapons. But what in this world don't?"

"Weapons. Like technology?"

"Something new, something complex and dangerous, but I don't know what. When I got out of the program, the CyberCops were waiting. They accessed the data, smashed my equipment, and left me." Odessa's about to set up the final access routes when *logjam* flashes on the screen. "Fuck. Must be satellite interference or a power drain."

As Odessa searches for the miscue, muttering under his breath as if words will make things happen, True thinks about *logjam*. A word that conjures up something. From his past.

Odessa punches a box underneath his console and *logjam* is replaced by *proceed with access plan*. Sighs, then says, "Yo, man, last thing. *You're* scaling the net."

"Me? Why not you?"

"I got to stay here and make sure you get your ass out, both cheeks intact. This is one complicated ether-route."

"What about Reiner?"

"Why the fuck should Reiner go through? You're the one with the skills. You need me to tell you I think you're good? You're good. Excellente, man. You got flair. A natural. That's rare."

"I can't go."

"Well, I ain't going. Like I said, this is a two-person setup. And Reiner doesn't do shit like this. She's from the old school. Does everything primary source."

"How old can her school be? She's, like, thirty-five."

"Try sixty."

"No."

"Fuck, yeah. Surprised you didn't know. Which is another reason she can't go. All that plastic surgery and drug therapy's weakened her heart, her insides are rotting. You know how much shit she has to pump into her body to stay the way she is? Time moves forward. Try to stop it, it'll fuck you up. Look inside her and you'll see someone hurting worse than you and me."

"She told you this?" True's irrationally jealous.

"No. You think I'd work for someone I didn't check out? Reiner's background wasn't easy to find, but it wasn't hard either."

"What else you find out?"

"TUS." *The usual shit.* "But trust me, she can be trusted. Otherwise I wouldn't be here."

"She's never rocketed through electric space?"

"Never. She'll trip a trap, get us all smoked."

True can't face going through virtual reality again. He'll never get out.

Reiner breezes in. "I smell scoop. Let's get started."

True tries to detect age lines, bloodshot lines in her eyes, wrinkles, gray hair. But Reiner looks a robust thirty-five. The drug therapy would bleed Fort Knox. No wonder she grows her own food.

"What are you looking at?" she says to True.

"Nothing."

"I finally got over to the phone bank and tried to access those tabloid stories on Sato. It occurred to me since WWTV records pieces right off the air—and I never heard of any virus that could attack broadcast tapes—I might be able to access them. The stuff is well-protected, as you know, moated against hacker fiefdoms, attack plagues, whatever. I thought they might be shielded from Sato's eraser plagues."

"But they weren't, were they?" True waits for Reiner to lie. She could have contacted WWTV, erased the stories herself. What if Odessa is wrong about her? Maybe he's living lies, too.

"No, I got them. They're just useless."

Reiner's legit. Either that, or she got word True tripped the security field.

"The stories are utter bullshit," she continues. "I mean they paint Sato as a crazy fucker, but that doesn't mean anything. They were way off. They even got his first name wrong. The only interesting fact was that it mentioned his association with the bosozoku. And you and I did have a run in with them. But every time something fucked up happens, they blame it on the bosos."

True knows the stories are useless; he watched the tape and arrived at the same.

"We're ready to rock." Odessa hands True a headset. "Got to go dinosaur. You haven't worn a head jock in a while, right? Tough. The power keeps snuffing. Since this is a delicate op, and we can't let anyone notice any power drain, we got to use this."

True holds the headset loosely in his hands. Doesn't want it.

Reiner flicks at Odessa with her fingers. "Why are you giving it to him? I'm going in."

"Fuck no. True goes."

She grabs the headset. True doesn't resist.

"Reiner, Reiner, Reiner," Odessa says in rhythm, "This is some heavy shit in there. I know you haven't jacked in, and now is not the time for sightseeing. Dig? Let my man True go through. He's been there before, knows the shit. Does it like you sleep."

"I pay the bills. You guys are just guest stars in my reality."

Odessa slaps the console table. "Reiner! You ain't going to come back if you go in. That's the real deal, babe. You want to fry your brain? Your heart'll explode. I know you ain't no bodacious thirty-something pussy. You double that, and your insides are begging for time off the time block. True goes. It's the only way."

"You think I'm going to let some VR junkie fuck this up? We've come too far. Besides, you hear our friend True here talking? He doesn't want to go. He's scared of what he'll do in there, aren't you, True honey?"

True keeps quiet. Feels like he has no balls, no brains, no basic reason to argue.

"Fuck. Reiner?" Odessa throws up his hands. "Fine. Pay me."

"After the job's done."

"If anything happens, how am I going to get my money?"

"I've taken care of that. True has it." She hands True her

WWTV specially encoded debit card. "The ADC code is inside the gift I gave you at the airport. *Wakatta*?" She pumped the code for her automatic debit card inside his wrist-top. True has the number right there. For all Odessa knows, it's scratched onto some trinket in her apartment.

Odessa reaches across True for the headset. Reiner won't let go. "You're making a mistake, but that's your problem. But if you want to go inside, I got to readjust it a little." Reiner gives it up. Odessa shrinks the size.

"Me and True are going to pull you out at the first sign of trouble. While I handle the hardware, he's going to be watching the action on the monitor. He'll see what you see. There's a micro-camera and two-way mike in the headset. Don't talk back when you're inside unless you want to come out. Some security phalanx might pick it up. Just listen." Odessa clutches his head, feigns shock. "I'm asking *you* to keep your trap shut and listen? We're totally fucked."

Reiner blinks. "Up yours, Odessa."

Odessa checks the headset connection. "If my man here says for you to move left, you move left. If he says to leave something alone, no matter what it is, you listen. He knows the deal inside this cyber-ghetto. I'm going to be busy monitoring for trouble."

"OK, Mommy."

She puts on the headset, gives the thumbs up, and Odessa punches in the commands. On the surface, it's a deceptively low-tech console. Just a screen, control board, headset, wireless connectors; True, Odessa, Reiner. Power radiates from the pulsing box at Odessa's feet. Odessa's personal design and architecture, billions of bits of memory and instructions, strands of DNA coding, binary pathways, circuits, mind paint, and electric protoplasm.

She's walking on a path paved with zeros and ones. Although her feet move at a constant rate, she's picking up speed. A frown.

True grabs a plastic can of Sapporo out of a floor fridge, pops the lid. Odessa gives him the eye and True hands him one, too. *This is going to take a while.* "That's normal, Reiner. Just binary codes, junk mostly. Keep forward."

Reiner nods, then flies.

Up ahead, a topographical map of the world, mountains of data anchored on flatland. The two biggest are the U.S. and Japan, followed by India, once the world's number three software producer. Now, like Pakistan, it's dead, just its data scavenged after the war.

"That's right, Reiner. Fly to Japan, and when you get to that enormous mountain of data, jump to the top," True says.

Reiner looks like she wants to say something.

True senses fear. "Don't worry, Reiner. You'll find it easy to jump. I know it looks big, but there's no gravity except the gravity you make."

She jumps too hard, overshoots the data, but drags a foot on the tippy top. Stops, looks down.

True knows what she's feeling. It's coming back. Stomach whirls, head twirls. He takes a long sip of beer. Swishes it around his mouth, reveling in the flavor, the chill on his tongue. Swallows, says, "There are doors and windows, Reiner. Whatever you do, don't open the door labeled Business Transactions. That's a good way to get speared by laser bolts. We're going in a window. The doors are too dangerous. You need a password or to be able to finesse it. The window marked Publications is a good one."

Next to him, Reiner mimes opening a window. Is this how he looks when traveling data streams? Grasping at nothing except what's in his mind?

She crawls in the window. True notices how damp she is. Motions to Odessa.

"If she's sweating now, she's going to be flooding my console in a few minutes. Give her this." Odessa hands True a bottle with a hyposhot on the end. True guns it into her arm. Fluid replacement. True's mind shuttles back to when he was found dehydrated, close to death, the last time he binged on VR. It's good he didn't have one of these hyposhots; otherwise, he'd still be inside.

Reiner looks around the publications room, billions of books with their titles stretching to infinity up, down, forward. Each section is labeled.

True sees her mouth *eigo*, Japanese for *English*. "Wondering why it's in English? Thank Odessa. Smart software."

"Brilliant software." Odessa continues to scan.

So far, so good, but True knows the real deal's ahead. "See that trap door? Open it and take the dataslide down to Real Estate Publications. This is all legit research, so no worries. Yet."

Reiner takes the slide at a thousand miles an hour, categories arpeggiating downwards. Since she's thinking real estate, that's where the software takes her. There are a series of doors labeled Prices, Available Real Estate, Condominiums, Co-ops, Houses, Buildings, Land/Plots, Rentals, Transactions.

True says, "Go into Transactions, and when you get inside there should be a number of hallways you can take. Whatever you do, don't take the one labeled Recent Transactions. We're going in a different way."

Reiner opens a door and True watches her confront a series of snakelike tubes corkscrewing into silver- and gold-gilded clouds. "Take the tube labeled Land Transactions, Past

10 years. It's next to recent Land Transactions. Jump. Think Tokyo."

Reiner soars upward, screaming past places—Beppu, Hiroshima, Kyoto, Nagasaki, Osaka, Sado, Sendai, stops at Tokyo and prepares for entry.

"Wait!" True snaps. Something's not right.

Reiner's hand remains poised.

"What's up?" Odessa's scanning turns up empty.

"Bad feeling. Notice we haven't seen any traps, no cops, no other researchers? If someone is expecting trouble, they'd be right here. And Reiner's DNA's on file, so she could end up flatlined if she opens that door. Another worry I have. Was it a coincidence we found that Matsuo Realtor guy phased out?"

Odessa rubs his lips. "OK, I can deal with some introspection. But what the fuck is she supposed to do? She can't react as fast as me or you."

"I say we follow money streams from Osaka; no, wait, make it someplace quiet, like Sendai." True knows he's right. Doesn't bother for Odessa to agree. "Reiner. Don't take the Tokyo door. Step down to Sendai. It's safer."

She's gasping, the gravity-free environment, the ethereal nature of VR taxing her mind and body. Shivers and slivers of bewilderment. It's not her world. She doesn't know the rules.

Odessa takes her pulse. "I'm bringing her back."

Reiner overhears. Mouths a loud *No*.

True shrugs. "Open the Sendai door. You can't secure everything."

She slips inside.

"Head up to Regional Banks, then Collateral, Reiner. Open the drawer." She does. "Now slide inside. When you find Sendai property purchased with the assistance of a Tokyo-based bank, get on. You're in for a wild ride."

Reiner is looking pale. Even with fluid replacement, her mouth is sticky. Sweat greases her blouse, and True detects gray hairs, age lines, crow's feet, sour breath.

True's seen enough. "Pull her out."

"No money then." Reiner's voice a croak.

"Don't talk." True knows if she comes out, he goes in. In that case, it's possible; a little steroid therapy, some surgery, and Reiner'll be as good as old.

Odessa rings his words with warning. "Start looking more perky or you're coming out."

Reiner forces a smile. She likes to win, no matter how small the battle. Locates a loan for a VR Sex Playground, financed by Sonwa Bank, and is about to hitch a ride on Collateral.

True shakes his head. "No, Reiner. A good journo follows the money. Get on the Transactions stream."

Shooting to Tokyo's outskirts, where money trails have slowed to a baby walk. Heavy traffic. People on these streams, Japanese bank managers mostly, checking up on projects. In the distance, Tokyo's skyscrapers beckon, cracked, the quake reflected in their tumult. Thousands more skyscrapers in the data stream than in real Tokyo. Data's already bigger than the real.

Reiner's gasping. A temblor, then her own aftershock. She's taken too long to go so little distance. True looks to Odessa, who shakes a warning. Seems if Reiner wants to die, that's her biz.

A few virtual meters before Reiner, a laser slices her stream.

"Get out of there." True's shouting.

Odessa's scrambling. "Get her off that stream, they'll cut our access."

"Reiner! Jump onto the outgoing Collateral stream."

Just then that stream is severed. Reiner's astronauting out of control, barreling upwards. Lasers streak across ivory backlight and the monitor washes white. Reiner slumps in her chair. True removes the headset. Ladles her to the ground, amazed to find her breathing. Odessa zips the console shut so no one can trace Reiner to them. Grabs a beer and dabs at Reiner's lips with it.

She licks at them and her eyes juice awake. Whispers, "I'm too mean to kill. And too smart. I got a lot of gray matter."

Odessa pours her a heady glassful. Hands it to her. "A lot less gray matter in your brain, but a lot more gray matter on your head."

Reiner struggles to face herself in the mirror. "What the fuck? I'm old. What happened?" She pinches wrinkles on her arms, tries to expunge liver spots on her hands with spit and shine, flakes off skin. "I don't want anyone to see me like this."

"I don't want to say I told you so, but I told you so I told you so I told your ass so. Lucky you got any brain left." Odessa hands the headset to True. "Next."

What choice is there? Reiner almost killed for this, Aslam assassinated, Rush dissolved into pigment. Time for True to confront his demons.

He takes the same trail as Reiner, but instead of idling over binary ones and zeros, he soars. Hands at his sides, he's going like a million kilometers a minute—over data-mountains and information peaks, through and between archival skyscrapers, under mucousy clouds of energy. Feels more than sees what he's doing. Instead of Japan, he shoots to New York.

"What's he doing?" he hears Reiner ask Odessa.

Odessa's response to his boss: "Shut up and learn."

True locates a list of Sato American Subsidiaries, pulls out the dossier of a well-known trading company, and attaches himself to Petty Cash Funds. He surfs this wave all the way to Japan, into the heart of Tokyo's most powerful keiretsu.

True feels Odessa's approval. "Into the belly of the beast through a tiny incision. Keep it up."

He doesn't acknowledge, keeps skirting the wave, then squeezes into Sato's corporate headquarters, into their financial data. He's there in like thirty seconds. Reiner took ten minutes and didn't make it to Tokyo. True's consumed by Sato's murky world of investment, he slows here. No mistakes. Odessa's software doles out topics as pictograms. True floats by icons for Net Profit, Gross Profit, Investments, Taxes, Real Estate. Searches no further. Inside he must choose between Corporate-owned Real Estate, Outstanding Loans/Potential Collateral, Newly Acquired Assets. True jacks in, lands smack dab in a fat stream of Tokyo land transactions.

True can see by the logjam of data that Sato's land holdings are growing at a spectacular rate. Eyes peeled for trouble, he rips the handle off Government Regulations (for reference only). Follows the money trail contribution to contribution, the real deal, accounted for by the corp itself. A quick review convinces True that Sato is behind retaining Tokyo as the capital.

Skirting Land Transactions, True's present location, is an electric highway: money, funneled into the country from abroad, backed up out of sight. Sato's selling assets abroad, depressing real estate markets in the U.S. and Europe, and crushing them in the Third World. Japan: the first corporate nation, Sato at the helm. Major shit, True thinks. He'd better get out.

A sign blinking *logjam* captures his attention. So much money flows into Japan Sato can't process it. A two-day wait for processing. He looks at the sign, blinking lonely; out of his eye's corner, notices unprocessed money being leaked to the Luzonia Effort. Here he sees insurgents flailing, killing each other. Their expressions: terror, confusion, what the? Weapons testing. A TV screen, a news conference. The Sato corp announcing the purchase of a number of R & D companies, none True recognizes. He'll analyze it later with Odessa's tape of this.

On his way out, he stops at the logjam. A name from his past, before he lost himself in worlds like this. Waits for it to become clear. It doesn't.

Odessa's impatience cuts through True's meta-world. "Why you just standing there?"

True starts the climb back to Odessa's apartment. He's feeling comfortable now, almost doesn't want to leave, but isn't tempted to tempt fate after what happened to Reiner.

Suddenly, there's Eden. Does a double-blur. Yup, it's her, drinking True in with fierce eyes.

What are you doing here? True thinks.

"I'm here because you want me here."

Odessa's voice, a galaxy away. "It's your mind, True. Get the babe outta your mind, man. There's an interactive defense mechanism in there. Twisting your thoughts. Get out!"

"Are you going to listen to him, or to me, your heart?" She takes his hand, places it to her heart, pulsing hard. A long rush. She takes his hand, holds it to his temple. A tremendous jolt. "Hold that for me, would you, dear?" Manufactured dyke laughter. Deafening, all inside his head. He rubs his temple; something hard and metallic is lodged inside. Watches while Eden floats to clouds and stops to wave with her new girlfriend. True speeds out of Sato's world, into Tokyo's investment streams, then out of Tokyo. Nuzzles inside a love text, hiding behind sticky declarations of love.

Before he can take the last ramp, Odessa yanks him out.

Odessa's hand on Reiner's limp wrist. "She's dead."

Evil reality crashing down on top of him. Reiner's lifeless in her chair, mouth and eyes open in surprise. True searches for a pulse, for a puff of air. Gives up and shuts her eyes. Reiner looks ancient now, her body relieved not to have to stem the tide of time. Even in death, she ages years in minutes.

Odessa's studying the foreign object in True's head. It's hardly noticeable—almost could be a zit or some other skin malfunction. "She was saying something about not trusting the chick in there, when she just upped and died." Odessa taps True's temple. "How the fuck did that get in there? This ain't no fastfood restaurant where you get it to go. This is virtual reality."

True rubs it. Can't explain it.

CHAPTER 18

"Pay me. The job's done, and I'm allergic to death."

True ignores Odessa's demands, as he largely ignored them for the frantic hour it took to get to Hatanaka's condo. Odessa's pacing the tatami. True wonders how many times he'll have to go back and forth before kernels of rice flake off.

"Give me my bread. You, Reiner owe me."

"When the job's complete, like Reiner said."

"Nothing more complete than when your employer croaks."

"I need you. The key, obviously, is this chip in my head. You're the only one I know who can access it. The guy we're going to see knows more about Sato than anybody. He'll be able to fill us in. After you access the chip, you get paid. Otherwise, Reiner will have died for nothing, and there's nothing worse than dying for no reason."

Odessa kicks at the tatami. "I don't get paid, I can't get out of here. I can't just jack into some bank's assets. I'm history in cyberspace. Everybody's looking for me."

"That explains the two-person hookup and why you didn't head in yourself."

Odessa points. "That's right, cowboy."

All those caveats Reiner brushed aside were for naught. Even then, they never expected Reiner would die. Now that she had, they were both beginning to question their own invincibility.

Hot's voice filters into the room. "Come in, True, and bring your associate. You'll find me next to my bedroom, outside collecting sun."

"Reiner's dead," True says to Hot, who's in his garden among glorious scents and colors, a panting breeze.

Hot nods. "I know."

True's eyebrows arch. "Oh?"

A thousand year-old sigh. "You are here, you have brought someone else, and Reiner is not. The only conclusion I could arrive at was that Reiner was incapacitated. She is not a woman easily incapacitated. If you are here and she is not, she must be dead."

In his chair, Hot is not regal. Tiny and frail, his pajamas hanging to the floor. He groans upright and walks stiffly to a mini-shrine, pulls a twined rope, claps his hands as he bends his neck in prayer, throws a coin into a bowl.

"What the fuck is he doing?" Odessa asks.

"I am praying for Reiner." Hot finishes, breathing heavily from the exertion, then sits back down. "You may pray as well."

Odessa shifts the weight on his feet. "If we're going to pray, let's pray for our own asses."

The garden is lush and beautiful, much grander than Reiner's backyard plot. Many trees; only one, a tall, thick-trunk oak, suffered any quake aches.

Hot says, "I assume you believe I will be able to tell you why Reiner is dead?"

"We know why. It was her first time in the net, and she got smoked looking for info on Sato."

"Sato. And what is it you wish to know about Sato you couldn't learn in the information void?"

"I know Sato's the one buying the land. And I'm pretty sure he's the one who masterminded the capital remaining here, and all because he wants to set himself up as some corporate king."

"It seems you have solved a great many mysteries. I cannot fathom what it is you expect I know above this."

Hot's nerves are jouncing. Why, True wonders. "Did you know Sato was the one behind this?"

Hot's expression doesn't change. "I had my suspicions, but no, shall we say, hard proof."

"What is Sato doing with weapons sales to Luzonia?"

"This is, I presume, a related question. And the answer is, I believe, he is building ties to other nations in order to solidify his position globally."

"By selling off his assets abroad, and, I assume, urging other Japanese corps to do the same, he's shaking the economic foundations of Europe and North America."

"He knows what he's doing."

"Why is he doing it?"

"I think it's self-evident. Sato is the most powerful man in Japan. With his ties to other nations, he will shortly be, as you said, crowned corporate king."

"Sounds like a bad movie. What kind of military hardware was he selling to the ethnics and Luzonian platoons fighting the establishment of a Muslim state here?"

"Why?"

"Because it's right here." True taps his temple.

Hot's eyes inflate. "You must leave."

"Why?"

"Get out of here. You are in possession of information many would kill for. I refuse to be involved."

A grim voice from the garden atrium. "But you are involved, Uncle."

Both True and Odessa seek a place to run. The garden walls are too high to scale, the only path to freedom lies between them and Sato—who's accompanied by a bodyguard, whom True instantly recognizes. The bosozoku. Clad in leather, chains, and hoop earring du jour.

Sato moves toward Hot, who's babbling, slaps a hand over his mouth, squeezes the sagging skin.

"You called him Uncle, but he's really your father-in-law." True takes on a conversational tone.

"Yes, we Japanese use 'uncle' as a term of endearment."

"Charming."

"Uncle needs his rest, don't you, Uncle?" Sato reaches over with his other hand, holds Hot's chin. "I should have killed you when I took over your business." Hot's breathing becomes spasmodic. "Instead, I let you live in disgrace. But no longer." A hot river of Japanese language, then the old man's neck pops and crackles. Instant death.

Sato wipes his hands with a handkerchief. "From the moment I was introduced to you at the Karaoke Kafé I was certain we would meet again."

"You talking to me, or him?" True indicates Odessa with his chin.

Sato holds out his hands, as if trying to determine which object is heavier. "You. Although his talents escaped me at the club. *Oi de*," he grunts to the bosozoku, who flicks on his DNA scanner. Holds up the viewer for Sato, who reads aloud, "Born Darryl Raspberry, goes by the name Odessa Flashfire. Also a cornucopia of cyberspace monikers such as Peace, or 16ea3e, among many others. And I thought you were merely a house musician. You lead a complex life, Mr. Flashfire."

"I prefer the simple life now."

"It doesn't get much simpler than this. According to these records, every corporation in the Global Fortune 1000, which includes my own, is offering a substantial bounty for you."

"Must be an input error."

"Dead or alive."

"You don't get a bonus for bringing me in alive, do you?"

True catches the hint of a gold molar in Sato's mouth. "You have a marvelous sense of humor. Just for that, I will let you decide how you will die. I could have you lasered, have my guard break your neck. He's quite proficient at that, although Ailey-san has managed, to this point, to elude him."

"What if I worked for you? Lots of info I could get my hands on for you."

Sato clicks his tongue. "What use are you to me?"

The bosozoku stirs.

"No, man, no no no. C'mon. I am the *man* in the infonet. Let me show you what I can do. On spec. You don't got to pay—"

The biker whips Odessa with a kick that heaves him into a cherry tree. Blossoms rain down, covering him with petals, and

Odessa, shocked by probably his first-ever bout with non-virtual pain and anguish, puts up a hand in self-defense. The bosozoku stands poised to complete the task.

"If I hacked the Global Fortune 1000, imagine what I can do for you." Odessa's shaking, squeezing his words.

The speed triber looks to Sato for further instruction, who nods. He picks up a shovel, prepares to swing it down on Odessa. True leaps over and hugs the shovel's blade, pulls it and the biker down on top of him. Hears the crunch of his own bones.

Odessa is frantic. Last chance. "I know how to get to the CyberCops. I can get inside every online network around the world. I can smoke your enemies, steal their data, or alter it any way you say. Kill us, you're letting a golden opportunity slip away."

The boso's pinning True's throat to the ground. True's gurgling, his fight draining away. Sato nonchalantly taps his charge on the shoulder and the pressure subsides. True staggers up for air.

"I accept your offer, Mr. Flashfire." Sato speaks with the biker in Japanese. Then says, "My assistant will take you to your work station. One mistake, however, and I'll have you killed. Do you understand?"

"Yeah." Odessa struggles to stand. Touches True with his eyes, trying to express everything they went through in a glance. True nods. What else can Odessa do? He prays the hacker doesn't do his job too well; that would mean major global trouble in the coming years.

The speed tribesman leads Odessa past the hunkering oak and some chrysanthemums, through a gate, away.

"Now that's over with, you have something of mine." Sato taps his temple.

True rubs his own temple. "You're going to kill me anyway. Why should I give this to you?"

"There is no choice." Sato plants his foot, menaces True with the other.

"If you harm me, how do you know you'll be able to access the chip? I got it in a virtual world. You have to ask yourself, will the chip function outside my reality? If you knew the answer, you'd have killed me by now."

Sato plants both feet. "It doesn't matter whether the chip can be accessed. Do you think a confluence of coincidences brought us to this point? You have been used. Used by my enemies. And I am going to use you right back."

A boiling hypothesis. "So you can't risk killing me just yet."

"Not yet. But I believe we can reach a mutually beneficial agreement."

"If I give you the chip and let you plant another chip, I assume a red herring, you'll let me free?"

"No. The deal is you let me replace this chip with one that will destroy my competitors."

"What do I get?"

"A few extra months among the living, although it would depend on how soon they locate you. I won't interfere. It benefits me to make it appear that you cracked my data defense. The more difficult you make it for them to catch you, the more they will believe nothing is amiss."

True's been marked since before fleeing Luzonia, has been doing somebody else's bidding, perhaps living out the computer profile Aslam alluded to. Was Aslam also set up by Sato?

"I'm offering you a chance for survival, such as it is." Sato calls in on his ring transmitter. "I'm paging my number one technical assistant." He motions for True to join him inside. "Let's leave the sun. It's hot today, and I don't like cancer treatments."

True's eyes scramble to adapt to the darker room. "How do I know you won't smoke me the second you get the chip?"

"You don't. But as I explained, you will be working for me."

"Like Odessa. What's to stop me from warning your enemies?"

"One of my subsidiaries markets a drug for torture victims to help them put negative experiences behind them. Most conveniently for me, you will forget any of this happened."

"Have I ever had this drug before?" True searches his memory. So many pieces are missing. Is it VR that stripped them from his mind, or has he been used like this before?

Sato stretches out on Hot's bed, keeping an oblique eye on True. "If you'd had this drug, you wouldn't remember. And you won't remember. So there is no reason to tell you."

True sits on the corner of the bed. "In Old China, before the place shattered into a dozen ethnic enclaves, there used to be these farmers markets. You could get almost anything you wanted. Vegetables, spices, clothes hangers, abortion pills, meat, books, computer software. One grand bazaar. I went there once and saw these puppies and cats in cages. I know how they feel about being caged. It's awful not having control over your life."

Sato clasps his hands behind his head. But he's listening.

True continues. "I decided to save at least one of these animals from a life in a cage. Who knew when someone would buy one? I bargained. The lady was ancient, a century old. It took a while, but we agreed on a price. When I handed her the money, in the days when cash was still common, she took the puppy out of the cage. I could only watch as she broke its neck. She thought I was buying dinner."

The doorbell gongs. Sato stands. "We'll have to discuss your psychological problems later."

A few moments of pressed silence, and True hears stirring outside the door. When he sees who's there, his heart clutches. But before he can panic, Sato flashes behind him and butterfly-wings his arms back. For greater leverage, he plants a shoe in his spine. When he pulls there's a sickening crunch. Scalding pain from within his bones. True tries to collapse in agony, but Sato props him up. The pain almost drives True from sanity.

"He's giving us the chip." Sato's voice, calm and metallic.

Eden produces a scaly knife, holds it to True's eye, but instead of blinding him digs the knife tip into his temple, twisting the blade. Blood pouring out of him, onto his shoes, the floor. She holds the chip up to the light, and True sees halogen beams glint off the blood and diamond-bright silicone. Sato tosses True to the floor. True, his arms broken and shoulders separated, stays in a heap, tormented by pain and betrayal, watching helplessly as Eden licks blood off the chip and analyzes its construction.

"He's all yours." Sato takes the chip. Leaves True alone with his wife.

Without a word Eden is standing over him, flops him over on his back. The broken bones hit floor. Needling fire. Torment. She stretches her body on top of his, kisses him deeply, her lips spongy soft. "I love you, True. But love isn't the only thing." She bolts upright and comes down with the knife. Stabs him in the chest. True barely feels the impact but sees screaming white. Cut. Stab. A burning sensation when Eden reaches into his chest to remove his heart. Holds it up and tosses it aside.

True's slipping away and the last voice he hears, would ever hear, belongs not to Eden or Sato; not to Aslam, Reiner, or even Rush.

But to Piña. "Holy fuck! Oh shit. Oh shit. What the hell is this?"

This is so unfair, True thinks, sliding toward hell and all stops between.

PART THREE

VIRTUALLY TRUE

CHAPTER 19

True's in a netherland of consciousness, no landmarks to help measure the hours that fritter life away. How long, he wonders, has he been staring at the psychotropic pattern beamed overhead? It whirls, turns in and folds out on itself, like origami, or a 3-D rose in time-elapse, shooting from bud to bloom. Brilliant shades: red, orange, purple, flow into flecks of gold. Mes. Mer. Ized. Happy-happy-relaxation. Happy-happy-love-yourself. Happy-happy-self-esteem. Happy-happy-relaxation. It's not important where he is or why he's here.

He blinks brittle eyes, manages to regrasp his gaze. He's in bed. A hospital room. Ecru walls, a bare floor, nothing except a bedside table. Trouble focusing on objects only steps away. Paranoia rips through. He must be in Japan. Envisions racing to the door, running down the hall, outside, where he'll have to stay on the run. Escape from Sato and his salary samurai, hide from his corporate ninjas, fly away, far away from Eden who betrayed him again—left him lonesome to pick up the pieces of his shattered life. Why isn't he dead? He remembers Sato wishboning his arms, cracking them into gravel. Eden crushing his heart. The torment is too great. He wants to run, hide, cry, and be loved, all at once.

Most of all, he wants to know why he's alive.

True's eyes are back on the swirls, and paranoia is supplanted by euphoric tingling. Wrenching free means terror's return. Is he being brainwashed? Dosed on the drug Sato claimed would make him forget? But how could True remember something he's sure to have forgotten? Something else tugs at him. This psychotropic personality enhancing pattern is one he's experienced before, back when his virtual reality addiction crashed his mind. The same 12-step psychotropia therapy course. And although these patterns accomplish in a few minutes a day what takes psychiatrists years, True detests them. They certainly didn't prepare him for life out of VR's fold.

It's part of the new psychology. Hypnotic suggestion via broadcast patterns, an extension of the media-plagued world he knows he contributes to as a journalist. An FDA-approved method of public brainwashing. He closes his eyes to block temptation. Last time in test-band therapy, his appetite increased and test-taking skills improved while his need for FREEze and VR vanished; all welcome changes, he has to admit. But there was a downside. His savings went pffffft as his need for things material rocketed. Suddenly he hankered for a sports car, manufactured by an American corp in an Asian McLand, cutting-edge music techiae, and the latest in apartment furnishings. Step 12, Social Interaction/Romance pushed True into video-dating, requiring a whole new (expensive) wardrobe, available from participating online catalogs. He curses his corporate-sponsored health coverage. Luckily the psychotropic effects wore off when his insurance ran out.

And a handy bonus: If True agreed to change sexual orientation, he'd receive free psychotropic test pattern software upgrades for life. Standard governmental policy across North America, Europe, and Asia, a means to muffle the population explosion. But True doesn't wish for this, clinging to the belief that someday, somehow, he and Eden would be together again.

Instead? He touches his temple. Scarless skin. Was the chip really extracted? And why are his arms and shoulders pain-free? He eye-contacts the pattern again, but struggling to a sitting position busts him free. Checks his body—no injuries. There's a water pitcher on his bed table, next to a dusty glass. As he reaches for it, a door splays open. True drops the pitcher, which clatters. Through his haze, he recognizes a familiar silhouette. His throat spasms.

"Ailey! You need a doctor, or are you just being dramatic?" Rush drops True's wrist-top on the table. Not the one Reiner gave him. His, the one destroyed on the plane with the Japanese boy. True knows it's his. The same scratches, battle scars. Personalized objects always feel that way.

True waves him off. "No."

Rush puts the pitcher on the nightstand and looks at the screen. "Ohhhhh, the happy psychotropic test pattern. I know that one."

"Turn it off."

"What?"

"The psychotropia. Turn it off."

"You sure? From what the docs say, maybe we should jack your ass into this permanently."

"Turn the damned thing off."

Rush shrugs, flicks a switch at the foot of the bed, and the pattern is sucked into white. True's enraged at himself. He fell back into his virtual reality nightmares and couldn't get out. What else accounts for the fact that Rush is alive, more alive than True, and his old wrist-top sits a foot away?

Rush, spooked. "You don't know what the hell's going on?"

"No."

He sits on the edge of True's bed; his body with its multiple plastic installments, liposuction, hormones, and muscle grafts, is stiff, unyielding. True prepares for worse than worst.

"You fucked up, Ailey. One minute you're working on a story for me, the next I can't find you. I give you a few days, figure you're digging something up. Next thing I know you're here. The docs say some no-legged black market woman found you rolling in your own shit."

True's face sunburnt by shame.

Rush clicks his tongue. "You were practically dead. At first, I thought you picked up the plague that's going around. But turns out it was a virtual overdose. Your death certificate would have read you died from dehydration. I'd write your obit, say you OD-ed on entertainment."

"How long?"

"In VR? Fuck if I know. The network brass in New York told me you'd been cured."

"Where am I?"

"Nerula's psycho hospice."

"Never heard of it."

"It's a wing in the National Hospital. Only those with private insurance plans get in. You're lucky our corp's generous. If it were up to me, I'd yank your coverage. Already you've raised premiums for everyone else. I wouldn't even give you back your wrist-top, but the legal department informed me we're contractually obligated to. By the way. You have to verbalize receipt."

After Rush confirms True's DNA, True's officially retendered his wrist-top. "What was I doing for you last?"

"Last time we talked, I called to tell you to get your ass over to my place."

"Why?"

"So I could fire you."

"For ... ?"

"Hanging out with an enemy of the state, getting me in hot water when he croaked. You're supposed to cover news, not make it."

True blinks. Minuscule gray, black, and green dots spread, then coalesce.

"Now, because you're under treatment again, I can't fire you. They say this thing you have for virtual reality is a disease, like drug abuse or alcoholism or schizophrenia. Personally, I think you just have a weak character."

True closes his eyes, sees nothing but the maroon of backlit eyelids. No dots, no nightmare. A good sign. Opens his eyes again. Rush is still there. Another good sign. Kind of.

"I'm not the only one who questions your character," Rush says. "The chief of police contacted me. Bong Bong claims you owe him something."

"Don't pay Bong Bong. His info was useless. Besides, you give in now to him, you'll be paying him the rest of—"

"You are in no position to offer advice, VR man." Rush clutches his stomach. Grimaces. Then, "WWTV's lined up your old shrink."

"Oh, god. Dr. Powter."

"Yup. Dr. Powter. It's a shame."

"You're telling me."

"I don't mean about your shrink. I mean because I had, like, the greatest idea for a story. Our ratings would've kissed ozone. But ... " Rush lets silence snowfall.

True's curious, despite himself. "What story?"

Rush shifts near. "You weren't here last year, but you've heard of the annual Urban Survival Tournament?"

"Sure. A race through Nerula's worst slums. Idiots from around the world come here to die. You go in with only the clothes on your back and are left to the mercy of shanty folk, who aren't known for displaying mercy. So?"

"You know how we cover it?"

"All the networks get together and chip in for the cost of a hovercraft, then share the footage."

"They used to give some of the contestants wrist-tops to feed live pics back, but they outlawed computer assistance when people cheated."

"What's your point?"

"I wanted to hire our own hovercraft. A WWTV exclusive."

"Exclusive what? All the footage is the same. Contestants run, they get shot, stabbed, raped, their clothes ripped off their backs, and the hover-cam captures it for posterity."

"With our own hovercraft, I could record *your* experiences. None of the other networks would have that personal angle. Why, we'd rake in the ratings." Rush's excitement ebbs. "But you're not going anywhere. And when you do, it's strictly stateside."

"Too bad." True looks at Rush like he's the sick one.

"Of course, if you run the race next week, I'll make a deal with you. I'll recommend you get one more chance here. Otherwise, you go back to New York. And you know they'll fire you just as soon your treatment's up."

"The choice between corporeal death and career death? Is this why you dropped by?"

Rush's eyes glance off his hands, which are caressing his belly. "I had to come down anyway. I got some stomach ailment action, bilharzia—something else, too, docs say. Figured since I was here, I'd drop my idea off with you. It's in your hands."

True spirals toward sleep. He hears Rush's words cut through his inner dark: "Soon as they can, they'll get rid of you. Work with me. At least you get another chance."

Under a quilt of guilt, True sleeps. Aslam's face, older, with crow's feet, crackling skin, peers up at him, asks what he's going to do about his murder. True wonders about the earthquake and the capital staying Tokyo, Sato scarfing up land, and the microchip he would have killed for.

"What chip, Ailey?" Rush still at the foot of True's bed. "What the hell are you talking about? And you really think the Japanese are going to keep their capital on a bed of rubble?"

"How long was I out?"

Rush scoffs. "Out? You're way the fuck out. But you closed your eyes for about a second."

"You read my mind?"

"I listened to your words."

Letters melt down the walls. True strains to read them. Rush flickers in and out. A spider web unfolds and True studies the filaments that wind through the maze. Random letters sit in rows. Don't make sense. A message there, maybe, but he can't decipher it.

Rush is gone. There are the psychotropic test patterns, and

again True's not sure whether he's slept or not. He does know one thing. You can't control time. Like Reiner, who in his imagined world was unable to stem aging tides; and himself, who experienced virtual weeks in real days, time clicks along. All you can do is ride the wave. But don't try to control it.

He struggles to right himself. He must turn off this psycho-cleanser. Like his need to get high with Reiner that imagined time in her apartment. Couldn't turn it down. The only time he feels good is when the test pattern pulls him into its vortex, strengthening his feelings for himself. But it's as fake as his imagined trip over the last couple of days. At least, he thinks it was a couple of days. Maybe it's been a week, a year, a lifetime since Rush left. True checks his wrist-top for the date, but gets sidetracked. This psychotropia has to end.

True lunges for the foot of his bed, reaches underneath for the off switch. Jabs at the button. Nothing. Artificial happiness smiles on. True realizes the switch is programmed to reject his fingerprints. Anybody else can turn it on and off, but he—the patient—can't. He falls back to the bed, lets his eyes get sucked into the pattern. Let someone else run his life for a while.

The test pattern dissolves, replaced by a familiar face. "Hello, True. I'm glad you've decided to accept me. Ready for another session?"

"Dr. Powter." True studies the gray stubble prickling a pudgy face. True hasn't met him in the real but imagines that a cannibal would find he tastes medicine-y. "It's been a long time, more than a year."

"A few hours, True. Don't you remember?"

"No."

"Good. You're getting better."

"How so?"

"Because the issues we dealt with were extremely unpleasant for you. That imagined electronic expedition you took illustrates many of the problems you are having in your life. For example, imagining that your wife embraced lesbianism tells me you are angry with her for leaving you. The assassination of your colleague with the same type of device that did *in reality* kill your friend, Mr. Aziz, is probably your way of dealing with the lack of justice in the world. You do not care for your colleague, Rush Gelding, do you?"

"No."

"There is a chasm between—" Powter stops short. "Hold on. I have another call." The screen stalls, cluttered with special offers for psychotropic software. Buy three, get a free therapy session with internationally recognized Ph.D. Dr. Christopher Powter, best-selling author of *Simply Getting Better*. What a quack, True thinks. Powter comes back. "I am sorry about that. Now, where were we?"

True shrugs.

Powter scratches his chin. "Chasms. There is a chasm between reality and your expectations in life, which are derived from external sources."

"Media."

"There are many issues you are facing. You feel you lost everything of importance the last time you fell into this electronic addiction. Now you feel you have wasted a second chance. This virtual vacation you took is constructed of symbols. You told me you suspected it was an interactive software program; so it was you, in fact, who made up the whole story, playing out these issues in your mind."

"I told you that?" True feels manipulated. Knows there's more here, although it's fruitless to argue. The picture is murky now. It will, he hopes, clear up soon. "Why Tokyo? Why Reiner?"

"Those two elements do not seem to add up, given the nature of your traumas. Then again, didn't you see your ex-wife—"

"She's still my wife."

"—excuse me, your wife interviewed on TV after the quake. Yes?"

True has to hand it to the doctor.

"But then again, you seem to have so many issues to work out, there are bound to be a few that are not so easily solvable. We can attempt one of two methods. We can try to work through each problem, which would take much time and money, and frankly your insurance would probably run out before we finished."

"No discounts for long-term customers?"

"No."

"Or?"

"Or we can just erase it. Purge you of all of these bad memories and start you on another life."

"Sounds like the easy way out. Actually, it sounds like a lobotomy."

"Oh, no. You would be more intelligent than you are now. We would have to, of course, create new memories for you, ones not so traumatic. Then you could be a productive member of American society again."

And not a drain on the insurance industry, True thinks. "What's the unemployment rate now in the U.S.?"

"I'm not sure. Somewhere around thirty percent."

"What am I supposed to do with all this free time I'll have as this productive-unproductive member of American society?"

"We can deal with that when we come to it."

True cups his hands behind his head. "Let's hold off on any long-term treatment plans for a bit. I need to think about this."

"Well, that is your prerogative as patient; however, my professional advice would be to get started as soon as possible."

"Afraid the insurance will run out? You are—"

Powter's image flickers and sparkles, dissolves, bounces back. "There's a logjam of data squeezing into Nerula. How do they expect me to do my job in when these third-rate third-world nations can't even keep up their satellite feeds?"

"Logjam?" True speaks to the disintegrating image.

"What are you talking about?" Powter's image now strong and clear. "You zoned again. I'm going to prescribe more time with these psychotropic patterns. There's a new one that should ground you better in reality."

"Logjam, Dr. Powter. I remember now."

"Our session is over. We shall talk tomorrow," and Powter vanishes, his face edged out by new patterns and colors.

True stares where Powter was, sees the letters—perhaps the word—*p0yiwk*, blinking. On. Off.

p0yiwk. What does it mean?

True wakes up, his arms squeezed by electrical restraints. In a bed across the room is another patient, muttering in gibberese. Peering over True is Rush, who, for the first time True can remember, looks concerned about someone other than himself.

"Why am I in restraints?"

"You don't remember?"

"What?"

"I left you to get a bite to eat at the cafeteria, and you were wandering the hospital, trying to break into the plague section, screaming you had to escape to Tokyo. Why Tokyo, Ailey?"

True rifles through his memory. "I don't know."

"I'm no shrink, but judging from what you were ranting about, I'd bet you're obsessed with Tokyo, Reiner, someone named Eden, and log rolling. You have a thing for Reiner? You wouldn't be the first."

"My subconscious is telling me something's there."

"Listen, headcase, I wouldn't even trust your conscious if I was you."

"How much time passed since the last time you stopped by?"

"What do you mean?"

"How many times have you visited me and over how long a period of time?"

"This is the first time."

"What about when you first came in and told me how I'd fucked up so much?"

"About an hour ago."

"What about Dr. Powter and his therapy sessions?"

"You won't see Powter until you get back to New York. In the meantime, he prescribed more patterns. When this 12-step is done, we'll fly you home and Powter will do what he can."

"Who's in the bed across the room?"

"The plague is out of control. The hospital is putting all the psychos together in order to free up rooms for plaguees."

"You scared?"

"I'm inoculated. So are you. WWTV stands by its employees." Rush stands, cramps up. "My stomach feels like someone's grabbing at my intestines." Rotten eggs in Rush's wake.

Not just bilharzia, True realizes.

Rush plants his thumb on the ID scanner and the door spits open. "Ailey! Think about the Ghetto Tourney deal. It's good for you, good for me, good for the network."

After Rush leaves, the pattern snaps shut, and a familiar face shuffles into the void.

CHAPTER 20

Reiner peers down at him from the screen, says, "I know we've never met, but I've admired your work. I just wanted to offer my sympathies. Addiction can strike anyone. If there's anything I can do, let me know."

She's the same as in True's dreams, the same unrepentant toughness barely camouflaged under steroid therapy and plastic surgery; the same voice, mannerisms. True marvels at his imagination, how it picked up on her entire essence.

He squirms under the restraints. An idea. "You know what you can do? Check into Tokyo land transactions since the quake. Find out who's been grabbing up the land."

"For what possible reason?"

He's too aggressive. As well as he feels he knows her, she doesn't know him. He want to slow down, but the words gush out. "A hunch. Before I ended up here, I interviewed a Japanese refugee at the dock—old guy—told me he'd been forced to sell his land for dirt. Said it's happening a lot there."

"Who'd buy worthless land?"

"When they rebuild, it'll be worth trillions."

"Only way that'd happen is if they keep the capital here."

"Exactly!"

"Bullshit. That's American paranoid delusional jingoism presented as a Japanese conspiracy. All due respect? In bed with restraints on, you aren't what I'd call a reliable source."

"Reiner, come on."

"You act like you know me. I only called to offer condolences. You were a damned fine journo, and I was sorry to hear this is how you ended up."

"I'll tell you who's scarfing up the land. It's a corrupt circuit named Sato. Runs the Sato corp."

"Tsuyoshi Sato?" The look on Reiner's face—like she calls on a good will mission and this poor shit still thinks he's a reporter instead of a head case.

"A martial artist," True continues. "Controls an organization of salary samurai and corporate ninjas."

Reiner can't control herself anymore. "Sato's a skinny, whiny salaryman who inherited a fortune. He's harmless. Hasn't worked a day in his life. Certainly isn't made of the stuff to pull off what you say he did."

True's desperate. The restraints don't promote his cause. "Listen, Reiner. Just check into it. Do it for me."

"It's a waste of time."

"You won't regret it."

"What I regret is calling you, Ailey, sorry to say."

"I know I can trust you. Before, I didn't, but I was wrong."

"Before? Before what?" Reiner rubs her eyes, tired of the conversation.

"There's so much at stake."

"Bye."

"Reiner, wait. Please, wait."

Her patience is stretched taut. "What?"

"Check into recent land transactions. If you can get through the screens, you'll see Sato's behind it all. He's exerting intense pressure behind the scenes to get the politicians to keep the capital in Tokyo. You'll see."

Reiner rolls her eyes and the screen zips shut. True looks across the room, sees three more beds, a slumbering log in each. The wall unshuts; more beds are wheeled in.

The plague rages on. So does True's mind.

A new pattern replaces Reiner's snapshot. Psychotropia, mind candy, min-max: minimum effort, maximum results. True stops fighting. Let it work its numbing magic.

It's deep night; snores and deep breathing accompany True's thoughts. Finally he's unshackled from psychotropia; an opportunity to try and make sense of things.

"p0yiwk." He reaches for his wrist-top and plugs in this haunting code.

No reference in data banks relating to p0yiwk.

True types it again—the wrist-top responds in kind. He stares at the glowing keyboard. Whispers "Pee zero why eye double-you kay. Pee zero why eye double-you kay. Pee zero why eye double-you kay."

It's important, knows he must decipher it. *Pee zero why eye double-you kay*. It feels vaguely cryptographic.

He's out of step with reality, a little off line. Things aren't what they seem.

He stares at the first letter, *p*. True is out of step. Things aren't what they seem. *P.* Step. True looks at the letters on his qwerty touchpad, the steps around the symbol: The letter *O* is immediately to the left. Diagonally up to the left is *0.* Clockwise shows a hyphen or a dash, to the immediate right a bracket. Then quote marks, a colon or semi-colon, the letter *L.*

He thinks through the issues that dog him: Tokyo, the earthquake, Reiner, Bong Bong, Rush, Aslam, land transactions, capital and capitol, psychotropia patterns, Dr. Powter. But *Pee zero why eye double-you kay* seems a world away. He counts up the number of symbols: six. True is out of step. Trust your intuition. Six symbols. Six letters.

Tokyo, earthquake, Bong Bong, Rush, Aslam, none are constructed from six letters, although Reiner is. So's Powter. True tries to formulate a cryptogram to solve the puzzle, but no matter what, no matter how many spaces there are or in what order he places the letters, neither Reiner nor Powter equals p0yiwk.

A step away. He stares at the pattern, starts words beginning with letters surrounding the *p* key. After minutes, maybe hours, True solves it.

"p0yiwk." When True takes each letter down diagonally to the left, the message spells "logjam." *LOGJAM.*

Logjam? He thought about it in his virtual trip, also during imagined sessions with Dr. Powter. It's more, much more, than too much data piped into too small a space. It means he suffers from mnemonia. He runs a trace on the word, pulls up a number of entries from past newscasts, looks at the name of the reporter who filed them: True Ailey. He watches footage from a year ago, of himself: healthy, capable, not diluted as now. True watches, fascinated, as he breaks a story that ended up breaking him.

"Shirley Logjam's nightmare began long before she knew she was living a nightmare," True begins in his report. "With echoes of Nazi atrocities in last century's Second World War, Logjam was a human guinea pig. Her company, International Soft Where?, a developer of complex virtual reality systems including the popular *Street Ninja*, tested its most experimental and dangerous virtual reality systems on her.

"Now Shirley Logjam is dead, her mind and body destroyed by her devotion to her work—a devotion not even she knew she had."

True has no recollection of this report, yet there he is, providing footage and narrating a grisly tale of electric intrigue. He gets to relive a lost part of his life, like finding a dusty journal.

Shirley Logjam died of liver failure. The autopsy showed she'd been abusing FREEze, a meta-amphetamine commonly used in tandem with virtual reality games, enabling the abuser to be fully absorbed by mirror universes. "At first glance, it's a typical story of FREEze abuse. Except one major difference: Shirley Logjam was no drug addict. She was murdered."

True accesses all the broadcasts, background notes, edited-out portions, footage never aired. What he finds possesses an eerily familiar quality. Three days after the death of Shirley Logjam, her husband turned up at True's door claiming his wife was murdered. After investigating, True discovered her company had been testing its virtual reality products on unsuspecting employees, drugging them and detailing their responses.

His report numbed a public already numbed by technology. The trial, in which the American Defense Corporation, among others, stood accused, was an offshoot of True's report.

In his notes, he discovers that International Soft Where? is an ADC affiliate. True searches for a connection to Sato, but there isn't any apparent one; ADC and Sato Corporation are direct competitors. Enemies.

True checks the dates: days before he fell into virtual voids. Even his notes from the period are a haze, and the closer to his hospitalization, the hazier they get. He watches, transfixed, as he floats into a court room, watches as the CEOs of the defendant corporations refuse to cooperate, threatening to move their operations abroad, and the American people pressure their representatives to force the special prosecutor to drop the charges. Remembers de Bris told him the charges were dropped.

He compiles a lengthy list of corporations, including ADC and MedTekton, the plastics company. True asked de Bris whether MedTekton was one of the companies on trial. They weren't, this is true; but bank data shows ADC and MedTekton have megs of money zapping around one another's accounts.

The question sticks. If ADC is behind his latest electronic escapades, what makes True certain Sato's the key? Why'd his latest elect-trek take him to Japan, to Reiner, Eden, accessing Sato's chip? He's about to over-and-out when he hears a familiar voice: "True. It took you long enough."

The wrist-top. Aslam, grimy in camouflage. Behind him, barracks for rebel forces on the move. He's chewing on a straw. "One of the hardest things to manufacture is this drinking straw. It requires near-perfect quality control, which you don't find in fucked-up places like this." Aslam in the virtual flesh, talking into a wrist-top, WWTV-issue, pans his jungle locale. Scorched trees and earth, stationed near a cave with an assemblage of bunkers, collapsible aluminum nut-and-bolted together. Aslam knots the straw, holds it to the lens. "This is the last straw, True. The last straw." He snickers soundlessly. "I told you that computer model was something." Aslam pops the straw knot in his mouth, chews on it. "So I'm dead, you're listening to me, and you're on your way to figuring things out. Least, I hope so. It's been a hard road, my friend, and for that I'm sorry. If I hadn't had to include you in this shit, I wouldn't have. But there was no other way."

From fifteen days ago.

"Besides, you owe me. You know you do. Pay-back time. Brother-to-brother. It's cast a shadow over our friendship ever since it happened. We never talked about it, though I wish we had. But at least I won't have to listen to you fuck things up, apologize or something, like that's what I want, which is total bullshit. You know what I'm talking about. Pakistan, India, the war." Like Aslam's right there, bedside; only in memory, really. "A trade. You for Anjou and Imran. Only at the time I don't know it's a trade. Just trying to do the right thing, you know? You're in jail, Anjou and the kid are with her family in Lahore, and I get electric fever: I'll spring True from jail, have the wife and kid meet me at the border, where you and I'll be waiting, and we'll all flee ever happily into Free Tibet. A good scheme for escaping nuclear war, which was just hours away."

Guilt claws at True. He knows the story already. Lets Aslam finish his purge. "But they don't make it. Rumors of nuclear war were driving people to panic. A lot of traffic accidents. I guess that's what happened. Maybe she was killed by bandits feasting on the anarchy. All I know is they would have made it if I'd been with them." Aslam's complexion turning strawberry rash under his jungle tan. "Except I was with you. And you made it. No offense, True, but it was a bum deal for me. When Anjou and Imran were dissolved into radioactive dust, some of me died with them. Faith is all I got now, True. Which is why I need you."

True flashes to this time, the angry mood, the border's desolation spiraling up to the Himalaya's breathless peaks, waiting, waiting, waiting for Anjou and Imran. Launch time all keyed in. Ready. 10-9-8-7-. Have to escape, far away from this nuclear MADness. But Anjou and Imran don't show, and when True and Aslam can't afford one sec more, True has to coax his wasted friend over the border, away from the war and the ashes of his family.

Aslam keeps on. "I don't know how much I will have told you. Some military corp contacted me after my platoon was smoked by a weapon that nullifies everything you do. I can't explain it, but we were powerless against it. They offered major bucks if I tracked it down. Lots of perks, money. Figured I'd use the corp's resources to get you to track down the design codes, then take them for myself. I know I can biz with you. You didn't really believe I'd leave the insurgency? I wanted to smoke those fucking ethnics with a taste of their own. I also needed to take care of biz, in case, you know, I got smoked. So here I am. TCBing. I don't know who the defense contractor who hired me is. Could be Boeing-Mitsubishi, American Defense, maybe GEC. I didn't get to pose too many qs."

True begins to sift fact from virtual fact. Too much coincidence in all this. Are there things to be learned from his intuition?

Aslam looks to night's sky, stars hazed by artillery smoke. Peers into the camera, at True, grins. "Did you catch any of those promos your shitty-assed anchor Rush Gallstone ran?" Aslam mocks Rush's inflectionless promo voice. "'Coming next week: I risk my life bringing you a rare live interview with the blood-thirsty leader of the Muslim Insurgency, Aslam Q. Aziz. A WWTV exclusive brought to you by Rush No Balls.' What a glitch-master. Just to piss him off, I'm not doing the interview. I got what I needed. Which is to leave you this message; a heartfelt request, actually. Find out what this corp technology is all about and share the wealth. A Japanese corporation's got it. The Sato Corporation. I don't know how they got it. Maybe it's in WWTV's video archives. But you'd have checked that already since you're here with me now.

"That's all I know. The rest is in your scoop-worthy hands. Your mission, which you have no choice but to take, is to restore the corporate balance of technology. I know, I know. If I had the technology, no way I'd pass it on. But I'm dead, so tech-transfer is the next best. Do it and we're even. The cosmos is clear. But don't let me down."

Muffled commotion, insurgents scrambling to face Mecca. Aslam's flat, moody expression. "Prayer time. Goodbye, handsome best friend. Too bad things always get worse before they get better. The story of our lives."

After saving a copy for himself, True erases Aslam's video note from WWTV's archives. Then sets to retiring his debt.

After daybreak True's still energized. He doesn't want to sleep because with sleep come nightmares and he's had enough of those, so he accesses his wrist-top's jazz program.

Drums beating.

Insistent.

Incessant.

Wood striking skin.

Splashes of cymbal

circling vultures of sound.

Tribal sounds from the jungle. And True focuses on the rich tones of the bass. The music's foundation. Chords pound on a piano, hands splayed; clusters of tones weave throughout, threads of a magic carpet.

Sheets of sound.

Coltrane's shrieks of sound.

Pleading for understanding.

And healing.

Peace.

Knowledge.

Above all knowledge.

In defiant stillness True listens to "Resolution" from *A Love Supreme*, John Coltrane's ode to God. Lost in the music, surfing on the waves and pulses of notes, his mind reeling from the power of the tenorman's passion, his search for truth winding strand for strand with True's.

Reedy gasps, squeals, squalls. Oblong cycles of notes. Pentatonic scales. Brush fires of sixteenth-note runs spiderweb with Elvin Jones's percussive fabric, the skimming of drumsticks on cymbals. Tones of terror intertwine with McCoy Tyner's cascading chords and rhythmic thunder. Over grave bass tones and tomes, a dark, plaintive cry is issued. More shimmering cymbals and gravel bass notes, contained within the confines of Trane's vision—his *jazz-schauung*—the elixir of life, the fountain of art, the driving force of his music. And his life.

"Resolution" ends. "Pursuance" begins. The melody, a jagged line, brings to True's mind a mountain range's peaks, connected by Trane's magical sense of lyricism. And the mountains urge True on.

The Pursuance of Aslam's murderer.

The idea will not fade.

Trane pursued the ultimate truth.

True will pursue the truth.

Elvin Jones locks into a triplet fill, sparring with Trane's throaty cries and McCoy Tyner's chordal ripostes. Jimmy Garrison strums taut strings: buzzing Tibetan monk chants in double-note harmony, reminiscent of exotic far-east vocal boxes. And there are the mountains again. True feels those towering hills. Remembering the cold cell in those mountains that once held him, one tiny window funneling in a string of light. True slept on a dirt floor. Scant food, shit on the floor—his shit—ankles gripped by shackles. True lost hope, his spirits sank lower with each hour. It was then Aslam walked into his cell and back into his life.

True remembers he laughed. Over mind's edge. "My old friend Aslam." True was only obliquely aware of his incoherence. "My old college buddy Aslam. What a great place for an alum—an alumni reunion, buddy."

From his ground perch, True watched as Aslam, then an officer in the Pakistani army, marched over—he can see the mud-caked boots even now—and kicked True. There was a breathless flash of white that came from somewhere inside his head, the shock of pain. Darkness blanketed him. When he woke up, he wasn't chained and was sleeping on a mattress. The scent of clean sheets made him cry; so thankful for little things. A pillow, pillow case, blanket, cleanliness. Someone had bathed him while he slept, and at the time, it was all True needed to be happy.

"Psalm" ends, the final song on *A Love Supreme*. True checks the time—the hour is sifting into dawn. He knows he has to sleep, but is afraid to dream, afraid to be alone, afraid to be with anyone.

True types a new drummer into the program, substituting Tony Williams for Elvin Jones. But keeps the rest of the John Coltrane Quartet intact, even though he's sure Tony Williams never recorded with Trane. But True wants to hear something unique. Tony Williams, always on top of the beat, sticks skimming along like flat-sided stones on a lake. The infinite space between two beats. Some drummers play right on it, others a little on top, like Elvin Jones, but a few sprint ahead, as if they alone pull the music along with them.

Tony Williams's conception of time is unique.

True's conception of reality is unique.

Because what is reality anyway?

Where are the boundaries?

Once, he thought he knew.

And the song he chooses for the computer to assemble from the billions of bytes of artistic data it absorbed, all the players' solos and recorded works, all of their tendencies and theoretical underpinnings? Knowledge of their substitutions, altered dominants, diminished and augmented scales, triads.

The song?

What's the song?

"The Promise."

But before the music runs out, Reiner calls and True's taken away.

Her first. "You were right about the capital, the land transactions, everything. What now?"

"What do you think?"

"I'd suggest you get your ass to Japan."

"I couldn't agree more."

"Are you really ill?"

"I'll explain when I see you."

"How will you get out of the hospital?"

"Leave it to me."

CHAPTER 21

Urine-warm rain slants down from smudged clouds, runs off through cracks and fissures in the pavement. Pumice and coral walls, barriers built to hem in shanty dwellers, sponge water until stained with greasy patches. Mined from surrounding reefs, coral is nature's barrier against wave erosion. In Luzonia, it's also ground, mixed with flour. Buildings and bread: two reasons Luzonia's coast melts away. White flakes flop down with the drops, like snow but not snow, spewing from an abandoned rubber factory constructed before Luzonia's rubber trees were stripped away, processed, exported, gone forever, point-zero-zero-zero-one percent repatriated as foreign aid: as windshield wipers, weapons, sneakers, surplus condoms, useless shit.

The factory's been converted into a crematorium. The plague is out of control, thousands of bodies a day stuffed into ovens. The gagging aroma fills True's head. He wonders why his scent mechanism works after his VR-FREEze-mare. Probably because he's tiptoeing on shards of fear.

True and Rush stand crammed at the starting line of The Urban Survival Tournament, set outside the tunnel where the truck was stuck. It's True's neighborhood, a place he knows, but through the tunnel exists an unknown purgatory. A martial artist practices "Bruce Lees," rooster squawks and kicks, his heel brushing Rush's well-ordered locks. Rush ducks, collides with a female bodybuilt. Biceps roaring, she collars Rush and flings him down.

Rush picks himself up. "Lot of fucking help you are, Ailey."

"I'll be sure to count on you later."

But it's good to be outside again, even rain-soaked and surrounded by these combat-tested loaves of violence.

Rush holds his press pass as a shield, hoping to avoid more ignominy. "Give me the wrist-top. You can't take it inside. It's against the rules."

"Give me a minute. I don't like to part with it." True tugs at the bright red sweatshirt Rush gave him. It flows loosely from his nail-file frame, the fibers coated with a radar-enhancing material so Rush can track him from the air.

While Rush gripes, True wonders how his hair stays so perfect in rain. "It cost me a lot of money to get you here to the starting line. Bong Bong is convinced your death will bring him personal honor or something. I'm definitely going over budget this year."

"You deducted the shirt from my salary. What are you complaining about? Besides. Think of the ratings."

"Yeah." Rush says this dreamily.

"Think of the money you'll save on my salary after I'm dead."

"Yeah." Rush's smile flips to a frown. "Not that I want you to die or anything. Hang in there as long as you can. The more footage we get of you, the better. You win, that'd be the best scenario of all."

"You honestly think I can complete this course without getting my face ripped off?"

Rush squeezes True's limp bicep. "No."

The joint network craft hovers overhead. Background footage sweeps.

Rush holds out his hand. "I better get to my ride, get out of this rain. Give me your wrist-top."

True unclasps it, dangles it for Rush to take. Before Rush can grab it, a street urchin snatches it and tucks into the crowd. Rush shouts after him but the boy vanishes.

True says, "You have all of it on file anyway."

"It's WWTV property. Now I have to requisition another. Now I'm really going over budget." Rush goes to his waiting hovercraft.

True works his way into the contestant pool, his eyes darting left and right. He's careful not to rub elbows or step on toes. Already fights break out between those with too much pride and too little brain, all with lots to prove, this their only means to prove it.

There are announcements—the usual warnings and explanations: no outside equipment; the winner is the first contestant to wind through the ghetto unassisted and come out the other side alive. A 21st century game for a 21st century media market. The footage will be grisly. True wonders whether this is actually better than being glued to a hospital bed, psychotropic patterns beaming above. He looks around, sees Bong Bong lounging on the bridge walkway. A black umbrella shields him from the downpour. Bong Bong waves, calls down, but True can't hear him. He wonders where Pidge is.

Cannon fire. The start. True's pulled along in the contestants' current, through the tunnel, deafening and dark, then out. As soon as they clear daylight, bricks, bottles, and rocks whistle down. True covers his head, keeps pushing forward. Steps aside, lets the rest of the pack shoot by. At his feet is a school of cockroaches, water bugs, other festering insects, feeding on the slime and garbage. A teeming congress of rats nearby, too. He wonders about their reputation as being able to survive atomic blasts and feed on the toxic waste, that they'd outlast humans on earth. But True's seen roaches or rats only where people congregate. Maybe vermin need people like journalists need misery.

True sprints down the main artery, well behind now, counts off one cross street with his fingers, another, another, another, as the contestants shatter into smaller groups, working in teams in some instances to fend off attacking Luzonians. True hangs a right with a small herd of other contestants, scoots into a doorway where he stays hidden as the tumult crescendos.

From here, he watches the martial artist fend off a gangpack, his feet spinning like turbine rotors, crashing into jaws and ribs. Until he's speared. The pack pounces, rips the clothes from his body, checks for gold or silver in his teeth, carves organs out of his body and sticks them in plastic baggies with ice. You can't strip a car or computer that fast, True thinks. The Urban Survival Tourney, the organ trade's grandest supply show.

He waits minutes more, overwhelmed by the frenzy, sees the female bodybuilt beat and stomp her way down the alley until her brain is crushed by a well-aimed brick. She's consumed by a teeming mass of teens who pick her clean. Leave the rest to the roaches and maggots. More die while others fight on. Only a few able to advance to the next block—the next game level. Obstacles pop up at every turn: ghetto survivors, pockmarked by radiation burns, scars, and blisters, brandish weapons. Artillery debris and bricks fire down. Old-style bullets smash into hearts, heads. Makeshift spears pierce natural body armor.

True's waited long enough. Hops over a pile of corpses, their organs sliced out, their innards dripping, and takes another left. True's heading away from the finish, sees Rush's hovercraft above, imagines his supervisor's confusion as he circles back toward the start. Keeps his back to walls, ducks under windows, is wary around doorways, notices that although people here are poor beyond poor, they all have TVs, tuned in to the event as it happens—graphs, stats, interviews, replays, comments from last year's winner.

A rock glances off True's head. A boy, couldn't be more than ten, jumps on his back, and True shakes him off. Keeps running. He's gasping now, out of breath, didn't think about that when he filled out his entry app. Near the tunnel he slows. A gang blocks the street he needs. They brandish metal rods and clubs, home-made knives, jagged glass blades, spears made from remelted metal. True's panting, his sides cramping. The mob moves forward. No hurry. True searches for a way around.

Suddenly, there's Pidge, as if the cops rule here as they rule outside. Pidge sprays the ground with jus de betel nut, hits some ants, which are attacked by other ants only because they are different now, forming teeming balls. True checks behind. There's even greater tumult there. Pidge sidles forward, stands face-to-neck with True. Above, Rush's hovercraft, action-catching.

Pidge holds out his hand. "Cash card?" True shakes his head. Pidge taps True's pocket. "No." Pidge snaps his fingers, points to True's sneakers.

"You're going to have to kill me."

Pidge's eyes glow yellow with threads of red. He draws his pistol. True looks to the gang, watches their fluttering hand signals, fingers flickering and snapping, waving like humming-birds. In seconds, in a flurry of furious activity, Pidge is dead, rent limb from limb, his neck sliced ear to ear, his spine split.

And this is the extraordinary part for True. They don't gouge out Pidge's organs. Instead, they choose retribution. Dwellers fly out from behind doors and windows, from all around, and beat on Pidge's corpse with fists, feet, rocks, bottles, garbage, bricks. When they're done mashing him to ground meat, they take turns spitting on what's left. Rush's hoverer hums upstairs, capturing the moment for posterity.

True follows the gang down the street into the winding ghetto-maze. At the farthest point from the finish line, True sees a man dressed the same as he, the same radar sweatshirt, the same build, skin tone, hair. His twin goes in the other way while True follows his guides through a criss-cross of homes, blade-narrow alleys, and tunnels. True squeezes through a hole in the shanty wall. Scrape, scratch.

On the other side Piña's lazing on her skateboard. "Pidge bought it, huh?"

"Thanks."

"That's free. Piña owed the motherfucker." She heaves a shirt at True.

"*I* almost thought I wasn't going to make it. The double Piña chose? Perfect." True takes off Rush's radar shirt, puts on the new one.

"Even made sure his underwear matched yours, stains and all."

"How did Piña stage my death?"

"Stage? We x'ed your double. Only way it'd look real."

"You killed him? Why?"

She shrugs hammy deltoids. "So everybody thinks you're dead."

"But what about the guy?"

"He was dying anyway, plague or something."

"Piña's saying he'd have died anyway? In what, six months?"

"Two." She pats the skateboard. "Get on."

"I've got to check out something in my apartment."

"Piña cleaned it out when they took you away. Got everything you need. This too." She tosses True's wrist-top to him. True accepts a microchip access from her, copies the wrist-top contents onto it, then hands it back. She gives him a coin envelope. "This, too. Piña hired a hacker who said this is the only thing that doesn't fit right in your home system. Told Piña it's bizarre shit, so watch out."

True flips her his wrist-top, pockets the microchip access and coin envelope. "Piña better be careful, too. Whoever has my wrist-top won't be of this world long."

"Decisions, decisions. There are so many motherfuckers Piña'd like to give it to."

True studies the zigzaggy part dividing her yarny hair. "When Piña rifled through my apartment, she see, like, any blood-red holograms of me?"

Piña hacks up phlegm. Actually she's laughing. "That's from a TV show. 'The Program Contact.' About spies and shit." She pats her skateboard. "Get on."

"Thanks." Almost free now. A little giddy. He leans down, kisses Piña's cheek, and is amused to see her break out in a rash of embarrassment.

CHAPTER 22

Tokyo is the same except for the aftershocks, which True didn't include in his virtuopia, which should have told him things weren't what they seemed, but he missed it and now he's back, hoping he'll score higher this time around. Although plenty of buildings are charred and streets are buried in rubble, it isn't as unbearable as his version. Most Tokyoites have swarmed into police-protected refugee camps or moved in with relatives and friends in other cities. Scriggly kanji-signs decorate doors of abandoned dwellings.

True and Reiner at WWTV's Tokyo Bureau on the top-floor of a battered building. She's nothing like her broadcast icon. Not in her mid-thirties, not the statuesque, stiletto-tongued TV anchor. More like late sixties, hair soaked gray, age spots tinting hands, dry, curling skin.

She pats the couch, indicating True should sit. "I know what you're thinking."

True sits and surveys the office. Lightning-bolt cracks are

haphazardly caulked. He wonders about the quake's capriciousness, why WWTV's Tokyo bureau is left standing while buildings hugging it—like the convenience store, the sushi shop—have collapsed. And why some city blocks were consumed by fire but not Reiner's. Futons rolled up, crammed in a corner. Reiner must sleep here, her home probably ground to dust mite food.

Reiner falls onto the sofa. Creaky breaths. "I use an icon because a different broadcast image works to my advantage. I go undercover, no one knows it's me."

"Does it help the ratings?"

"Who wants to see an old lady?"

"Where's your dog, the black Lab?"

"How'd you know I had... oh, you saw the initial quake reports I did. I picked her up outside the office here. Got an aid worker to take her to Osaka. Tokyo's no place for pets."

"Did you read the data I dumped into your computer system before I left Luzonia?"

"Like a cheap thriller. Assassinations, secret weapons, plots to get you addicted to drugs and software. Where do you want to go from here?"

"Ever hear of a technology that can predict the precise time of an earthquake, or a machine that can cause one?"

Reiner presses an itch in her back. "No. Haven't run across anything like that. It could be Sato's superstitious. Decided a few years ago to pull out all his investments in the probability that a major earthquake would swallow Tokyo. Bankers and brokers don't like to admit this, but they knew that when a big one hit Tokyo, the global economy would rumble. Lucky it didn't happen when Japan was an economic superpower."

"Like in the 1980s and early '90s. Sato ever show such foresight before this?"

"Not that I know of."

"He have any investments in a company with the kind of technology that could topple a metropolis?"

"Doubtful. I read through all the available information, and there was no explosion or anything like that. Just four fault plates rubbing up against each another. Your typical earthquake."

"Typical except in its magnitude." True by the window now, overlooking the sprawl. There are those signs again. "Why are so many buildings covered in scraps of paper? Is it a religious thing?"

"Change of address forms. Signs informing anyone who cares where the occupants went. Communications are still down."

"They look like kids wrote them. I thought it might be some sort of cultural superstition. Like the purity of children, maybe."

"Nah. The signs are by adults. Penmanship's been deteriorating since last-century's introduction of the PC."

"Did you run a trace on International Soft Where?"

"I can give you an abstract or you can ask Odessa, who's got the sum."

"I want to meet him, in person. Let's stay away from communicating over satellite feeds or microwave cables, at least for important stuff. Is he far from here?"

"This way, please."

A door a few steps down. The room is crammed with computing equipment—micro-microchip boxes, wires, transformers, consoles stacked and neatly sorted, shining lights and whirs. Some of the equipment's so antiquated it's not even blue-book. Some of it is custom-made. Some warped beyond high-tech. All of it hooked up and running. A stirring in the midst of this techno-mélange. Odessa, dressed completely different from the one True "met." He wears an off-white velcro-down shirt, blue jeans, sneakers, his hair mowed conservative, no jewelry.

Odessa stands, reaches out a hand. It's soft, except for the fingertips, which are type-cast. "We've met."

"We have."

"Not what you expected, but people change."

Reiner comes over. "When did your paths cross?"

Odessa's eyes don't stray from True's. "I played a prank on him." To True: "Sorry about locking you into that pol's speeches. I was pretty arrogant back then."

"Doesn't matter now." True wonders why Odessa is here. Did he hack the wrong corp, is he fleeing? Or did he only imagine this in Tokyo's mirror? Memories or imaginings? Reality or his own creations?

"Reiner tells me you've been hooked into something cutting-edge. Don't suppose you brought something I can use."

True reaches into his pocket, hands Odessa the chip Piña gleaned from his home computer. Odessa jams it into a tiny porthole and sits. A screenless wall of images shoots up in front of him. He studies the code, then immediately shuts down. "There's a virus in there, and by the looks of it, a pretty nasty one. I've never seen it before. I hope my containment systems can handle it." Odessa types furiously. Stops. "I'm going to need time to let the systems work on it." He spins around. "There seems to be a virtual world inside a virtual world in there."

"I didn't know that was possible." True rocks on his heels.

"Makes two of us. But I can see from the code structure there's a virtual world in there. Inside that virtual world is a gateway to reality."

"Huh?" Reiner says.

True tries to fathom the idea. "So, I was in virtual reality. I didn't know I was there. When I snuck into the net to look for incriminating evidence on Sato, I was *actually* in the infonet. So the information about Sato is true. And the chip I accessed from Sato is real. But then I passed it on to someone else before I left virtual reality."

Odessa nods. "That's right. Reiner fed me the data you sent. I'd say that electronic escapade you took was real. Whatever it was you took, you really took."

"Somebody sent me in to grab that chip from Sato."

"They used you. You were tricked into traveling through a real database to cull heavily guarded secrets. It's a smart piece of engineering, but the program couldn't do it without someone with an innate ability to navigate through tricky dataspace."

"And the software program offered me a built-in incentive. I thought I was saving my own ass."

Reiner: "Odessa. By reading the chip, can you replay everything that transpired?"

"It depends on this virus. The funny thing is, I can't tell if it was planted in there as protection or it just ended up in there—possibly from some incorrect coding." Odessa ponders a pause more. "Might even be alive."

"Alive?" True mouths.

"Not alive per se. Alive in the sense that even when not plugged into hardware, it grows. I know there were a couple of powerhackers onto a generation of software that could become more intelligent in time. This interactive program, by being able to tap into your mind, it could grow. In a sense, you've customized this software. Your thoughts, ideas, experiences may have spawned greater complexity."

"So ... " Reiner looks at True. "*He* is the virus."

"Yeah. And the thing may have continued to grow even after you were disconnected."

"Can I be stopped?" True's skin sprayed with cold pickle juice. "Should I be stopped?"

"I don't think we want to stop you—your virus-mirror, actually." Odessa checks the readout. "We're in luck. There's an automatic self-destruct program within the software, but the virus blocked implementation."

"It wants to survive. My will to survive has interacted with the software codes. That's where the virus came from."

Reiner slaps her thigh. "And we wouldn't have it unless this happened. So, there's our answer, how we can ensure this virus is kept under control."

Odessa brushes his scalp with his palm, indicating Reiner's gone over his head.

Reiner frowns. "Don't you get it? If you wanted to survive, if someone offered you a place you could go that was comfortable, where you could spend the rest of your life, would you go?"

True understands. "Hose it into another database, a place where it has room to grow. Just make sure it doesn't leak."

Odessa slacks over the console. "How come I didn't think of that?"

True wonders what the characteristics of a virus impressed with his thoughts and memories would be. Would it wreak havoc, erasing hard-fought data, leaving a trail of empty in its wake? Would it soak up info, add to the glut of statistics strangling humanity? His choice: virus as truth serum. Stamp out some of the deceit crushing the world.

True to Odessa: "Before you start, do you have PR on International Soft Where?"

"The American Defense Corp subsidiary, yeah." Odessa pulls it up. "ISW handles weapons programming for ADC. They were established ten years ago as a licensor of different technologies. They rely less on developing their own software than on buying up promising operations. Here's a list of small companies they've bought or absorbed."

Reiner places a hand each on True and Odessa's shoulders. "I've got to file some stories, so I'm going."

"I'll stay with Odessa." True's eyes hopscotch down the list. "I'm sure I can make myself use—" Stops at the name Six Days, Inc. "Forget it. I'm going with you."

Odessa looks up. "Find something interesting?"

Six Days, Inc. The world is indeed a small place. Six Days, Inc. Of course. It makes perfect sense. No wonder he was targeted. No wonder the software he was enveloped in was so intimate about his inner workings. So obvious he wants to kick his own ass.

"Interesting isn't the word. Try extraordinary."

CHAPTER 23

True's studying paper scraps glued around the entrance to a downtown building, mostly in Japanese, some in English, Arabic, Chinese, Korean. Through glass he sees inside. A cavernous hall, families in tight rows, possessions heaped in corners. Some sleep, others play cards or mahjongg or talk, living on standby until the corps and bureaucrats decide what's next.

He's searching neo-Tokyo's White Pages, translating non-English into English with his wrist-top, keying on words that he hopes will jostle his memory. A kimono-clad obaasan, bird-wing bow tied in the back, is eyeing him. Her face is powdered ghost. She points to a paper that's been creased, recreased, finally posted.

"A peace crane." Her English is creaky and unaccented.

"What?"

Heavy sigh lifted. "It was origami, a peace crane. But now... " She indicates construction rubble across the street. "Who are you looking for?"

"A friend."

"Have you found your friend?"

"No."

She crooks her arm. Points around the corner of the building. "Everybody waits. Perhaps you will find your friend there waiting as well."

"Waiting? For what?"

The woman starts her leave. "Everything. We must wait for everything these days."

When he arcs around the building he understands. A mega-line of people and various containers. In the distance, fire licks at a cluster of apartments, warm wind sheeting down. True asks a man with gray hair crowning his skull what the line's for.

The man has jaundiced teeth. Wispy strands jut from his chin. "When there is a line, you wait. There is bound to be something you need."

True walks down the line, glancing at faces, sensing the collective fatigue. He keeps a running tally, mouthing as he walks: Japanese man, Japanese woman, Japanese woman, probably Korean. Mirroring the kilometer-long line. Ten minutes later, there she is. He knows it's her by her hair's red highlights, accentuated by real sun, and the way her jeans nuzzle her.

"Eden, it's True."

Eden whirls. True knows he should have gone slower, broken it to her gently, but there's no time. "True. What are you doing here? How did you find me?"

She drops a water jug. True picks it up, hands it back, then sweeps with his hands. "Do you know what you're in line for?"

Her eyes, matte hazel marred by allergy red. Poets say the eyes are the mirrors to the soul; but True, who has seen more dislodged eyeballs than he cares to remember, knows it's the face, the context, that is beauty.

She says, "Water. Food. Gas. If you walk to the front of the line, people get nervous you're going to cut ahead, so you have to get in a line and wait, see if there's something you need."

"You could be waiting for nothing."

"Theoretically."

"Somebody could have started this line for no reason. What if there's nothing up there? What if this line leads nowhere?"

"Why would anyone do that?"

"It's difficult to say sometimes why people do the things they do." True wishes he could love her again, wishes he could go back. He scoops up a small piece of concrete, rubs his thumb against the grains. Bits sprinkle. "I wouldn't have been able to find you if it hadn't been for that newscast."

Eden's crying. True hears murmurings, knows someone's translating the play-by-play. Her sleeve soaks up tears. "I did the interview because I knew you'd see me."

"Why didn't you look for me?"

She studies her shoes, or maybe the water jugs. "I started to. I called WWTV. They wouldn't tell me where you were posted, and you weren't on the air at all."

"I was shooting footage for Rush Gelding in Luzonia."

"I didn't know."

"You didn't want to know. I wasn't hard to track." He thinks of Aslam and Bong Bong, ADC, and Sato. Tracking True has been easy. Until now.

"I felt responsible."

"You were the dealer. I was the user. You could have cleansed yourself better by staying."

"I was scared."

True senses the man behind eavesdropping. He withers him with a granite stare.

She cries, nods, and bounces on her feet. Idiosyncrasies he once loved. "I made you sick."

True remembers the teenagers in Luzonia's ghettos, how they'd take two cats, tie their tails, hang them over electric cables and cheer until they clawed each other to death. "You work in international aid?"

"I fix donated computers. Make systems run on antiquated or recycled equipment."

"A noble profession. After I was committed, what happened to your work?"

"Six Days, Inc? It was bought up by International Soft Where? I tried to destroy my work after I saw what it was capable of. But they sicced lawyers on me. They told me all my research was proprietary, so I didn't own it. They gave me some money and I left. What else could I do?"

"ISW is owned by American Defense Corp. Right?"

"Right."

"You know of any connection between ADC and Tsuyoshi Sato?"

"I don't know anyone named Sato. I've only been here a few weeks."

"Thanks. See you around." True turns to leave. She squeezes his arm. "You're so thin."

"No one gave me fattening-up money to keep my mouth shut."

She lets go, shakes. "They had my research. They had the power. All I had was me. Me!"

"Me me me me," True arpeggios. Can't believe how cruel he is. Doesn't care. "I just went through another VR trip.

Someone set me up. If you'd stuck around last time, maybe none of it would have happened."

"I'm sorry."

"Yeah."

"It's all I've got besides—" She breaks.

"Yeah."

She gets it out. "Besides being in love with you."

"Yeah, well, I think you didn't love me enough."

"Do you think being apart has been easy for me? Every day without you is a day without happiness."

"Happiness is an elusive goal."

"We can be happy." A chapped lipped kiss.

But True walks anyway. For a while, as he puts distance between them, he hears her sobs, then only imagines them, and these memories haunt him all the way to Reiner's. But that's fine. It's natural. It's life.

CHAPTER 24

Odessa's replaying True's virtual escapades on a monitor, tweaking the color and clarity when necessary. True watches the schizo-split screen images of him alone: one side clenching air, writhing on the floor, the other side playing out his VR tale. Odessa freeze-frames True delving into Sato's mainframe, after Reiner's icon speeds toward old age and death.

Reiner jabs True's shoulder. "Your opinion of me was pretty goddamn low."

"It wasn't all me. Your death advanced the story I was playing out."

Odessa zooms in on the chip True stole. Analyzes it on screen. Flips it over; cuts away sections to see inside. "Racist view of me, too, by the way. But your thoughts are your own."

"No, they aren't; otherwise we wouldn't be watching them now." True parries embarrassment, wonders what Reiner or Odessa's thoughts would be like, but decides no one should have to go through what he did.

Odessa runs a coded sequence under the image. "See, you're back in reality, right there, or virtual reality at least. That really is a chunk of Sato's property right there."

"Can you tell what's on the chip?"

"Not yet. That'll take a lot of code crunching and time. It's scrambled, and remember I don't really have it. I only have a virtual representation."

"Did you run down background on the relationship between Six Days and International Soft Where?"

Reiner coughs. Doesn't feel comfortable out of the information loop for long. "I did. Six Days was known for brilliant VR software R & D and interactivity. It was a small, innovative public company. Owed its existence to seed money from a secret source."

"Sato's corp, by any chance?"

Reiner lips a popping cork noise. "You're full of surprises True, in all worlds. How'd you guess?"

"There had to be some connection between ADC and Sato. How did Sato lose Six Days to ADC?"

"Hostile takeover. ADC planned it carefully. Slowly had International Soft Where? buy up Six Days stock, then convinced a Sato shareholder to turn over his shares. Coincidently, the guy who sold his shares to ADC is dead now."

"Anyone we know?"

"No one important. Just a pawn, I think. As a result, ADC was able to scarf down everything, including the pissoirs and mops. The big deal was the interactive R & D. And that they were backed by American courts."

"Because of all that corporate maneuvering, ADC knows me better than *I* know me. A lot of their R & D was tested on me. They used that to get me to steal from Sato for them."

Odessa moves the chip into a different program. Jabs at it with analytic software.

Reiner ahems. "Since we know Sato's economic behavior before the quake was eerily clairvoyant, what do you think? I mean, he sold everything that would sustain losses in a major quake yet kept construction company investments, power companies, food, and raw material import companies. He knew about this quake before it hit."

"You think it's a quake-prediction software?"

"Has to be."

"No."

"You think it's a quake-make weapon?"

"No."

"Then what?"

"First I go back, take a look-see."

Odessa's attention away from his work. "Into Sato's database? Yeah."

Reiner scowls. "You're not going to risk your life in there again, are you? Haven't you done enough mind candy? Why don't you stick to real reporting?"

True eye-rolls. "Real reporting means getting the job done. I have to get inside. Find out what Sato knows."

Since Sato's defense systems are hampered by frequent powerouts, it's easy for True, initially, to slice through. Odessa rides shotgun from the outside while Reiner watches via monitor. True somersaults beyond Sato's investment portfolio, skips by blocks of companies propped up by Sato money, leaps over to Sato's personal log. Locked—access denied.

"It's tricky." Odessa's voice from somewhere inside True. "I know that encryption device. Two wrong codeword guesses, you're braised journo. Give me a sec. I can crash it."

"How?" True mouths. Doesn't want to tip off his presence.

"It's based on my invention. Scratched my initials in the design so I could always gain entry." Odessa lasers a string of code, fiery light. Nothing happens. "Shit. One guess left."

True climbs away, up to Investment Portfolios, and peers down.

"Don't be a pussy, True. I'll get you in." Odessa fires again and the door swings open.

True sails down and is about to squirt through when he catches a whiff of trouble. Datamines: saucers in designer raspberry, pink and yellow, a screen of them floating inside the door.

Odessa's inner words again. "You've only got a couple minutes. Get shut inside, you don't get out. These mines are armed and ready to rock, except for one of them. Don't know which, yet."

True floats over, studies the mines from assorted angles while Odessa searches for the key to breaking through. Twelve of them, three in a row, four columns, fill up the door. Except for color (all are in the pastel family), and the rate they rotate, the mines seem identical.

"Got it, True. The winner is... the light blue mine near the bottom-right corner."

True looks. There is no light blue mine near the bottom right-hand corner. A light cherry one, a lime one, a powder concord grape one, no blue. True points, shrugs.

"You don't see a blue one, do you. And I don't even know if the data are based on color or location. All I got from the codebreak is it's the light blue one, lower right corner. Someone's jiggled it. A quake precaution. Smart. Very smart. Get back here and I'll work on it. Fuck me fuck me fuck me. But don't worry. I'll get it."

True stays, looks at the lower right hand corner. A red one, almost too bright to be pastel. True thinks. When blood hits oxygen it turns red, but inside the body it's blue. True still hovers.

Odessa taps on True's inner ear mike. "Don't even think about it. Don't worry. I'll get it. But you're going to have to chill your enthusiasm a while."

True remains in space. Reaches for the mine.

"True. You're being rash. OK. I'm telling you. Get back here. Don't do this. True? True?"

At the last instant, True grabs the mine diagonally left, pulls it out.

Nothing happens.

He waits some more, but nothing happens, so he shoots through.

"How'd you know?" Odessa's yelling, excited. "Never seen anybody do something like that. Your rep is deserved. Reiner? You ever seen anybody—of course you haven't, because you're not into this kind of thing, but let me tell you, your colleague is microdude of the net."

True still in the matter at hand. He heads to Recent Entries, senses Sato's presence everywhere, his idiosyncrasies, taste, business acumen. True skims the data and skims *over* the data—the entries are arranged by date, size, and content—checks the content abstracts and selects R & D Testing, Misc. Lists of various tests conducted the world over, divided by Technology Type, Testing Site, Test Results, Investment Yield Projections. He selects the Site category, scrolls a list of countries where Sato R & D Testing was or is taking place. Luzonia. True dives into this file, follows roads paved with bricks of info, stops when he gets to one labeled Virtual Reality Weaponry, Luzonian Interior, dated a recent day—three weeks prior.

He picks up the brick and looks in. Watches insurgents fire from tight bunkers, gunpowder and laser juice in the air. In a wink their world turns topsy-turvy. They fire wildly. Splotches of them disappear. Abstracts confirm the success of the test. Confused, True access a log of Fortune 1000 meetings. Meetings, private sidebars replete with threats and accusations. Sides broken into two camps: Sato's and ADC's. Private memorandum, from Sato, confirming Luzonian R & D test results. Computer models predict success against Sato corporate foes. The reality of this virtual reality discovery outstrips his wildest electrical musings. What he's discovered is deadly.

Light pulses, bleached whiter than heaven's white, shoot by his ear. Odessa shoots intercept missiles. "Out of there, True!" A plasma blob paddles by. Odessa fires manually, tries to knock the tracers off line. Only has to miss one, though, for True to be ex-True. He feels Odessa's furious salvos, the mice clicking reminding him of monsoon rain pummeling plastic roofs.

True thinks *escape hatch*, like in cartoons, settles for the door he came through, but the mine screen is back online, undoubtedly with a different code. An errant laser grits the door behind the screen three-quarters shut. True slips up toward the screen, but slicing lights pin him down from behind.

Odessa from somewhere inside True's brain. "Reiner. Go in. Take this mine deactivation software in to him. I can't reach him through the interference. When you get near, shoot it to him."

True can't hear Reiner. A barrage of lasers caroms off the wall, over his head. He's trapped, aware that Sato's

CyberSecurity are on the way.

"Just get in there!" Odessa's screaming.

Then Reiner's voice in the back. "I've never been in there before. I don't know how."

"I'll back you up. You have to cover him or he's dead! Reiner! Fuck! She ran out. True? Can you hear me?"

True doesn't think Odessa will hear him anyway. He hugs silence.

Odessa, panicking: "Who the hell are you? What are you doing? Put that down. No-o-o-!"

True assumes things on the outside aren't going well either. Hopes Odessa and Reiner are all right. The door inches shut as lasers fire unabated. True thinks about risking a hit, but knows he wouldn't survive. Is it better to die in Sato's log? He jumps into a pond of investment algorithms, hopes he can lose himself in the digital data, although he knows all Sato has to do to flush him out is apply them. True elbows an equation out of the way so he can rest more comfortably, then peers up through the numbers to see the door opening, heaven's light streaming inside.

A familiar voice, a familiar aura, a radiance enters this void. True sees Eden, towing a shield of scavenged binary code. She feathers down, takes True's hands, wraps them around her waist. Using the screen as protection, she pushes through a phalanx of CyberSecurity leaking through the door and deactivated mine screen. They are too far away by the time anyone can fire. Into a safebox room. They funnel through a prism, up so fast True suffers mental bends. A crushing roar in his ears. Blackness.

True wakes up on the floor of WWTV's Tokyo Bureau, arms and legs wrapped tightly around Eden. Odessa's shaking him alive. "Are you copacetic or what? Should I leave you two alone to get better acquainted? Who is this hacker extraordinaire?"

Reiner's in the corner, her hand muffling her mouth. Failure doesn't set well with her. When she sees True looking her way, she says, "True. I'm so sorry."

She swings through the door.

"Who is she?" Odessa looks at Eden, shakes his head.

"My wife." True gently nudges her awake.

"You're one lucky man. Weren't for her you'd be smoked, served on a platter with bagels, cream cheese, and shit."

True, Eden, eyeball to eyeball, limbs snaked through limbs. "How did you know where to find me?"

She licks thick lips. "Finding you was easy. The hard part was rigging a software screen from binary junk in less than a minute."

"Why'd you find me?"

She sits up. "The only way I can make things right is to get that software back from ADC."

"Before that, we have something more pressing." True calls Reiner.

A shuffling sound outside the door. Reiner leans in.

"Get ready to record, Reiner. You have a story to air."

"No. You. It's yours. I'll do the grunt work."

"I've got to do a little research before we air, but then—"

"What?" Eden, Reiner, Odessa's voices overlapping.

"War."

PART FOUR

VIRTUALLY REALITY

CHAPTER 25

True watches Eden teleshop for computer parts through the net, virtual price comparison at chop shops ringing Asia— Singapore, Hong Kong, Chiang Mai, Bombay. She trades a vintage transducer and infolink carrier she tracked down in a Thai junk shop for Setup-and-Go hardware from a Nerulan rounder. Plows the profit into super-speed, brain's-edge data blasters, transmitters, surveillance software, debugging algorithms, virus detectors. She's running ten deals at once. He understands this is what she did for international aid, piecing together computer systems from ancient history, holding these crackpot inventions together with electrical spit and virtual glue. One 24-hour cycle and she has the core tech. Boxes, packages by courier, have been arriving all morning. On her way to constructing a hacker's wet dream—her words.

It's comfortable and comforting to be with Eden. Familiar with her tiniest nuances, how she craves aromatic coffee, can't face morning without it; how when conducting a deal over the net she splays her fingers, the crook of her thumb a triangular well; how she puffs at tickling stray hairs. In the shower he remembered how he missed her hothouse cheeks, crystal collarbone, her yearning breasts. Yet their love-making is unsatisfying, as if he was making love and she was making love but *they* weren't making love.

The sound of the telelink, and Slovo de Bris's face sparkles in wall-length 3-D. "I can't believe you called and left a message. I thought you were dead."

"Just lying low."

"Why did you contact me over conventional lines?"

"Eden's rigged up some surveillance protection."

De Bris has again ballooned due to unchecked gluttony. An IV drip for his arm. Home liposuction. "Now that I know you're alive and I should be happy, what the hell do you want?"

"You catch Reiner Jacobi's story?"

"Incredible."

"It was my scoop."

De Bris knows better than to question. "Just when everyone gives up on you, you uncover the biggest story in years."

"You helped."

"A tiny bit—if at all. But I'm confused. Why give up the glory? Your career isn't exactly cutting-edge."

"It's better no one knows I'm alive. There's more."

De Bris idly checks his IV drip. Taps the tube. Milky white glue goo inside. "Like?"

"Tell you later. But I need you to answer a question about Aslam's autopsy. You said he'd been exposed to various intestinal ailments. What were they?"

De Bris sucks up the pre-referenced data, comments as he reads, "Bilharzia, no surprise. They eradicate it in Africa only to discover it in Southeast Asia. Never heard of a case in Luzonia, though. That was thought to be too far south. Dysentery, giardia, and malaria, which isn't intestinal but I figure you should know."

"Check your WHO environmental factor charts. Exempting Nerula's shanties, where in this city could you contract any of these?"

"According to the literature, the malarial mosquito is Luzonia's national bird. You get dysentery at any restaurant where the waiter's keeling over. That's it, far as these charts go. They haven't been updated in years, since the U.S. withdrew funding. Anything else?"

"No."

"Answer me this: Jacobi reported that while ADC was testing VR programs to use as weapons, it was also developing an army of clones. But something happened to the first batch of clones, and this is what escalated tensions between ADC and Sato?"

"Right so far."

"What happened to the first clone batch?"

"I'm not sure. Sato probably launched a pre-emptive strike, somehow infected them with a virus. Find out what kills one, you can kill them all. This prompted ADC to plot stealing Sato's prize weapons technology: virtual reality systems. This was the weapon Aslam hinted at, but I was too slow to figure it out."

"Where do things stand now?"

"Latest word is that war's imminent. Sato's been plaguing ADC's clones and ADC's been ripping off Sato's VR weapons technology. It's a standoff."

"The first world corporate war." De Bris's eyes far away.

"The Global Fortune 1000 Board tried to mediate, but neither side is having it. Both ADC and Sato are lining up support. Could get bloody."

"What kind of support?"

"Well, for example, banks on ADC's side are funding the war effort. Why? Because they underwrote the R & D investment—a series of low-interest loans—for cloning an army. When the infection crippled the clones, the banks were threatened with default. It could cripple them, too, so they continue to funnel money into ADC."

"Owe a bank a thousand dollars, it owns you. Owe it a thousand million, you own it."

"Right. ADC retaliated with a series of hostile takeovers of key Sato assets, including Six Days, a software company. ADC pushed the U.S. Government into backing their claims—kind of a corporate-nationalistic manifest destiny. Round two: ADC by TKO."

"And the quake?"

"I don't have that answer. It's conceivable Sato knew of the potential of conflict with ADC years ago and acted accordingly, selling assets to plow into a war juggernaut."

"You're onto something bigger. Tell me."

"Not until I'm sure."

De Bris's wheezing picks up. "Fine. Don't tell me. Knowing you, it'd hazardous to my health anyway. But take some homespun: Don't let anyone else enter your mind."

War in full fury. True experiences the news coverage on the majors. Standard analyses, interviews, air surveillance pics from long-range zooms, nothing from ground view. True sees Eden dig through plastic peanut packaging, looking for a piece of hardware. Some packaging material soaks in solvent; a gelatinous accident, she explained. There only until she can locate a hazard-waste disposer.

Eden now at the console, the War Room, as she calls it: "Sato retaliated minutes ago by taking over ADC holdings in the Southern China Republic. Sato's private army went in with mercenaries from sixty countries." Eden's mouse-clicking is breakneck. "WWTV's Tokyo bureau is situated near a tempting Sato target, an R & D firm."

True hails Reiner, fills her in. "You're taking a huge risk."

"That may be, but we're not leaving. We can handle things. Besides, Odessa's onto something. He left hours ago and hasn't returned. He wouldn't tell me what it was, only that if he's right, none of us would ever look at things in quite the same way."

"What's that mean?"

"I don't know."

"Anything peculiar happening?"

"No-o-o-o. Yeah. There have been scattered reports of people disappearing."

"Kidnappers? Extortion hunters? People leaving town?"

"Who knows. Lots of rumors, though."

"Call me when Odessa gets back."

"What are you going to do in the mean time?"

"Talk to Rush."

Actually, not talk to Rush. True taps into the Nerula bureau's telebank, kneads his way into the database, plugs in Odessa's security breaching software, and is into the network so fast he has to double-check he's really in.

Hackers. Indispensable in this neo-world of digital fabrication. The software instructs him to narrow the choice of conversations, and True, who isn't sure what he's angling for, codes in dates from a month before Tokyo's quake, hyphen, the present. All WWTV network calls are recorded, to protect against libel. Key phrases encapsulate content. True scrolls through every conversation Rush had until the day of the quake, and beyond.

Most of them are sugar substitute: a hairdressing appointment; telemarketing firms; some of True and Rush; Rush and WWTV editors; and accountants; Rush and Reiner; rows of *misc.* calls. True pulls up the abstract of Rush/Reiner's conversation. A split screen, Rush one side, Reiner the other. The conversation is short, Reiner informing Rush of her hacker, Odessa Flashfire, and if anyone comes to Tokyo, she nominates True, but prefers no one. "My disaster. Find your own."

True scans the *misc.*, a bland assortment of personal calls. Didn't Rush do anything journo-related? At list's end are a dozen calls with no identifiable second party. Callers with sophisticated identification protection technology or whose voices were never ID'd, sources with stories for sale. Rush declines; budgetary constraints. Some rely on an auto-translator. They speak Luzonian or another tongue, Rush responds in English, and via technology, True eavesdrops. One call from outside Nerula but not originating stateside or from Japan. True keys in. No icon, just blank air, Rush on camera, talking back. The voice: Aslam. *The insurgency wants to make a major announcement. We've decided to pass word through you. I'll give you an exclusive.*

I'll send my number one man.

No. You. Alone. Or no exclusive. True can feel Aslam smirking through cable feed. *You'll be sorry if you pass on it. Big time careers have sprung from less.*

Rush stroking his chin, hedging. *How do I know you won't kidnap me?*

Why would we kidnap you? We are revolutionaries who need you to spread our message. You are a journalist who needs a message to spread. We need each another.

You have a very pragmatic world-view, Mr. Aziz.

Practically pay-for-view as the need arises.

Rush tells Aslam he'll have to mull. Later, more calls from Aslam, settling on interview content, rendezvous-time, coordinates; Rush finalizing, OK-ing footage from the insurgency's PR firm (for use in the promos), then a six-hour research link with WWTV's database from Luzonia's interior. After Rush's return to Nerula, another flurry of calls. True accesses the latest one, from twenty minutes ago—Rush on one side, blank, the other, originating from a nearby pre-millen phone booth. No ID, no voice print. A sophisticated ID block.

Rush scratching at uneasiness, talking back. *OK. OK. But no more talk over the link. Come by. Now. You'll get what you want. But this is the last time.* Rush hangs up, brings gray static to bear.

True calls to Eden. "By tapping my wrist-top, can just anyone key on my location?"

She's touch-screening, tap-tap. Holds up a finger, so wait. Tap-tap. "Not unless you want them to. You can transmit your location to anyone you want. You can also send out a false signal. That's always fun. Reroute it through any toaster oven in the country."

"I'm going out."

Eden unhitched from her post. "Where are you going?" From her, an unusual query.

"Checking into something."

"There's so much we need to do here."

"It's important."

"Not more than tracking the war effort."

"You're upset. Why?"

She pulls aside. "While I've been scavenging computer equipment from every second-hand crap hole I know, you've been on the telelink."

Curiosity prickling. What *is* she up to? "Journalism isn't exact. There are no special algorithms you can rely on to pull a story together. There are lulls and breaks, followed by spasms of activity. That's the reality. That's why I'm going."

"I'll go with you."

"What's come over you?"

"Nothing."

"Then"—True kisses her forehead—"I'll see you in a while."

He's at the door and Eden's sulking at her computer, trackpad-tapping with furious hands.

True's relieved to be away. It's not supposed to be this way, wasn't like this before.

The streets are grim, sun-dappled plague-ees in degrees of decay. A body sweeper, a black truck that scoops up corpses, converts them to fuel, is spewing charcoal wind and bleached flakes. A perpetual motion machine. Chaotic queues at the phone bank, those in front hold off the rest. True thinks about asking to see a phone log—perhaps there's a signature—but mayhem is not conducive to careful record-keeping. In the same building next door is a new VR shop. 3D-posters jostle for position on the front plexiglass, ads for hardware, primo-violence software, sexicles, one special offer: *Dial internationally from next door, take 10 percent off any software.*

A familiar sari stepping out. "Baba, I am surprised to see you. You are legendary in the shanties. Like a cat with nine lives. How many are left?" Her cancer spots have faded. Business must have picked up.

"Lost count, Rajput. Were you able to de-glitch that imaginary lover software?"

"I was indeed."

"What did you buy?"

She shows four packages: "I borrow a little from one module, combine it with another, shape it with a third. With the proper recipe, I'll have sizzling autumn sales."

"Aren't they copyrighted?"

"Do you see any CopyCops?" She tucks the package under her arm. Speaks in pianissimo. "Would you like a taste of pure FREEze?"

"How can a synth drug be pure? And no."

"Perhaps a real woman this time? Or if you are intrigued with organ donation, I can arrange a buyer." She writes an imaginary $-figure in her palm.

"That's below market value."

Leavening shoulders. "This is why we haggle. I propose a price, you tell me it is too high. Haggling helps us to feel comfortable with each other and our transaction."

"Just the same, I'll pass."

"Then until we biz again." Her sari billows as she leaves. True zooms in on the Rajput while at the same time messaging Piña, who's reduced to a cube in the upper right-hand corner.

"You got your ass back here." Piña smiles broadly. She's in

her arcade. VR static, missile whistles, and laser fizz, sadistic sex as ambience.

"Lying low, but I'm into some odd-frequency ozone. Can Piña meet in, say, a half hour?"

"Where are you?"

"Near home but on my way to the shanties."

"Tailing someone?"

"Yup."

"Piña'll send word. A guide OK?"

An in-situ drug deal in progress. True has to accept that her business comes first. "Fine. The guide rendezvous is over the tunnel. Track me over this channel."

"Ooooh. New equipment? That what you been spending Piña's money on?"

"No."

"Most guides can't read, so Piña'll say, *Take care of the guarang.*"

The Rajput cruising up the tunnel paths.

"The tailgate party has begun." True follows the Rajput to the shanties over landfill picked clean. Milling at the entrance, a small figure in a long, black coat. Face obscured by a hood. Just two green-olive eyes. "Piña's guide?"

Nodding cloth. True projects the map so the guide will know where to go. Through the hologram True sees a house on fire, its twig-like foundation crumbling to earth. "We're here." True points to a dot in the holoscreen. "We want to go there." In the spleen of the shanties. "Can you speak?"

The hood shakes, no. True's voice synth repeats the question in Luzonian. No again. At least True won't have to listen to idle chatter. They follow the Rajput past huts that are luxury-less except for TVs. The Rajput enters a home fused from refrigerator crates, a fire curling from a hole in the floor. True accesses the volume visualization software and, through a series of clever algorithms he doesn't understand, strips away crate layers until he sees inside. He filters the conversation through the translation program.

The Rajput is hugging a boxy Luzonian woman, who clears a place for the Rajput to sit. The sole chair.

"God has given me a great gift. You were able to get the money," the woman says. "Now with both payments, I can get AIDS medicine."

"I have a black market connection for that, as well. I can fulfill all your commercial needs."

"Is this drug expensive?"

The Rajput emphasizes the cost by sucking air. "I can get the medicine for the same money I received on your behalf today, if we add it to the initial payment."

"I am grateful." She falls to her knees. The Rajput allows her to kiss her hand.

There's something about the woman that uncorks memories for True. Has he seen her face on TV comms for ceiling fans? Escort services? Adobo sauce?

The guide holds a laser pistol to True's head. "Off." True, caught off-zone, spins down the VolVis program. Gun still itching, the guide unclasps True's wrist computer, stuffs it into a pocket. "OK OK OK. You are not stupid as I had thoughtfully considered."

That syntax. Who else?

Bong Bong pushes back his hood, bites a smile. "Good afternoon, ladies and germs. Good costume? But not as good as these softwares you see through walls with like Superman."

"You're welcome."

"I have voices in the shanties, people loyal at me. They seen you escape, pull the switch with another to die in your place."

"I didn't know he was going to die."

"Then you are even less of a man. Come. We will converse with this Rajput."

CHAPTER 26

Bong Bong jabs True's spine with the barrel of his laser. They trudge through the slums, up to the shanty's sole landmark: a clock tower, constructed a few governments ago to illustrate the point that a cure for poverty would take time.

To the end of time, True thinks. "I've never seen the tower up close."

Bong Bong stops pushing. "It's nice. Good for tourist. All over, clocks. Lots of clocks."

More than lots. Coated in time pieces solicited from 240 nations. And, as far as True can tell, none of them match. Thousands of seconds, none in synch.

"Well, India had its Taj Mahal, Thailand has its Grand Palace, Tokyo the Emperor's residence, why shouldn't Luzonia have a clock tower that doesn't tell the right time?"

"The right time is there." Bong Bong points to a clock on a ridge.

"Guess you just have to know where to look."

Bong Bong knees True through a door at the landmark's base. It takes a few breaths before True's eyes adjust to the dim. Patchouli in the air. The Rajput brandishing a knife. When she recognizes who it is, she tucks it away. There's creaking in the ceiling beams. Bong Bong spits Luzonian at the Rajput, who marionettes her head, and hands her a pistol, which she pegs on True. Bong Bong travels up the rotting steps.

"He wants you to keep me covered?"

"I'm sorry, Baba, but when you are a lone seed you must float with the wind."

"And Bong Bong's the one blowing, right?"

"A veritable hurricane."

"He thinks someone's up there?"

"It may perhaps be rats or other such vermin."

"I should have known you weren't telling me the truth about the beggar girl. It wasn't until I saw her mother it made sense. She traded her daughter for money."

"Not for money. For medicine."

"She sacrificed her daughter to save herself."

"To save her husband."

"A brave man, to be sure."

"If he perishes, the family perishes. He has work."

More Bong Bong stomps; de-lurking the clock tower.

"Trading in an eleven-year-old is defensible?"

"I have seen too much death in my life to be upset by something as this. War cost me a whole people."

"Was she aware of her sacrifice?"

"I do not know. I only ask for what I need to know. Why do you have the privilege of criticizing? You are guarang. A little rich, I think. Your country has never been invaded, you have never feared you will not have enough to eat. Or a roof to protect you. How can you possibly understand what it takes to survive these days of hell?"

"You're guarang here, too."

"There are different flavors of guarang. Guarang on package tours, who never venture from comfort. They know nothing of the real world. Other guarang stay at home, live their lives in isolation, as if other cultures do not exist. They soak up the world's limited resources but add little. Then there are the do-goods. The worst guarang. Before the Paks obliterated my people, we one year received surplus wheat from America. *Ah, American wheat,* everyone said. *Now we will have wheat forever.* More wheat than we could imagine. There wasn't enough room to store it, so much of it went bad. And since this wheat was free, our farmers could not compete and went out of business. The next year we starved. But no help this time from your government. They told us we should be more self-reliant."

"You were pleased my friend was assassinated."

"I was ecstatic a follower of that gutter religion died. This time I was able to make a mixture of business and pleasure."

Bong Bong alighting. Breathing hard, he snatches the pistol from the Rajput. "Nothing nothing nothing. Some bugs. I squashed them." He wraps True's computer around his wrist. "I want to see that movie. Get it?" Bong Bong elbows True in the shoulder. The Rajput stands cautiously by the door.

True plays back the meeting between the Rajput and the Luzonian mother. The Rajput's eyes narrow, terrified. Well, so's he.

Bong Bong aims. "Stand against the wall, both guarang."

True joins the Rajput, shirt to sari.

"Baba. You are upset because of the Muslim? Billions of

Muslims have died before you or I were born. I was merely facilitating a transaction."

"Translation: Someone wanted Aslam dead but knew conventional techniques wouldn't work. He had corporate sponsors, which made him even tougher. That's where you and Bong Bong came in. You needed to recruit someone to get close to Aslam so the DNA-coded missile could lock and unload. Simple."

The Rajput eyes Bong Bong, who headshakes a warning.

True plays his hand. "You might as well tell me. Bong Bong isn't going to let either of us live. He knows you've been skimming. What else explains the payment Rush handed you, a payment Bong Bong didn't know of? You can't extort in Nerula without going through Bong Bong. Right, Bong Bong?"

Bong Bong cackles in a distinct hyena dialect. "This is very interesting to me, but I do not have time. On behalf of the law enforcemental agency at Nerula, you are sentenced to death. Blah blah blah. OK. That's it. That's all I remember from these constitutions."

True is bumming silence. Bong Bong whirls, fires on the Rajput who spasms and avalanches to the floor. Her head is a meld of blood and brains. Dead on her side, arms pinned underneath, folded in prayer.

"More organs." Bong Bong nudges her with his foot. "That's why I aim high. Also this." He pockets her debit card. "People steal from me, they die. That's it. Now. The show we all been waiting for. These softwares."

"It may take a while. I'm just learning myself."

"Then I kill you, hire the hacker. Maybe I kill you anyway."

Re-escape: True fires brain blanks. "I can show you stuff that'll blow your mind, Bong Bong." True grabs the wrist-top.

Bong Bong brushes True's hand away. "I hold this computer."

"First thing, you turn it on. You do that by—"

"Don't speak down at me." Bong Bong talks through tight teeth. He jabs at a few buttons. Nothing happens.

"The *on* switch is here."

Bong Bong grunts. The 3-D screen fills up their vision, and True pulls up the program menu. He's not familiar with everything Eden added. "What do you want to see first?"

"To see through walls is handy."

"But it's complicated. Better to start with something simple, work our way up."

Bong Bong's glands emit suspicion.

"You have the gun, Bong Bong, and the wrist-top." True selects a psychotropia file—why Eden included it, he doesn't know—and the happy psychotropic pattern beams overhead.

Bong Bong grinning scar to scar, his eyes scotch-taped to the pattern. He's far away, recounting life's happier moments. "Guarang. I was born in these slums. We were poor. Have you ever seen such poverty?"

Yes, many times, True thinks. "No."

"It kills you. Nothing to eat, nothing to play with except for garbage."

If this is Bong Bong's happy side, what would greater introspection yield? True wonders. *Greek tragedy?*

"I was seven. We had a gang. The Magnifico Seven, like an old movie. I found some glue and we went to the roof to sniff. It was hot. Wet like it always is."

"Jungle sweat."

Bong Bong looks with wild eyes at True, then his gaze settles back on the pattern. "Jungle sweat. Good." Clasps True on the shoulder. Implying: *You're not so bad, guarang.*

"What happened on the roof?"

"The roof," Bong Bong mouths. "We make the suicide pact. Why live like pigs when we could die into our way? We got high, high as stars, then held hands and ran to the edge. One-two-three we jumped. Aaaaah—"

"How high?"

"We were fucking high."

"The roof. How high off the ground?"

"Five, six stories."

"I haven't seen a building in the shanties that high."

"Before the wars, guarang."

"What did it feel like when you jumped?"

Bong Bong's eyes spring tears. "Like heaven. We were flying, and the ground came toward my head and I seen the building shoot into the sky. But I was caught by the tree. That's when they had trees here. Even flowers. People grew food sometimes. Pickled vegetables. The branches scratched my face. Maybe I broke some ribs. But it saved my life. I rolled down the hill. When I stopped I seen the Magnifico Seven, OK, six, all dead. Then I knew nothing could kill me. Then the wars. I was thirteen. I killed many enemies of Luzonia. Except a few times, I was OK. That's why I am the Police Chief. All my enemies are dead."

Not all, True thinks. "What about your parents?"

Bong Bong cocks his head. "My father? I don't know. Dead when I was some baby. My mother was aliving until last year. She was like durian, outside hard and spiky, but sweet and delicious inside."

To True, durian is the most vile fruit he's ever smelled or tasted. "You miss her?"

True leans on the door. When Bong Bong closes his eyes, sighs deeply, True tries to bolt. But True bangs his knee on the door, which smashes into Bong Bong's wrist, cutting off the psychotropia. True sprawls onto the deck, rolls down abridged steps, Laurel-and-Hardying into the dirt. He looks up to see Bong Bong in bent-over spasms of delight, his weapon juiced and ready.

"That is your best? How can you guarang control the earth's money? That amazes. Surely you are no man, American. Your cock may be big, but it's soft." Bong Bong squeezes an eye.

Fire rains down from the clock tower roof. True rolls away from Bong Bong's errant shot, which scorches a chasm into the ground. Before Bong Bong can re-shoot, he's engulfed by heaven's flames. A few drops spit on True. Bong Bong wails up to the moment his life is done. The flickering dies when there's no more flesh fuel.

Piña skateboards in from behind the curious. Checks out the smoldering remains. "Who's that?"

"Bong Bong."

Piña's eyes bug. "No shit? Bong Bong? You did that?"

"I thought Piña did."

"Must've been someone pissed off at the cops. Man oh man. Look at that. Napalm. Some serious shit. Everyone'll be talking about it. Piña's going to hire the bitch who offed Bong Bong. Holy fuck!" She steals another look at the corpse, then True. "Every time Piña sees you, you look like shit."

"Piña brings out the best in me."

"Piña's got something for you. At home. Important. OK?"

True needs a medkit for his splotch burns, but Piña's never let him down. On the back of her skateboard his burns must endure wind sting.

Napalm. The scent of terror.

But he's alive. A miracle.

Piña grapples to a truck and they speed through the tunnel, past True's apartment, to Snakeskin Alley. The mall.

CHAPTER 27

Piña's home, weepy on the outside, garish, odd on the inside, a basement floor-pad hugged by armored gates. True's often passed it en route to her arcade, but didn't notice. Piña props her skateboard against the door and swings in on her hands. A gym takes up most of the room's core, barbells of iron and sand trapped in plastic doughnuts, a bench, pull-up bar, ab-flexor. Trash scavenge, stuff not manufactured in years, spills over platforms, tables, wall- and ceiling-mounted cases. Posters of female bodybuilts, muscle-accordion bodies tapering up to zit-sized heads. Ropes, deep-sea fishing nets, porthole pegs cover walls, hang from the ceiling. Legs are a distinct disadvantage traversing Piña's air trails.

True limps to Piña's bed, waits while she shimmies up coiled ropes, swings to a ceiling-mounted cabinet, rummages through, comes away disappointed, scales the shipping net and falls to a trapeze. She sails to another cabinet—True hopes the one with the medkit. A little ultrasound for his knee, some skin-repair for his burns, he'll be fine. But no. Piña slides down a rope with an armful of rusty-lidded jars, drops to the bed, one bounce, two, three, slips the jars onto the night table. The concoctions smell earthy, mud, burnt leaf, and minty.

"No medkit? Ultrasound? Skin graft bandaids?"

She pinches his leg. "Off."

"Huh?"

"Take your pants off so Piña can see the burns."

True stands, fights the urge to wince. "I'll fix myself up when I get home."

Piña pokes him in the stomach. True falls back. "This shit's better. Natural. All that ultra shit graft-crap eats out your insides. This shit'll fix you up."

She pulls his pants over his knees, then feet while True grinds his teeth. Piña massages in goop from one jar, gobs on a second coat from the other jar. An inexact science, True thinks. She wraps a coin in toilet paper—like a chocolate kiss—lights the end, places it on one of the burns, then smothers the flame with a drinking glass. She repeats this for each burn on his back. The suction pressure increases as the oxygen is consumed, forming a vacuum, resulting in blood being pulled toward the wounds. True tries to sit up. Can't.

"Shut up and stay still." Piña goes back across the room, concocting some witch's brew. Tail of newt? Eye of okaapi? Her face is almost angelic as she blows a stray hair from her eye. Her torso, as pumped up as her poster idols, is latticed with scars, blotted with tattoos. She remembers something, takes the monkey bars to a rope, then up to a metal wire, which she slides down using a leather belt. She stops when her hand smacks a ceiling cabinet. Takes out a vial and is back in her chair in two flashes.

Piña waits fifteen minutes, then's back to yank the glasses off, one by one. She tips them back, holds them up to True. "See this puss? That's bad shit from your body."

True checks his burns. A little tender, but OK. "Much better."

"Thirsty, right?"

"Yeah."

Piña hands True a mug containing radioactive hues. "Some beet, garlic, carrot, parsley, onion, and tomato. Good for your blood and health."

True, craving vitamins, quick-gulps it, the garlic and onion particularly potent. Tingling. "That's a powerful remedy." True once read you could overdose on beet juice. Maybe he was too hasty in rejecting homeopathic remedies. But then he's hit by the shakes. "What did you put in here?" He drops the mug. His limbs are dead weight. He thinks about running but can't even stand.

Piña picks up the mug. "A new synthnarc Piña's been marketing. Don't need virtual reality on this shit. You'll feel good in a few minutes. Better than you can fucking imagine."

"What is it?" His jaw is clenched.

"Like Piña told you. A synthnarc. A little lude for a nice, hard stiffy, some methyl-A for that loving feeling, some synthetic coke, and a little THC for enhancement. It's selling great. Piña calls it 'Lovers Ouroboros.'"

She pulls back a strap, points to her shoulder blade, to a tattoo, the snake of everlasting destruction and regeneration, a circle of paradox. "It's a new marketing strategy. On the street or in Piña's arcade, you want some Lovers Ouroboros, you point to this."

The room, the nets, the ropes, cabinets, posters, and his own thoughts rollercoaster. Did Piña kill Aslam, set up the whole thing, take out on an assassin's contract? Is True next? Or is this some organ donor's nightmare? Blood boils under skin. True tries to say something but the thought butterfly-flutters only an instant, then's gone.

Then deep haze. Liquid ecstasy.

True wakes up, hands and feet bound to bed. Piña's suctioning off glasses. She notices he's awake, but won't look. The last glass slurps off. Piña unties him, feet, then hands. He massages his wrists and ankles. Piña sits at bed's edge, pretends he doesn't exist.

"Why?" True's mouth is martini-parched.

Piña steals a glance. Says something to herself, mouths "fuck," takes his hand, kisses it, the hint of a bite. "You're different. You're like real-life what they got on TV. Piña don't know nobody like it. You're guarang but more delicate than other guarang, like a bird or something. True's good for Piña. Not a psycho or boy whore. Piña's in love."

True remembers the way his molecules marched after the first drug hit. Piña took control. Squeezed his arms until they popped purple. Choked and close-fisted him, pretzeled his arms behind his back while he: *No! Stop!* but she kept on, sucking pleasure from his agony. She fucked him savagely, her steely arms clamped around his waist, tighter closer to climax, squeezing, then damp groans as soundtrack to her crushing grip, asphyxiation. He tries to deny it, but he too experienced churning, pining sextasy.

He's helium-headed, uneasy on his feet. "I have to go."

"Piña'll help."

"You've done enough."

Quiet. Then rusty rasps. Piña's tears.

He should have seen this coming but then thinks, just like the victim to blame himself. Her chiseled physique heaving tears makes him think of time as a sculpture, how it's shaped by the individual. He has things to do before it's too late. To shape his own destiny.

True opens the door to distant, muddy explosions.

True calls Eden from a public telelink bank. She offers no hint of their earlier scuffle.

"Prehistoric equipment. Not even visual, just sound," she says.

" I hear war sfx. Any battles nearby?"

"Where are you now?"

"Town's center."

Her fingers a blur on the touchscreen. "Go north three clicks. There's a Sato installation under fire from ADC clones. Maxi Khoompootla's been transmitting footage of the build-up."

"Who are Sato's proxies?"

"Mercenaries."

"I'm on my way." He waits for her to tell him not to go. Nothing.

True wishes he had his wrist-top. Imagines it's melded to whatever's left of Bong Bong.

CHAPTER 28

From the side of the road, True watches the American Defense Corps clone army division march in sharp rows. Human technology patented, raised in vats, trained for a purpose, strictly regulated by Global Fortune 1000 by-laws. True wonders if he gets close enough if he'll see warning labels printed on their feet. Directions for battery replacement? Voltage and safety instructions? Clone faces are drained of fear, that part of the brain distilled into licit—and illicit—drugs. Headsets relay instructions: where to go, what to do, when to fire, attack, their whole operation supervised by one grand military strategist; who, so far as True knows, could be a either a supercomputer or some drugged-up video game stud.

True spots Maxi Khoompootla across the boulevard, scanning the troops. Maxi has lost stones since last True saw him. Or did he imagine Maxi? No, True was in real-time at the refugee center. True dodges thrusting clone boots and slides through. Sidles up to Maxi, notices a festering wound on his arm.

"You should have that laser burn looked at."

Maxi's head is too big for his twiggy body, eyes peering from beneath an oil-skin hat. Not the same robust Maxi of weeks ago. He laughs. "What? This little bewdie?" Points to the wound. "Looks like chunder, don't it?"

"Chunder is … ?"

"Vomit. Spew, mate."

"Looks like a laser wound. We should find a medkit."

"Nah. A whore's lurk. Cut me when I wouldn't pay up. No worries, mate. 'Sides, got to fossick for war footage. You know how it is."

"You've dropped a lot of weight."

"AIDS. Put off using the vaccine, but she'll be right soon. Thought you were dead. Bit it in the Urban Survival Tourney."

"A premature report. Aren't you worried about being so close to the action?"

Clones continue to flow, thicker now. In the distance, fortified bunkers leading to an industrial park. Luzonians and tourists have lined up along the boulevard. A fin-de-siècle mentality—Mardi Gras even.

Maxi takes off his hat, wipes the sweat from his forehead with his elbow, puts it back on. "Clones are programmed to hit only assigned DNA targets. And weapon tonnage is strictly limited by the Global Fortune 1000. No nukes, no big blows, no civvies are to be hit. Those are the rules."

"Those are mercenaries by that factory down there?"

"Yeah."

"Their DNA's been scanned by satellite?"

"Righto."

"Sato's mercs?"

"That's it. Bunch of bloody no-hopers. Couldn't find the loo in a pub."

"What are the clones attacking?"

"A sneaker factory."

"A sneaker factory? If the mercs want to run, they'll have the right footwear."

Maxi laughs, sounds like a squeaky screen door opening, closing. "A lot of factories down there, but Sato's a majority investor in that bugger there. The rest are to be left alone or ADC'll have to pay restitution."

"Could get expensive."

Maxi doesn't hear him. "Can you believe this bulldust? Corp warfare? It's finally happened. Why aren't you recording, mate?"

"It's your scoop. Working on something else. Mind if I watch your screen?"

"Don't come the raw prawn with me. What's your biz?"

Where to start? "Had a run in with Bong Bong in the shanties. He got my wrist-top. I got out alive."

Maxi scratches his head through his hat. "Bong Bong's been bonked? You pulling my dick?"

"He's dead."

"That bloody ocker feel a lot of pain when he got offed?"

"Homemade napalm."

"Ouch!" Maxi reaches into his pocket. Takes out a wrist-top transmitter. Ancient: 2-3 years old, but it'll work. Eden can clean up transmission if need be. "I owe you, mate. Every journo who's ever been stuck in this never-never land does. Take a spare."

"Thanks." True sets up a link with Eden. Posts the images.

"I'm getting the pix. What do you want me to do?" Eden asks.

"Send them direct to WWTV head office in New York.

Tell them it's me transmitting." Technically, True is required to have all footage edited and approved by the anchor. But WWTV isn't going to turn down primo war footage.

The clones are collecting at the bottom, on an equal plain with the mercenary army. They are like a well-conceived business plan: neat, crisp, clean, in stark contrast to the rag-tag mercenary force. True's eyes blur over the thousands of cloned troops on the move, identical goggles and uniforms, the same height, weight, build, all bred for battle.

The mercenaries fire first, low-wattage lasers, the color of concentrated urine. True and Maxi film it, both automatically enhancing the color. One hundred percent attention focused on their wrist-top 3-D screens. True sees all the action via his wrist-top recording, feels like he's in an action movie himself, with his gangly sidekick Maxi. He can almost see the script unfold.

MAXI
(*ducking as airborne debris rains down around him*)
Whoo! Would rather cauterize me own wound.

TRUE
(*breaking his 3-D screen into 16 separate action
scenes, zooming in at will, fingers dancing
over the touchscreen*)
Here. Cover your wound with this.

PULL BACK TO REVEAL

TRUE, who's stopped typing long enough to rip a piece of his shirt off, handing the strip to MAXI, who uses it for a makeshift sling. Both back to filming, expressions grim.

CUT TO

THE BATTLEFIELD: from where they are, quite a distance, down the hill. They feel safe here. Other thrill-seekers mill about. A pickpocket works the crowd, mostly robbing tourists, legs ghostly white, their skin splotched by early-stage melanoma.

ZOOM IN ON

THE FACTORY, which is pummeled by CLONE artillery, bullets and searing laser-fire. A wall disintegrates, topples on some dug-in mercenaries. The noise is deafening, even from TRUE and MAXI's vantage point. Bedlam.

CUT TO

TRUE taking in the action on his wrist-top.

ZOOM IN ON

TRUE's screen, still divided into 16 sections with 16 different camera angles, 16 miniature battles playing out at the same time.

CUT TO

WITHIN THE SCREEN, a CLONE firing his laser at a BOY, maybe of Pakistani descent, maybe Indian, and the BOY is cleanly severed. Legs lie a meter or two away. The boy's arms are wrapped around his torso, his mouth is contorted in agony.

TRUE cannot mike his screams over the hubbub, but knows he can overdub them later. The factory is popcorned with artillery, splashed by lasers. It crumbles.

MAXI

Look at them shoes in the rubble. As soon as this is over, these Luzonian looters going to have themselves a party.

CUT TO

MERCENARIES on the run, retreating, and in some cases, circling back around the CLONES, racing around the hill and up the sides toward True and Maxi. The battle is now over the land under the factory and the CLONES have the upper hand. The sounds of battle, juked up on TRUE and MAXI's receivers, get louder as MERCENARIES swarm toward them, the battlefield shifting as CLONES take up positions on Sato factory land. A nearby factory—another company, another country— lies untouched. The CLONES secure the land, working smoothly, while other CLONES give chase to the MERCE-NARIES.

CUT TO

A laser streaking over TRUE and MAXI's heads.

MAXI
(checking his hat for damage)
That was too close.

                    TRUE
We have to get out of here. The mercs can
shoot whoever they want, journos included.

                    MAXI
Too right.

                    TRUE
They under the standard merc contract?

                    MAXI
That's right. They lose, they get nothing.

                    TRUE
Not much incentive for a neat little war, is there?

                    MAXI
GDAYGDAYGDAY.

                    TRUE
What?

                    MAXI
                (shouting red)
I said not from their perspective.

CUT TO

MERCENARIES flooding their only rear guard route of escape.
TRUE and MAXI are hemmed in on all sides. CLONES are fortified in front of them, protecting newly conquered territory.

TRUE

We've got to get out of here.

MAXI

How?

CUT TO

An explosion rocking the hill, and TRUE and MAXI stumble trying to retain their balance. A tourist is hit by whistling shrapnel, falls to the ground screaming. There's panic, as the crowd of onlookers races in five different directions at once. A CONVENIENCE STORE is hit and shortly after beer and soda fizz out on the street. Other liquids as well. A few desperate onlookers fling themselves on the rising tide of soft drinks, lapping at it with their tongues.

CUT TO

TRUE, enhancing the scope of his screen to 360 degrees. Behind, he can see that the MERCENARIES have stopped running and are massing behind them. The CLONES in front. Realizes HE and MAXI are seconds away from being caught in the crossfire.

TRUE

Sato's mercs are regrouping to take this hill.

CUT TO

TRUE, WITH A DESPERATE IDEA. CLOSE UP.

PAN BACK TO

TRUE, pointing at the CLONES.

> MAXI
> (*shaking his head in disbelief*)
> You out of your fucking Yankee head? Run straight into an army pointing lasers? That's hara-kiri, mate. Those clones have no soul. They'll kill you in a quick sec.

PULL BACK TO REVEAL

MAXI, looking to run toward the mercenaries. TRUE grabs MAXI's injured arm.

> MAXI
> Fuck! That hurt.

> TRUE
> You're not thinking clearly. Listen. The clones only shoot pre-scanned enemies. It's the mercs we have to look out for.

> MAXI
> Don't wait around on my account.

CUT TO

TRUE and MAXI running full throttle down the hill, into CLONE fortifications. TRUE feels he may not be the fastest man who ever lived, but then again, maybe at this moment he is. As they get closer, bullets and lasers piss across the sky, over them, not on them, from behind. The hill provides temporary shelter, a shield from the mercenary volley. CLONE lasers and guns are held, ammo not wasted. True and Maxi skid to awkward stops when a CLONE laser is fired. The smell of an electrical fire. TRUE and MAXI see a MERCENARY melted into a small pond. TRUE holds up both hands in surrender. MAXI holds his hat to his head.

TRUE
(*shouting hoarse*)

We're journalists.

MAXI

That's right, you bloody laboratory experiments. Show them your press pass, Ailey.

TRUE
(*hissing*)

Me? I'm not reaching into my pocket with a billion jigs of laser fire power trained on us. Show them yours.

MAXI

Give me back my wrist-top.

TRUE

Fucking usurious Ozzie bastard.

CUT TO

The CLONES, who don't even twitch at the sight of TRUE and MAXI. Breathing hard and heavy, sweat flowing down their heads into their eyes, stinging them, making them blink. TRUE and MAXI wait. Finally, TRUE slowly reaches into his pocket, wincing as the guns, unwavering, point at them, and extracts his hologrammed press pass.

> TRUE
>
> See? Journalists. Observers.

CUT TO

The CLONES, who don't waver. From behind them, TRUE can hear explosions, then the buzzing, hacksaw sound of a laser. Some of the CLONES drop, their armor melted to their skin. But they don't cry out, don't exhibit the human characteristics of pain. They are merely incapacitated. The thought crosses TRUE'S mind that it was a shame he couldn't have been a CLONE when his life with Eden fell apart.

CLONE lasers blind them, the sound of screams and agony of men and women in battle. TRUE turns to advancing mercenaries.

> TRUE
>
> Hope none of the clones makes a DNA miscue.

CUT TO

TRUE and MAXI sprinting into the CLONE stronghold. The CLONES ignore them, keep their weapons trained on MERCE-

NARIES. TRUE and MAXI swivel through the first wave of CLONES, dive behind some mortar and cement—the remains of the factory—and thousands of pairs of sneakers. The stench of melted rubber is almost suffocating. From behind the wall, TRUE and MAXI keep recording the action, catching the battle on screen, trying to remain calm as MERC and CLONE alike are maimed and killed.

CUT TO

TRUE's wrist-top screen, EDEN in the right-hand corner, sitting quietly in the apartment as the other 15 screens are taken up with vicious fighting, 15 tales of bravery and cowardice, violence and retreat, death and injury, lasers, guns and hand-to-hand combat.

> EDEN
>
> Are you all right?

> TRUE
>
> So far.

CUT TO

An explosion nearby, and hundreds of pairs of sneakers raining down on and around them.

> EDEN
> (*screaming*)
>
> True!

CUT TO

TRUE and MAXI, huddling under sneakers, dust, concrete, and glass floating down.

> MAXI
> (*tossing a sneaker away*)
> I got a bloody headache.

> TRUE
> Tell me about it. We're OK, Eden.

> EDEN
> Incredible footage. I feel like I'm in the middle
> of the war.

> TRUE
> Funny. So do we.

CUT TO

MAXI, grinning broadly, then wincing, although the smile stays intact as a whole platoon of MERCENARIES is wiped out.

CUT TO

TRUE. CLOSEUP. EYES WIDE OPEN, MOUTH AGAPE.

CUT TO

THE FACTORY, TRUE and MAXI, part of a world that's gone haywire. Suddenly, their positions change, the whole battlefield has shifted, kaleidoscoping, like falling off a motorcycle. In a blink of the eye, they are 10 meters from where they were before.

CUT TO

The CLONES, still firing on the MERCENARIES, who seemed to have all of a sudden increased in size, as if reinforcements have been sent in. And then CLONES begin disappearing, but not from mercenary fire. One second the CLONE is firing or moving to shore up a position, the next it's gone. Whole lines of CLONES disappear, like a shuffling deck of cards.

TRUE
(*Seems to understand something important*)
Maxi. We have to get out of here.

MAXI
OK, just a little more footage. Look at them disappear. Like they're dissolving. This is incredible.

TRUE
Now!

CUT TO

MAXI, who doesn't answer, wrapped up in the battle.

CUT TO

AN OVERVIEW OF TRUE and MAXI's WRIST-TOP SCREENS, as CLONES disappear in a domino-effect crossing screen to screen.

CUT TO

TRUE, running, waving MAXI on, as he heads out onto the battlefield

PULL BACK TO REVEAL

THE BRUNT OF THE MERCENARY ARMY, their guns trained on him

CUT TO

A TEENAGE MALAY MERCENARY, tattered and bloody, taking aim

CUT TO

TRUE wincing and running, looking suspiciously like a video game character

CUT TO

MAXI, still in the same spot, filming

CUT TO

TRUE, doing a quick 180, the MALAY missing him, then aiming elsewhere, as if he couldn't be bothered with TRUE, and TRUE racing back to MAXI

CUT TO

TRUE screaming at MAXI to get moving and

CUT TO

MAXI shutting off his wrist-top, muttering "Ready to rock and—"

CUT TO

CLOSE UP. MAXI looks at the camera, says "Holy Fuck," and photo-flashes invisible.

CUT TO

TRUE hitting the deck where Maxi was, hugging the ground, his nose nudged under sneakers

PULL BACK TO REVEAL

THE WHOLE BATTLEFIELD and the ensuing mayhem, as the battle intensity picks up, one long gun report and laser hiss, the air redolent with blue smoke, chemical lasers, burning flesh and hair, rubber and gun powder. There is a loud thud that seems to come from within True's head and his world spins out of control, the atmosphere's molecules breaking up into molecules, a Seurat painting, thousands of colors shimmying, shimmering.

There's another thudding explosion, the world shifts again, and True is lying on something soft, gooey. The stench of burnt flesh and hair is melted into his clothing. Something familiar lying by his head. The dregs of an oil skin hat. Maxi's wrist-top beside it.

True rolls out of the muck, frantically rubs at the viscous material. In his mind he's screaming, *Get it off! Get it off!* but knows he'll never get Maxi off his clothes, never get him out of his mind.

The battle is over as the clones chase the remnants of the mercenary army.

True in unfettered shakes. Looks over the battlefield. A clone steps around him, ignores him.

True picks up a half-melted sneaker. Heaves it at him. Misses.

CHAPTER 29

Eden gasps when True walks in, stained with vomit, dirt, and Maxi. "Are you all right?"

True nods stiffly, afraid he's on the verge of losing control.

The apartment is crowded with flowers. Roses. In vases, bouquets, planters, wrapped in plastic or displayed in pancake-thin origami. The air is thick with their perfume.

Eden explains. "Someone named Piña sent them. There's a note."

She draws a bath, strips him. He knows she's surveying Piña's chafes, the scratches running along his spine, the purple-olive splotches on his chest. Artillery, she may ask? But she doesn't and True doesn't say.

After he's immersed in the stinging water Eden takes off her panties, steps in, hiking up her skirt and lowering herself on him. She soaps his body, the arms first, gently; his shoulders, kneaded. She lathers his toes and works herself up his ankles, shins, knees, thighs. True's aroused despite his pain.

She encloses him in her, her legs rubber-banding around his waist. She urges his hands onto her breasts. The nipples push hard against her soaking dress. She rises, falls, tension and release, stroking him as she dances.

The tub is slippery and True slides along the bottom. As her movements animate, her fingers and toes curl behind his back. Husky breaths. She throws herself all the way down on him, driving almost inside him, pulling close. He's coming down from her climax. His nose is mushed into her cleavage and he's thinking about the cycle of life, how it's really just a cycle from childhood to childhood. Except in his case, his childhood was taken away from him, spent in a lab.

Eden's hair is steam-damp. She hugs him as if this is the last time. But her message is different. "I love you, True. I love you. And I'll always be there for you. I know you don't believe me. I know you don't trust me. But I'll show you. I promise."

Plagued by guilt. He has a lot of work but little time.

She submerges her hands, reaches for him. "Want to come?" Licks salt off his lips.

True turns away. "I've seen two men melted in just hours and I have to finish this story. Later."

He knows, although she pretends this is fine, it isn't.

Eden stands and water cascades down. She pulls off her dress, wrings it out over True, flings it in the corner. One foot then the other out of the tub. "What can I do to help?"

"Can you measure the difference between the amount of power generated and the amount consumed in Tokyo?"

"They'll be roughly the same."

"I don't think so. When you locate the largest users of electricity, let me know."

"You want to tell me what this is about?"

True touches a Piña clamp-bruise on his wrist. "Just do it."

She sashays out of the bathroom, as if to remind True what he's missing.

True towels off, grabs the medical kit, and runs ultrasound treatments until he can breathe without wincing and walk without limping. Piña's video-card was already viewed. He glances at Eden, who's wrapped in work, and opens it. A hologram of Piña, a different, digital Piña, coalesces from pink mist. She's elegant, a one-and-a-half-meter feminine icon in slinky designer wear, purring breasts, silky legs.

"Dear True. Forgive me. I love you. If you let me into your life, there is nothing we can't accomplish. I can imbue you with strength and resilience. You can share your sensitivity and intellect. Together we dance among the stars. Alone I am inconsequential. I love you, True, truly."

Piña's sucked back into the envelope. True wonders what she traded for help in composing her sonnet. He studies a pink rose, de-thorned. Which's unlike Piña as well, to alter nature.

Eden, with a thread of a smile, calls over. "I have that power data. You were right."

"About?"

"Since the quake knocked out hundreds of thousands of buildings, consumption is only five percent what it was the same time last year."

"But power output?"

"Is up. What do you think it means?"

"Can you knock out Tokyo's power in one jolt at my command? Make it brownout so nothing vital goes out. Even just for a minute?"

Eden weighs. "Difficult; not impossible. Strictly speaking, not in one jolt but in trillions of electrical pulses, which would amount to the same. They wouldn't expect it, that's for sure. They usually guard against tappers, not someone trying to kamikaze the system at five percent capacity. I could probably block the access cells. It'll automatically reroute trillions of times but I could hold it off for maybe thirty secs. Rerouting will intensify with each failure, so with the limited hardware I have here, that's what I can do."

"Set it up."

"What are you doing?"

"I'm going to finish what's been planned for me."

"Then?"

"I don't know." He swipes at a strand of loose hair. "Rush is going to be here any minute. When he buzzes, let him in."

"How do you know Rush is coming?"

"If he doesn't, I won't be able to complete my computer destiny."

Reiner's transmitting from the Tokyo bureau, three dozen monitors behind her offering views of the city's wards.

True tweaks the picture. "I like you better this way, without your broadcast icon."

"You're probably the only one. I coded a message to the WWTV board telling them the war poop was yours. I also said you were working on a story that would blow the ratings heaven-bound. They said they'd clear the boards on your cue."

"Thanks. It's almost ready. I hope." Reiner knows not to ask about a scoop before air time. "Any word on Odessa?"

"Tracked down an antique obaasan who said she witnessed a gaijin matching O's description disappear. Then again she swore the Emperor's her lover, so there's that. Still looking."

True doesn't say Odessa's dead, like Maxi. Could be wrong, so shhhhh.

She: "Did you catch the promos Rush made for your obit? He scored a ratings coup with the Urban Survival footage. I sent word you're alive so he has to post a worldwide retraction. He'll be irate."

First Aslam pulling his exclusive, now this. Rush's road to anchor nirvana is strewn with potholes. Pounding on the door. Eden lets Rush in, who steams over. "Ailey. You are such an asshole."

"Right on time," True says.

"Told you he'd be pissed." Reiner's beatific icon, her defense, now substituting for her on screen.

Rush stomps his foot on the carpet. A mushy sound. "You're not allowed to transmit footage without my OK. Those are the rules. You're not even supposed to be alive."

"What's that mean?" Reiner cracks her neck.

Rush blisters. "I saw him picked apart and transmitted the footage internationally. I've been nuked twice this month. I'll be filed under 'gullible' at the home office."

"You should have checked with me. I'd have told you he wasn't dead."

"Reiner, shut up. Congratulations on your scoop. You're lucky as fuck. An earthquake then a war while I'm stuck in this SE Asian toilet."

"True's the one who dug up the war scoop."

True's aware of distortions in some of Reiner's monitors. "What's happening?"

There's rumbling, whirlpool dots and strands of light, buildings and people exploding silently, disappearing. The ground shakes as portions of Tokyo are sponged away. Pastel phantasmagorisms splashing eerie.

"Is that an aftershock?" Rush asks.

True, frantic. "Reiner, get out of there. Leave Tokyo immediately."

More cosmic disturbance. "I'm staying, True."

"You'll die, Reiner."

She switches off her icon and Rush's eyes wiggle. He doesn't know this Reiner, the one unable to parry time. "I've lived a long time."

The bureau remains unfazed by the electronic squall, swirling, untangling pointillism. True says, "Even with provisions for low-tonnage weaponry, you know the risk you're taking?"

"I'm staying."

Another wrinkle in the cosmos. Reiner's face dances from silvery old to gilded youth, then back. On one of the monitors: a shuffle of people disappear. Flash into air. On other monitors, too. "Aw, True. I've been sitting on the greatest scoop of the 21st century, and I missed it. Why didn't you tell me? Oh, man. That really sucks. Sh—" Reiner spins into cottony fog.

Losing Reiner is no easier the second time. Worse, for this is real.

"What was the scoop?" Greed tinges Rush's words. *What's the digital equivalent to that,* True wonders, *what mix of 0's and 1's?* He rewinds, freezes Tokyo's ghost, the metropolis.

"Where's Reiner?" Rush lagging behind the brain curve.

"Reiner's dead, though she wouldn't be if you hadn't killed Aslam."

The brittle mask of a bad liar. "What are you talking about? Those psychotropic patterns pop a synapse in you brain or something?"

"You hated Aslam. He offered you an exclusive, then yanked it. I didn't even notice you were gone, since most of our work is conducted over the link. For a while I assumed you never went. But I was wrong. You know why Aslam did that to you?"

Rush, wary. "Since you're making this up as you go along... you tell me."

"He tapped WWTV's database with your wrist-top and codes. Then he had one of his commando hackers plant a message for me. I'm sure he sucked every piece of information he could out of there. Unfortunately, he probably found what I did: There's nothing in WWTV's database about Sato's weapon. As for you, you're lucky to be alive."

Furious blinks. "You're crazy."

"As a jungle insurgent, Aslam was exposed to a variety of stomach ailments, two being bilharzia and giardia. Bilharzia's new to Luzonia, giardia common in areas outside the city. Since you both suffered from these same afflictions, I assume you and he shared time and space."

"I never said I had giardia."

"Giardia's signature is sulfur belches and farts. When you visited me in the hospital, you smelled like hell's brimstone. Then I knew."

Rush catches Eden's eyes, holds, releases. He tunes in True again. "So what if I met that psychopath? What's that have to do to with you blaming me for killing Reiner?"

"It must have been humiliating and horrifying. You must have been scared when you found out all they wanted was your wrist-top and access codes. You were expendable."

"I thought I was going to die."

"But—"

Rush is third-generation talk show trash but chooses to tuck these memories away, as if nothing happened. "I begged them to stop."

"What did they do?"

Rush steals a glance at Eden, at True. Looks at his shoes.

"How long were you held?"

"I don't know how long it went on, but I was in the jungle a total of a day. Aziz got me out, drove me to Nerula himself, dropped me on the outskirts."

"It wasn't Aslam's fault."

"If it wasn't for him I wouldn't have been there."

Rush right for a change. "ADC contacted you, offering a finder's fee, one that would let you score a little revenge in the process. You jumped at it. Didn't it seem like too much of a coincidence? Weren't you suspicious?"

No answer, so no. True keeps on. "You subcontracted the deal to the Rajput, someone known for tackling jobs like this. You instructed her to find a girl to get close to Aslam. Why? ADC provided the plan. They knew Aslam's vulnerabilities—after all, he worked for ADC, too, although he didn't know it. The Rajput kept her end, and Aslam was blown to shit."

Rush's aqua velva eyes. Words from far away in his mouth. "I don't know what you're talking about."

"What you didn't count on is how sloppy reality is. First, you didn't know I was Aslam's friend and was with him when he died. So you had to get rid of me. ADC assured you all you needed to do was spike my water supply with FREEze and I'd be done for. After all, it worked before. ADC needed me to fall into virtual reality so I would go into the information net for them. But you didn't know this, and didn't want to take any chances. You hired Bong Bong to get me. Even after he couldn't get the job done, you thought you were home free after the Ghetto Tourney. But meanwhile, the Rajput kept coming back for more money, threatening to implicate you in Aslam's death. Bong Bong said he'd implicate you in *my* death. So you were being double-blackmailed. No doubt, the money ADC paid you doesn't amount to much now."

Rush calculating his next plodding move, his career floundering on cloudy denial. "No."

"I went through your logs. Aslam inviting you to the jungle. You confirming. The Rajput's calls, everything." Eden's hand disappears into the medkit. She's nonchalant so Rush doesn't see.

"I won't let you do this to me." Rush levels a laser pistol at True.

"Bong Bong's dead. So's the Rajput. You have nothing to fear from them."

"Bong Bong, dead?" Palpable relief. Then, "I can't afford a scandal. I'm this close"—thumb and forefinger brush—"to getting my own show."

"You're this close to implicating your ADC contact."

His-s-s-s. Eden jabs Rush with an air syringe. Rush falls, splashing laserfire. True's bed chemicalizes into viscous flames. Rush collapses, face down, asleep.

"What did you give him?" True checks Rush's breathing, pulse. Slow, steady, like Rush.

"Condensed valium. He'll be asleep for a while."

"Don't kill him."

Eden sporting instant shock. "Why would I kill him?"

"Just don't. We have to prep for broadcast."

❖ ❖ ❖

Nerula's sinking into civil war. The result of Bong Bong's death is a power vacuum; and the police, like a prisoner who's been garroted, convulse, flail blindly at the populace. Teens swarm the downtown. Soldiers, who haven't been paid in months, join the rampage. The military is sent in to quell the police: female versus male, the first gender war. But True knows this is inconsequential compared to his story.

He, Eden should get to the airport, but he has to file this last story, complete the model, itself a cycle of birth to decay. Anarchy leaking into his neighborhood. Eden clicking at 3-D power grids. True putting the final touches on his script. Rush slumping and snoring in the bathtub.

Eden's fingers tight in her palms. "Keep your toes crossed."

"Fingers, toes, legs, and balls. They're all crossed." True accesses the emergency broadcast link, plugs in his password. The computer scans True's retina and, five clicks of the clock later, grants access. A live feature, virtually unheard of in these days of touch-ups and make-overs. The last time? Reiner: earthquake coverage and the corporate war. Now it's his turn.

The computer requests his broadcast icon. *As is*, he types.

Ready. Testing. One-two-three-four-go.

"True Ailey reporting live from Nerula, Luzonia, with a WWTV exclusive." He feels his voice. A little on the upside of the pitch. He tries to relax. "As Tsuyoshi Sato and his corporation battle the American Defense Corporation, there's a parallel story, a story that will shake the world."

True has the sense that as he speaks, satellites dotting the sky are picking up his transmission, distributing it in nanoseconds, sending a ripple of shock that will swell as it spreads.

"Tsuyoshi Sato inherited control of a keirestu of enormous wealth, but he wasn't satisfied." A 3-D photo of Sato is lodged at screen's bottom. In it, he's drinking champagne, looking imperious. "Before Tokyo's massive quake, Sato disinvested himself of all companies vulnerable to loss due to a massive quake. He plowed the money from these sales, plus the windfall from large tracts of Tokyo real estate, into controlling shares in construction firms and import companies, two sectors that have thrived since the quake. He also invested heavily into R & D abroad. When the quake devastated Tokyo, Sato not only didn't suffer losses, he miraculously profited.

"But was it clairvoyance? Did he stumble onto a technology that accurately predicts these temblors? Or was he plain lucky? Whatever the case, after the quake, Sato's company, through a variety off screens, bought up much of Tokyo's land at bargain prices." A grainy photo of Japanese toughs standing near devastated residential sites. "If he hadn't had the political strength to push for the capital remaining in Tokyo, he would have been stuck with millions of acres of worthless land. Instead, he's amassed a fortune.

"But it wasn't only greed that drove Sato. It was the awareness his nation has plunged into economic and cultural malaise." Pie charts of declining output of the Japanese economy, 1980 to the present, illustrating the drift. "A declining exchange rate, an aging population, a lack of high paying jobs, the ascendance of regional trading blocs, the push for factories to be built overseas which sucked jobs out of Japan, all of this led to Japanese economic stagnation.

"Sato postulated his nation would never return to the world stage unless a disaster was the catalyst for economic growth. But not even Tsuyoshi Sato can cause an earthquake. Or can he?" True lets this soak in, then: "In a WWTV exclusive, this reporter gives you Tokyo as it really is."

Nonverbal clues of haste to Eden, who doesn't need them, already at work. First, nothing, as her pulses are parried. It's nighttime in Tokyo, lights yellow and tan. The camera pans over post-quake rubble. A few people mill around, sleep in doorways. True looks at Eden, his eyelids brushing eyebrows. Then a cosmic shift transforms Tokyo. Piles of rubble are congealed into skyscrapers and wooden homes. Bent cars are recast factory new, or like new, parked in neat rows. The earthquake is gone. Tokyo's people are left in bewilder-awe, expressions captured by WWTV robocams.

"There was no earthquake; only an illusion, a sophisticated interactive virtual reality program used to enslave millions."

Eden's relays are blocked, the city back to the usual illusion.

But it's too late. Everyone knows.

"True Ailey, WWTV, Nerula, Luzonia."

CHAPTER 30

True's message board reels under the weight of electric-mail—congratulations, criticism, conspiracy theories, offers of love, requests for advice for a career in journalism, threats of litigation, job offers from competing networks. WWTV's editorial board eye-needles a message through: *Dear Reporter. Keep up the good work. Regards.* No signature but promises of a plum job and pay raise appended. He deletes them all.

Eden is battling e-rain, billions of digitized messages sluicing through the cracks in her net site. She looks, shrugs at True. "Someone's overwhelming the e-shield."

True's been expecting this. "If it gets through, can he fix on our location?"

Eden slaps frustration. She can't believe they're vulnerable to message attack. "I can prevent that, but you never know what or who he has working for him."

"I'll risk it."

Tsuyoshi Sato's hologrammed icon blazes before True. It's blinding, resolute. "You are a remarkable reporter, True Ailey."

True skips pleasantries. "So there's no misunderstanding, you realize I'm funneling this conversation directly to WWTV's head office?"

Sato's icon is out of time, out of synch, reception deteriorating. Sato's mouth hinges, the words a fraction late. "On the con-con-contrary. We understand each other all t-t-t-too well." There is a waterfall of pastels as Sato's icon shatters, reforms. Some words are lost, but True gets the gist. "—exhibit more caution now than you did innnnnnn"—an electrical buzz, then—"reporting this story."

"Are you saying it's inaccurate?"

More nasty static, then "—only part of the story. You engaged in corporate espionage."

"I was tricked into delving into your information banks and taking your virtual reality technology by the American Defense Corp. This is all documented and in the possession of the legal board at WWTV in New York. Your tech—"

"—breaking up."

"What?"

"Your transmission is breaking—"

A slitting sound. Then True can't believe what he sees: Odessa and Reiner filtering into Sato's hologram. Realizes Odessa must have hitched on Sato's transmission. Sato seems unaware.

"I'll be brief. I had to balance the corporate power. Soon, someone will develop an inexpensive software to stifle this VR application. An illusion is an illusion only until people know the truth."

"You stole from me?"

"My crimes pale next to yours."

Sato is assimilating True's words. There's an irritating time-lag, bolts of interference. Finally Sato says, "You will die, True Ailey."

"How about you? Do you think your Global Fortune 1000 competitors will let you live? You're a marked man."

"The situation in Nerula at this moment, I'm told, is extremely-ly-ly unstable." Sato's mouth is moving but no sound. When his mouth locks, True hears, "Anarchy, blood in the streets. You have only minutes. It's a shame I won't have a hand in ending your pitiful life, but I'll rest easy in the knowledge that you are—"

Silence. True says, "What?"

Mouth movement and words are random. Sato fizzes from sight, sucked away. But his final words linger. "You will suffer for this. You'll be dead in minutes. Dead. Dead."

Buzzing silence. Electric glow.

"What an asshole," Reiner says.

True hugs Reiner's and Odessa's holograms. "What happened to you two?"

"Odessa got caught up in some informational Milky Way in Sato's database. He figured out what was going on and got out in time for us to rig a VR shield, which blacked out our conversation. A little later, I turn on the news and there you are cracking the story wide-open."

Odessa steps forward. "Right after you aired, every corp in the Global Fortune 1000 turned on Sato. Pulled the plug on the greedy bastard."

Reiner's expression changes to concern. "Now your advice from me. Get out of Nerula. Sato's right. It's falling into anarchy."

Eden close to him. She whispers. "We have to go."

"Not yet." He says to Reiner and Odessa's image: "I'll contact you later."

He strangles transmission and now it's just True and Eden, like it was before all this. With a difference. "There's nothing I can do about ADC. They're the big winners, but as Aslam told me, it was necessary to balance corporate power." True places himself between Eden and the door. No escape for either. "But I can uncover an ADC operative."

Eden stands defiant.

"I was like some video game icon. You formulated the computer model to predict my every move. How? Because you'd been testing VR on me from the moment we met."

"Don't do this, True. Don't ruin what we've rediscovered."

He notices a gold ring, swirling etchings, around her finger. Their wedding band. When did she put that back on? "I became suspicious when I found out your company, Six Days, Inc., had been a Sato subsidiary until ADC launched a hostile takeover. Backed by U.S. courts, they took over the company. The only reason ADC did that was because they knew you were onto some hot technology. They offered you... what? Money? Glory?"

"Both."

"But Sato's not stupid. He sucked out every byte of data from Six Days. All your work was inside Sato's infobanks. You had no way of getting it back. All you had left were the programs you'd tested on me—not the algorithms, not their formulas. You knew it would have taken years to recreate what you did. But there was an easier way."

"You." Eden twirls the ring around her finger absentmindedly.

"Get me to trip into those data pools for you, liberate the technology you'd invented. You constructed an interactive character model. The net result was ADC's plan to use Aslam to get to me. The model calculated I wouldn't allow his death to go unsolved. Aslam, meanwhile, was planning to steal the technology himself from Sato, although he had no intention of turning it over to ADC. He was going to use it on all enemies of the insurgency.

"You got Rush to dump one of your VR programs into my home entertainment unit and spike my house with FREEze. I chipped away at the mystery for you in VR, flowed into the infonet, actually leaving VR. Ironically, the only reality I experienced during that time was when I was skimming through Sato's database, stealing that chip technology. For ADC. For you."

"Are you done?"

"No. What I couldn't figure was why you snuffed Bong Bong. When I left you that day, you were panicky. Later I said I'd seen two men melted that day, but you didn't ask. You knew about Maxi at that point but couldn't have known about Bong Bong, unless you were there. You also never asked me what happened to my wrist-top or why I was calling from a local phone bank. I guess the computer model didn't take everything into consideration."

Millimeters separate her finger from her thumb: almost OK. "It's close, not perfect. Something I'll have to work on when I patent the upgrade."

"You said the plastic packaging spilled in solvent by accident. I know from covering terrorism that napalm can be made out of styrofoam soaked in kerosene. That's what you dropped on Bong Bong from the clock tower."

"I had to make sure you didn't stray too far from the model. I was unlucky I was put in the position of having to save your life. The Rajput shouldn't have called from the same phone bank twice; definitely shouldn't have bought off-the-shelf technology next to the phone bank."

True wonders what Eden finds more galling, the Rajput's calling from the same phone bank or that she bought off-the-rack software. "Bong Bong heard you, which is why he went upstairs in the clock tower. How'd you get up there?"

Eden flexes, mocks him. "I climbed out of the window, used the clocks for footing. It was easy. Bong Bong didn't check the roof. I only wished I could have seared that legless bitch."

"You used me."

She brushes this aside. "Everybody uses everybody. You've known for a while now, but you didn't confront me because you needed my help."

"I didn't murder anyone."

"If it weren't for me, you'd be dead. Bong Bong, Sato, ADC would have iced you."

"Why not kill me after I stole the chip from Sato?"

"You had to break the story. Much better coming from a TV journo than leaked to the press. It was imperative the leak wasn't traced to ADC. Who the hell would have believed it anyway, especially with all the bad PR in the States over the trial?"

True has nothing to add. It started with Eden. It ends with Eden.

She says, "Don't you want to see the computer model I made? See yourself, how well you played the game?" She gestures and four walls display thousands of cubed snapshots of True. A pyramid beginning with Aslam and True in 24-7, options branching from that conversation, True says yes to Aslam, True says maybe, True says no and storms out, True says no and stays, discusses it further. Hundreds of thousands of possibilities, the one True ultimately follows inked in red, leading to Aslam's assassination outside 24-7. This leads to other options, the real earth choice marching on while others peel aside. True's web of truth, possibilities, consequences.

Eden fast-forwards to his virtual reality trip, what occurred, what might have occurred, and True delving into Sato's banks. She skips forward again, and True and Eden are arguing over whether he should be going out to check out the phone bank. The model indicates no preconceived paths for this choice. The word improvising fills the room seemingly a million times. Then the action is picked up during the clone/merc battle, True and Eden on the telelink, Maxi dying, True face down in his colleague's sticky remains. Back to the apartment and True's summations.

Then True and Eden in the here and now.

"What does this mean?" True hears himself, once, twice, a million times asking the same question.

"A meeting point. Each point leads to millions of alternatives. The wall monitors show the paths most likely to be pursued. You scored well, since you're so logical, taking most of the broad boulevards." Galaxies of Eden faces say the same things in precise time. "It's the final level. Your future is up to you."

"Up to now, free will has been an illusion." True's life's unfolding as it's happening. Disconcerting. Imagines he could, with one well-timed stroke, ruin Eden's plans to superimpose her artificial universe on the real world. He sees the outcome of that via a monitor on the left hand side of the room. He's breaking her neck but can't bring himself to kill her. He's dead soon after. That path is no good. Watches another as he and Eden go away together all forgiven, live their lives intertwined. He dies soon after. Guilt.

Options play out. By gaining Eden he loses himself. By losing

Eden he still loses himself. He studies a series of empty images in the corner. What the computer model can't predict. A window of opportunity? If only True knew how to blaze through it.

"All games come to an end. Your time will come, too." Eden wraps her arms around him, nuzzles his ear. "I am on the cusp of great discoveries. I can invent almost perfect worlds. For us. Together."

"The model says I'll die."

"Not if you accept me and it. I know we've had our glitches, but that doesn't mean I don't love you. I want us to be together."

"Accept you, as a god?"

"No." She conducts symphonic air. "Like God."

the final frames of Eden's model, shanty orphans, tattered and violent, are busting down the door, instantly killing True and Eden. Inside reality, just True/Eden not dead yet fearful of the soon-to-be. Children's shouts in the hall. Heavy knocks, heaves, the apartment door creaking, collapsing in, a teen pack wilding inside, here to ransack. An end-over-end glass splits True's lip. He's dazed, bleeding. Eden is carted away, screeching "True! True!"

In the doorway, Piña's propped up on prosthetic legs. Shoulder-long hair frames a strong jaw, deep mustard eyes, ultra-high cheekbones. He never noticed them before. A designer dress hangs from her shoulders to her ankles, bruise-colored silk, strapless, formal, accentuating her muscley arms and tapering to her combat boots. Tattoos still there. Scars, too. Quintessential guerilla chic. Piña's had a serious beauty makeover. She bends down, her equilibrium off kilter, unused to balancing on two feet. Rubs away True's blood with her spit.

Pina's bleached teeth, a supermodel's surgical smile. "I told the motherfuckers I didn't want you hurt. Better get your ass up. Come with me. These bastards are cra-a-azy." She's doused in lemon, rose, gardenia.

"With Piña?" His speech is slurred through swelling lips.

"With me."

She takes his hand—she's almost as tall as he is, now—and they help each other outside, through the mayhem. Piña shouts and a path is cleared, for even in anarchy Piña is Piña, a force of terror. Her arm is wrapped around True's neck for balance, a life preserver in this sea of discontent. She leads him to her motorcycle, a street urchin guarding it, splayed on the seat, playing with the brakes.

Buildings are a-toast, the sky burnt charcoal. Shanty dwellers settle old scores and compose new ones, content to destroy what they can't shoulder. Piña and True rev through the disenchanted throngs to her apartment. She hollers over her shoulder, "Just bought a new VR system. The best money can fucking buy. Runs all the hottest software. We won't even have to go outside. Just us. And VR."

Piña kisses him as they skid still and park by the door. He falls inside Piña's home, she after.

And as the door shuts, True listens to the din from outside rush to silence.

THE END

About the Author

Adam L. Penenberg is a journalism professor at New York University who has written for *Fast Company, Forbes, The New York Times, The Washington Post, Wired, Slate, Playboy,* and *The Economist.* A former senior editor at *Forbes* and a reporter for Forbes.com, Penenberg garnered national attention in 1998 for unmasking serial fabricator Stephen Glass of *The New Republic.* Penenberg's story was a watershed for online investigative journalism and portrayed in the film *Shattered Glass* (Steve Zahn plays Penenberg).

Penenberg has published several books that have been optioned for film and serialized in *The New York Times Magazine, Wired UK,* and *The Financial Times,* and won a Deadline Club Award for feature reporting for his *Fast Company* story "Revenge of the Nerds," which looked at the future of moviemaking. He has appeared on NBC's *The Today Show* as well as on CNN and all the major news networks, and has been quoted about media and technology in *The Washington Post, The Christian Science Monitor, USA Today, Wired News, Ad Age, Marketwatch, Politico,* and many others.